MW00794926

ACCUSED IN PARADISE

PARADISE SERIES

BOOK 24

DEBORAH BROWN

BODIES IN PARADISE

Cover: Natasha Brown

ISBN-13: 978-1-7334807-5-8

PRINTED IN THE UNITED STATES OF AMERICA

ACCUSED IN PARADISE

Chapter One

The sun was shining, not a single cloud in the baby blue sky. Coffee once a week was now mandatory, at one house or the other, with our friends, Fabiana and Didier, the hot, dark-haired, blue-eyed French couple that were also our neighbors and business partners. This week, it was my turn, and I'd corralled everyone to take their mugs and sit out on the deck, which wasn't a struggle, since it was an amazing morning and all of us enjoyed looking at the beach below. Didier joined us late, as he'd stopped to sneak my cats, Jazz and Snow, a treat. They could be asleep in the bedroom, but once easy-touch Didier crossed the threshold, they made their appearance known, weaving in between his legs.

My phone rang, and I groaned inwardly, as early meant trouble. I glanced at the screen and attempted to cover my wince, and casually slid it across the table to my husband.

Creole looked at the screen, and back at me, his blue eyes dancing with laughter. "You know I love you, babes, but this is out of my skill set."

"Oh brother," Fab snapped. She grabbed up

the phone and showed it to Didier, who shook his head with a smirk. It stopped ringing, and she slid it back to me.

Then it started to ring again. Macklin Lane would never give up so easily. She managed a ten-unit beach property that I owned across town; circus ringmaster would be a fitting title. My not answering only meant that she'd continue to call until I did.

I answered and breathed into the phone.

"I know what you were doing—passing the phone around, seeing who had the tonsils or other body part to answer. It's just me; how bad could it be?" Mac unleashed a deranged laugh.

"Warning: you're on speaker." It seriously saved time not having to repeat every word, not to mention saving me from hearing a lecture on something I forgot.

"There's a problem that needs your attention. I tried to be the fixer on this one but got nowhere, despite attempting to cash in a few favors."

Favors were traded like currency between family and friends. They came with a no-griping clause—just get off your…and do.

"Hold on a second…" I downed my coffee. "I needed a shot of caffeine to fortify my nerves before you cut to the chase."

"Crum was arrested for the murder of Travis West," Mac blurted out.

Everyone's eyebrows went up.

"That's ridiculous on several levels. That they

barely knew one another being one," I said in disbelief.

"Shot point-blank in the chest—West, not Crum. Kaboom." Mac yelled the last word.

The men grinned.

Fab rolled her eyes. "Sounds messy."

"If the killer was that close, sounds like someone he knew," Creole said.

"To my knowledge, Crum knew of the man, but they were casual acquaintances at best," I said. "They had one confrontation. It resulted in a black eye for Crum, and if the esteemed professor was going to kill the man, it would've been then, not months later."

Professor Crum—first name "none of your business" I'd heard him say a time or two—had retired from a high-brow university in California. In order to get your resume looked at by the five-star college, at a minimum, brains—and a lot of them—were required. Years back, he'd moved to sunny Florida, Tarpon Cove in the Keys to be exact.

"Anyone who knows Crum knows that he likes to talk…not get his brains rearranged." I made a face. "He has his eccentricities, but he's not known for going off half-cocked."

Crum had helped me concoct a plan to get West to buy a lot that shared a property line with his mansion. The Taco Wagon had been parked on that land and, though not on the main highway, did a brisk business…until it blew up.

More than a few people suspected West of the arson, although nothing was proven. As for the owners, they just wanted to be able to sell the lot and retire, which wasn't looking likely with West breathing down the neck of any would-be buyers. My idea had been for Crum to do the heavy lifting, in that he gathered together a group of unusual characters, and staged an obnoxious spectacle on the lot in the hopes of motivating West to snap up the property to prevent them from becoming permanent neighbors. There was zero chance of that happening, but West didn't know that, and the plan worked, as the last thing he wanted was never-ending antics and crazies for neighbors.

"Agree with you." Mac snorted, loudly enough that hopefully she was outside and whatever flew out of her nose didn't do serious property damage. "But Crum's keister is in the slammer, and he goes before a judge in two days for a bail hearing. When he called, I wasn't going to answer—good thing I did. Told him we had bail covered and promised a lawyer. I assured him we wouldn't let him twist. You're not going to make a big ole liar out of me, are you?"

"Just because he's a pain in my backside isn't a good reason to ditch him when he's in trouble." I excelled in plan-making, and my mind was moving at a rapid pace. It shouldn't be hard, since I'd been down the road of getting folks out of jail more times than I could count. "Bail—

that's the easy part. Lawyer... Did you call Cruz?" Cruz Campion was, according to himself, the best criminal lawyer in the universe, although his billboards only mentioned south Florida. The man wasn't short on ego.

Mac hesitated so long that anyone else would've hung up, thinking she'd already done so. "Cruz's exact words were 'Hell no,' and I spoke to the man directly. He's still not over Crum shtupping his grandmother."

Cruz's granny had come to town ready to party with any man in sight—young, old, and preferably still breathing...except for that one. Somehow, it'd never occurred to Cruz to hold his grandmother responsible for her hard-partying ways instead of blaming the men she seduced.

"Too damn bad," I practically shrieked. Creole and Didier grinned, and Fab rubbed her ears. I managed to calm down...some. "After everything we've done for him and his zillion relatives!"

"There's Tank," Fab said. "He doesn't need to know he was second choice."

Fab had met Tank—AKA Patrick Cannon, but only in the courtroom—during a jail visit. She'd found him sitting behind the glass panel, waiting on a visitor that was a no-show, and saw that as an open invitation to sit down and chat it up, rapidly discovering that he'd been arrested thanks to mistaken identity. He was swiftly released, and it turned out that he was a criminal defense attorney who'd recently relocated to the Cove and opened a one-man office. He'd assured us that if the case was beyond his capabilities, he'd find us someone who could handle it and it wouldn't be a slouch either. He'd been as good as his word.

"Called Tank already. He's escorting his mother to an out-of-state funeral for a relative he never heard of. Sounded irked over the whole drama." Mac sucked up every last drop of her drink, judging by the noise. "Back to Cruz. I reminded him that when he asks, I deliver. Then I practically begged."

"Beg?" I snapped. "I don't think so. You're never to do that again."

"You could get someone to represent Crum for the bail hearing and then have Tank take over when he gets back," Didier said. "Make it clear to the other attorney up front that he's only filling in."

That was a good idea. I winked at the man, and he grinned back. "I'll take care of it. I'll have an attorney signed up by the end of the day."

"Hold your horses," Mac cautioned. "I have a warning for you. Some would probably call it a threat."

"What are you talking about?" Creole demanded testily.

"Let me guess—Cruz sent a message that Madison better not show up in his courtroom to strongarm him? His office, perhaps?" Fab surmised. "Am I right?" She nodded, answering her own question.

"If you show up anywhere, Cruz will have you arrested," Mac said. "Under no circumstances is he going to represent Crum."

"Why don't Creole and I pay the man a visit and see what we can work out?" Didier offered.

I reached over and patted Didier's hand, loving his fierce tone. "When does Tank get back?"

"A week." Mac whistled loudly.

I was afraid to ask what was going on now. "This requires a Plan B."

"More like G or Z," Fab mumbled.

"Are any of his relations currently staying in one of the cottages?" I asked.

"Another tidbit I'm to pass along—he's immune to blackmail." Mac sighed. "Cruz covered all the bases when he issued his stay-away orders. He didn't specifically mention knowing that four of his aunts and uncles checked in three days ago, but since he's got his nose in everything…"

"Let the relations know that I'll be over right before lunch and am requesting a sit-down out by the pool. Text me their names. I'm not Fab and can't get away with 'Hey you.'" I wrinkled my nose at the woman, who smirked back. "Not sure if they know about Crum; if not, mum's the word. I'm certain all the guests will be asking questions when he doesn't show up to teach half-naked yoga." Or whatever he had going on at the moment. He claimed variety kept them hungry for more. I'd taken a softer stance since he helped me out and tried not to squash too much of his fun, as long as it didn't venture into anything illegal.

"Before we hang up, there's one more thing…" Mac paused. "Take me off speaker."

"She'll just have to repeat it," Fab huffed.

"It's personal."

I picked up the phone and did as she requested. "You're okay, aren't you?"

"I'm not sick or anything. Just need to talk to you for a few away from Fab. You'll understand when we have our chat."

"No hints?"

"It's better this way," Mac said in an evasive tone.

"One more thing before we hang up—get Rude to teach this morning's poolside exercise class. If anyone could match Crum's level of outrageousness, it'd be her. Anyone asks about Crum, make something up."

"Good idea."

I hung up, set my phone down, and turned my attention to all the eyes focused on me. "All I know is Mac has a personal issue. You know that people will talk to me about anything." Having that ability made for more than a few awkward situations.

Fab rolled her eyes. It was hard not to laugh.

"I'm afraid to ask what you're planning." Creole nudged me.

"I'm making a mental checklist. You'll just have to trust me."

Creole and Didier groaned.

I grinned at them.

"Don't worry, guys," Fab said. "I'll go along with her and make sure she stays out of trouble." They laughed, knowing that between the two of us, the situation could easily explode.

Chapter Two

Fab donned a black sundress and chose a sexy pair of heels, since she had the talent of being able to run in shoes of any height. I selected slides that went with my rust-colored spaghetti-strap dress, both of which passed muster under her eagle eye. I accessorized with my Glock and she with her Walther. We'd found out on several occasions that it sucked to be caught off guard.

We hopped into the Hummer, and Fab took the direct route across town, each of us caught up in our own thoughts. She pulled up to The Cottages and slowed for a look around before cruising into the driveway and parking in front of the office.

"All appears to be quiet." I got out and scanned the porches of the cottages, glancing over at the apartment building I also owned. I'd hired Gertrude Banner, aka Rude, as the manager, and she ran the property like a drill sergeant, not the least bit embarrassed to get up in someone's business when she should be minding her own. It worked out well for me, since she kept any antics from getting out of control. Her maybe-one-day husband, Cootie, worked for the guys at The Boardwalk, a family-and-friends real estate venture.

"Have you put the finishing touches on one of your plans?" Fab asked as she rounded the rear bumper, joining me. "I know you're still fixated on getting Cruz to rep Crum, but I think you should go with Didier's idea—get another lawyer to show up at the bail hearing, and when Tank gets back, sign him up. We both know he's way easier to work with and doesn't have a snotty assistant to lecture us on our imperfections."

"Susie likes you better than me. So maybe…"

Fab furiously shook her head.

The thought of going toe to toe with Susie had me grimacing. Most, if not all, of our past encounters had gone south in a big hurry. She hated us showing up unannounced and was no less annoyed when we made an appearance at a scheduled appointment.

"I'm going to keep my promise to Creole not to engage with Cruz and let others do my dirty work. If they deliver, I'm going to pony up a night of fun and games."

"You're not the only one making promises. Creole made me promise not to let you veer off into a ditch. I nodded reassuringly; it was the best I had in the moment."

"Especially if said ditch has water in it. It would ruin my dress." I flicked my hand down the front.

The office door flew open, stopping short of

bashing a hole in the wall. Mac came storming out in a flowing red sundress with a big yellow bee print, her bright-yellow tennis shoes with bug faces on the toes—and yes, matching socks—slapping the ground, a red umbrella drink in her hand. "You better bring your A-game for this sit-down you had me orchestrate. They're so excited about the private tête-à-tête that if it's not good, I'll get the finger of blame." Mac continued in a huff: "I don't want to be subjected to all-around grumbling, first from the guests that didn't get an invite and then from the relatives, who will unleash incessant peevishness if the meeting's a snore and keep it up until they check out."

Our heads turned at the sound of a horn blast, followed by a taxi blowing into the driveway and screeching to a stop.

I glared at the driver, who dismissed me with a brief glance, his arrogance on full display. He couldn't care less what anyone thought of his driving or whether they wondered if he was drunk off his butt. I calmed some, figuring out that he was just a bad driver.

After a minute, the back door opened and Joseph rolled out, lurched over to the bushes, and barfed. The driver backed out the same way he arrived, his tires taking a beating as he squealed down the road.

I'd inherited two tenants along with the property—Joseph and Miss January. Each had a myriad of health issues that were supposed to shorten their life span, a diagnosis that had gone in one ear and out the other as they toasted each day with a shot of their favorite liquor and a smoke.

Mac went running over. "Do you have vomit on you?" she yelled at the man hanging his head in the flower bed.

Neither Fab nor I could hear the answer and silently agreed that we weren't moving any closer. The answer must've been no, as Mac helped the man to his feet and extended a hand to his girlfriend, who was handcuffed to his wrist. Svetlana had gone limp in places and was in need of air again. The sexy blonde would be upset to know she wasn't looking her best, though the skimpy outfit accentuated her curvy figure.

"If Crum were here, he'd get out the compressor machine, thingy, whatever, and get Svet pumped back up. Unless you want to do it?" I turned to Fab.

"I'll pass." Fab stared off after Mac but stopped short of offering to help get Joseph to his front door. If that offer had ever been a remote possibility, it was off the table when he stopped to barf again. "I'm thinking Svet's going to need a good scrubbing."

"I don't want to be late for my appointment." I tapped my wrist as though I'd put on a watch, which I hadn't, and took off in a near sprint to the pool, Fab hot on my heels. We got to the gate, and as I entered the code, I said, "You need to trot out the charm, no matter how lame you think my idea is. They're going to be more impressed with you sitting down for a chat than me. You come off all slinky and sexy; most don't know how deadly you can be." I smiled at the two men and two women sitting on the other side of the pool.

Fab grinned. "You can stop with the compliments; I'm not letting you out of my sight."

"Oh no." I lowered my voice. "Mac forgot to text me their names."

"You smile. I've got it covered." Fab took over, introducing herself to the foursome, and they introduced themselves, excited but also suspicious.

I was happy that they'd chosen a table under the thatched umbrella at the tiki bar, out of the sun. We sat across from them.

"I would like it if you would keep this first part in confidence," I started, having decided on the direct approach. They nodded and reassured me that they would. "Crum is in jail for a murder he didn't commit." Now I had their complete attention. "He's got a bail hearing coming up in a couple of days, and Cruz refuses to represent him because..." I crossed my lips with my finger. "Another tidbit we won't share with anyone." They all nodded. I swore they moved forward. "Crum and Grandmother Campion did the horizontal hula."

They were silent for a few seconds, and then they all started laughing.

Once they stopped, they exchanged raised eyebrows all around, and Ruth Campion leaned forward. "How can we help?"

"I have a proposition for you." They all nodded with enthusiasm without having heard a word yet, and I knew they were in. "I'd like you to get on the phone and complain to your beloved nephew that I'm throwing you out on the street." One of the uncles snorted.

"This will be fun." Cruz's Aunt Sara nodded. "We've all got his private number, and he answers unless he's in court. We'll yammer on and on." She clapped.

Butch Campion growl-chuckled. "What's in it for us?"

"You name the night, and a car will pick you up and take you to Jake's for a night of fun and entertainment." I'd need to get hot on the phone—no...in person would be better—and make that happen. Bribe my employees to bring their A-weirdness.

Sam Campion flung his arm around Ruth, who I assumed to be his wife. "We'll let the little missy here orchestrate everything and tell us what to say." He smiled at her.

"Make me the bad guy—tell him that I was absolutely awful. Then suggest that he call Mac to deal with the problem. If he had to deal with me, he'd probably just send someone to kill me." I flinched.

The two women rubbed their hands together. "This is going to be fun," they said to each other.

"We'll tell him to put a stop to our eviction, as we don't want to go anywhere else." Sara fake-sobbed, and it sounded like the real thing.

Fab was clearly impressed.

Mac came storming through the gate. "What did I miss?" she asked in exasperation. "It's hard dealing with a barfer." She flung herself in a chair.

"No…what did we miss?" Ruth asked.

"Joseph lost his breakfast. He shouldn't go to the doctor's drunk. I made him strip down to his underwear, hosed him off, and sent him inside. I rescued Svet—she's propped up in a chair in my office—and threw his smelly clothes in the washer. Don't worry—I'll run the machine through a bleach cycle when I'm done," she assured the guests.

"Once Joseph's feeling up to it, a little fresh air and sunshine might do him good," Sara said.

So would laying off the booze. I smiled lamely.

Ruth stood. "Let's go inside. We'll each make a call, so we can hear what the others say." She motioned their husbands to follow. "I'll report to Mac once we're done. Don't you worry—we'll do such a good job that he'll do anything to keep us from calling every five minutes."

"Thank you." I waved.

Fab updated Mac.

"That's a great idea. When he calls, and let's hope he does, I'll say that there was nothing I could do to stop you." Mac nodded, liking her idea. "Are you going to be able to deliver at Jake's?"

"My employees are always looking for a way to ratchet up the excitement. I have no doubt that they'll sauce it up. Let me know the night and how many. They can invite whoever they want if they can pull this off."

Fab pulled her ringing phone out of her pocket, glanced at the screen, and backed up to take the call.

"We probably only have a few minutes." Mac eyed Fab. "Gunz is negotiating—some would say strong-arming—the old goat down the street. He wants to buy the man's property."

I groaned inwardly. "Which one?"

"Opposite side of the street, down at the end—the house that looks like it's been kicked in the teeth."

"I know the one."

"I didn't think you'd want Gunz moving into your territory. Unless I'm wrong?" Mac arched her brow.

"You're not wrong. You have any clue why he wants to buy here? Usually he picks up foreclosures, auctioned properties on the outskirts of town." I mulled over what Mac had told me.

"If you want, I can arrange for you to meet the owner. I know him." Mac preened.

Who on the block didn't she know? But I didn't point that out.

"Eugene thinks Gunz is a greasy toad. The renters he's got in there are a pain in his...and he wants out. He plans to skip to the Villages and hang out with retired folks that still have most of their marbles."

"Fab is going to be on top of us in a second." I squinted at her. "Call Xander and tell him to research the property and get back to me. Pronto. He won't be offended, as he's used to everything being a rush."

Fab and I had hit paydirt, getting Xander Huntington as our Information Specialist. He never said no to any request we made, and he had an easygoing attitude.

"What did I miss?" Fab walked up, shoving her phone in her pocket and giving us an evil stare.

"Nothing," Mac said, which had Fab staring harder. Mac ignored her.

"Let me know if Cruz caves to my blackmail attempt," I said.

"I've got an idea that might make everyone happy...as much as can be," Mac said. "I'll call Susie and have her suggest to Cruz that he send another lawyer to the hearing, but it has to be a good one. That way, Cruz will be happy that he doesn't have to put out. And you'll be happy, not having to worry about who you're getting to stand in for Tank."

"Have Susie pitch the idea and claim it as her own," Fab said.

"Good one. I like your idea a lot." I nodded at her. "If it works, send Susie a thank-you gift and sign just your name." Fab tapped her foot, letting me know our presence was needed elsewhere. "Anything at all, call me."

The three of us walked back to the office, Mac going inside with a wave while Fab and I got in the Hummer.

Chapter Three

"Before you tell me about the job…" I pulled my phone out and called Xander. I also wanted to stave off her asking questions about my conversation with Mac, which probably wouldn't work for long.

"Mac just called and told me what you want, and I'm on it," Xander said upon answering.

"I have another job for you." I went on to relay what I knew of Crum's arrest. "Would you dig up anything you can find out about Travis West? I want to know everything. Also check out his law firm. Maybe we can figure who his enemies were—there was at least one motivated to get rid of him. Also, while you're digging around, if you discover a link to Crum other than the one we know about, forward that to me as well."

"I'll put together a file and email it over ASAP."

"You're the best." We hung up. I looked up and was surprised to see that Fab had turned into Tropical Slumber Funeral Home. Next time, I'd ask questions in advance, not that it would change the outcome. "So what's up?" I asked as she pulled up to the red carpet and parked. The parking lot was empty, which signaled no send-offs in the next few hours. The first sign of an impending service would have been the hearse sitting out front.

Dickie and Raul had bought the business a number of years ago and transformed the old drive-thru hot dog stand, which had already undergone several transformations, still further, turning it into a thriving funeral business. They strove to offer every trick you could imagine to send your loved one off to the afterlife and were always open to new ideas. The men boasted that they had requests for their services from all over the state.

"Drama," Fab said, as though that answered my question. "Raul called, frantic to see us. He didn't part with any details, and I didn't wear him down with questions. You know they both like it when we stop by."

The front door opened, and Raul beckoned us inside. Dickie popped his head over the other man's shoulder and waved. The two couldn't be more different. Raul—average height with a bodybuilder's physique—was the approachable one with an easy smile who handled their business affairs. Dickie—well over six feet, painfully thin, and uncomfortable in his own body—was the artist. We'd developed our friendship over the years, often traded favors, and never said no to any of their requests.

"I hope this isn't about us providing security

for another funeral," I said as I got out and followed Fab inside, claiming the plastic slip-covered chair next to the door. If one of the dead came out of the nearby hallway, I'd be the first one out the door. I nodded at Dickie, who appeared paler than usual, if that was possible. He held his hands in front of him, wringing them back and forth. I smiled reassuringly.

Fab poked her head in the main room and immediately backed out. She couldn't just sit down and get to the point of why we were here—not without a snoop around first.

"There's no one displayed for viewing," Raul announced. "Not until tomorrow."

The guys were used to Fab poking her nose in every room and waited patiently while she had a look around before taking a seat. "How can we help you gentleman?" she asked. "You sounded a bit frantic."

"We'll do anything we can for you," I said.

Dickie lowered his large frame into a chair with a loud sigh.

"We had a funeral yesterday. The deceased, Mabel Griffin, was wearing an impressive diamond ring, and well, when we got to the cemetery, the daughter remembered that she wanted it back. We opened the coffin, and it was gone." Raul unleashed a big sigh.

"Gone? You mean one of the guests..." I choked on a swallowed laugh. Fab sent me the *behave* stare.

"That's exactly what must have happened," Dickie said in a semi-shriek. "We would never–"

"I never thought for a second that either of you would pilfer from the deceased," I said.

Both men smiled their thanks at me.

"Start at the beginning, or better yet, the last time one of you actually saw the ring," Fab said.

"The daughter brought the ring to me before the service and wanted me to put it on her mother." Dickie mimed sliding a ring on his finger. "She and I went into the main room before any of the guests arrived, and I did just that while she watched. I thought maybe she was squeamish—most people are—but in the end, she leaned in and kissed Mabel."

I squirmed in my seat. Another glare from Fab. *Yes, Mother.*

"I take it that the guests were directed to file by and pay their respects?" Fab asked.

Raul nodded. "Neither of us thought about the ring again, since the daughter didn't mention wanting it back. It didn't occur to me to do a final check before closing the coffin, as we've never had anything go missing before."

"Were you the ones to transport Mabel to the cemetery?" Fab asked. Raul nodded again. "When did you reopen the casket?"

"We waited until the guests had dispersed."

"I didn't think about this before..." Fab spun in a circle, checking out the corners of the room. "Do you by chance have security cameras?"

Both men grumbled, "No."

"We'll rectify that the next funeral-free day you have." Fab nodded and scanned the room once more. "I'll get my guy to come out. I'm sure he'll add to my recommendations, and then we'll get everything installed. If this ever happens again…" She paused, seeing the horror on their faces. "Not that it would, but better to be prepared."

"Do you have any suspects?" I asked.

"Troopie said—" Raul started.

"Who?" Fab and I asked at the same time.

"The daughter. It's a family name—she was named after her father, Trooper," Dickie said. "He's also deceased."

"Neither Dickie nor I noticed anything unusual," Raul said. "But Troopie didn't have a problem coming up with a couple of likely suspects."

"You want me to go point my gun in their faces and hope one of them confesses?" Fab shot up the room with her fingers.

Dickie and Raul looked horrified.

I laughed, those silent admonitions to behave out the door.

"Troopie threatened to sue if we can't recover the ring," Raul said in a hushed tone.

"How do you know it wasn't Troopie who snatched up the ring and is now pointing the finger to cover up what she did?" I asked.

"We don't." Raul shrugged. "That's why our

first call was to the two of you. Our plan is to hire you to locate the ring and return it to its rightful owner."

I stared up at the ceiling, hoping no one could hear the groan that escaped.

"Do you have a picture of the ring in question?" Fab asked.

"I always snap a few pictures in case a loved one comes back, wanting a remembrance." Raul fished out his phone and flicked through the screen before handing it too Fab. She checked it out, and based on her movements, I guessed her to be forwarding the pics to herself.

"How many people did Troopie finger as the likely culprits?" I asked.

Dickie held up three fingers.

"Does that include Troopie herself?" I asked. "Stranger things have happened."

Dickie shook his head. He was quieter than usual today—must be the stress. He didn't like problems of any kind.

"You know..." All eyes turned to me. "Maybe the best solution is to have a lookalike ring made that can be passed off as the real thing."

"I'm guessing that Troopie's going to want someone fingered for the crime," Fab said.

"I hate to be a downer..." Fab snorted, which I ignored. "Okay, hot shot." I turned on her. "Your gun idea is the only one so far that's likely to produce results...unless you have another hair-raising idea that you're holding back on. Heads up: I'm not going to jail. My idea of a fake ring is better."

"Wait until you see the size of the stone." She sniffed.

"Did Troopie seem more interested in getting money from a lawsuit or getting the ring back?" I asked.

Dickie shook his head. "She seemed very sincere in wanting the ring back. She mentioned it being a family heirloom."

"Since there's only three names, we'll run our door-to-door scam. See what we can find out." Fab sounded proud of her impromptu plan.

"My lost cat again?" I made a surprised face. "I can print up a few flyers, since I still have a copy of the one from the last scam we ran. People are more sympathetic to my missing Poochy than our selling candy or making an attempt to save their souls."

"Please don't call your missing cat Poochy. Sounds fake," Fab said.

I saluted, biting back a laugh.

"Even if nothing comes of this, we appreciate that neither of you ever turns down one of our requests or refers to us as weird, like some people." Raul made a face.

"Anyone ever makes fun of you, calls you names, let me know. I'll send Fab to pay them a visit and beat the spit out of them."

Both men smiled at Fab as she air-boxed. "You have the names of the possible perps… What about their addresses?"

Dickie stood, removed a sheet of paper from his shirt pocket, and handed it to Fab.

"They're all women." Fab scanned the list. "And local."

"New plan." I waved, which amused Dickie and Raul. "We take your husband, have him take off his shirt, and say we're running a poll."

Fab laughed…and continued to laugh. Finally, she said, "You pitch the idea to him."

"You can bet I will. Our husbands are always saying they're willing to help anytime. Time to pony up."

"We'll get right on this. It may take a day or two, as we have a couple of other cases," Fab told the two. "I'll let you know as soon as we learn something, helpful or not."

More cases? If we had anything on other than Crum, this was the first I was hearing about it. "That reminds me." I turned my attention to the duo. "Crum's been accused of Travis West's murder. Anything you can find out would be helpful. Maybe ask your coroner friend? Not sure what he'd know, but it's worth a try."

"We're having the West funeral here the day after tomorrow," Dickie said. "A friend already delivered an expensive suit for him to be buried in."

"Can you get a camera installed before then?" I asked Fab. It was a better option than sitting through a stranger's funeral, which we'd done before but both of us tried to avoid.

Fab nodded. "My guy owes me, and for now, we just need one or two in the main room."

"Do you do a guest book?" I asked, feeling like I should know the answer.

"We certainly do," Raul said.

"Snap pictures of the signatures before you hand it over to the family," I said. "It would be interesting to know who shows up."

"If we hear any good gossip, we'll let you know," Dickie said. "Guests tend to air their feelings at final send-offs."

Fab stood. "Don't worry; we'll figure this out, and I'll keep you updated."

I rose and was halfway out the door before slowing and turning to wave. I didn't race to the car, but close.

Fab wasn't far behind me. "Did you have to sprint out of there?"

"Look, Pot, you wanted out as badly as I did. Once you stood up, that meant time to go as far as I was concerned."

Fab backed out and honked at the two men waving from the doorway.

I leaned back against the seat. "What a day."

Chapter Four

Fab flew out of the parking lot and cut over to the main highway, turning in the opposite direction from home.

"Another job? Client? What?" I asked.

"Do we have secrets?" Fab weaved around a slow driver, leaving them in the dust.

At least her treating the road like her own racetrack didn't make me sick anymore. "No, we don't. At least I hope not."

"Then what were you and Mac talking about? Don't say 'nothing.'"

"As long as you agree not to discuss it with anyone. Your husband would be okay, since when mine finds out, yours will know."

Fab held up her pinkie finger, and I linked mine through hers.

"This has to do with your favorite client." I took a long pull on my water bottle and went on to tell her everything that Mac had confided about the property down the street. "Your client wanting to snap it off the market doesn't sit well with me. Do I have a good reason? Not really. I just don't want him lumbering around the neighborhood."

"Hmm..." Fab mused. "It's weird that Gunz never said anything. I'd have thought he'd have called me, since he always has me check out properties, he's interested in. Why not this one?"

"My guess is that he didn't want me to find out, not knowing how I would respond. Just means I don't have to feel bad about snatching it out from under him."

"I'm surprised you're interested."

"As Mac was relating what was going on, I began feeling territorial. I hadn't previously thought about buying up every property on the block, even though I already own the two, but today may have changed my mind. I'll need to run it by Creole, but once he hears Gunz's name, I can't imagine he'd be opposed. His feelings towards the man are a lot like your husband's—lukewarm at best. They both think Gunz is always up to something illegal, despite his protests to the contrary."

"The upside to working for Gunz is that he doesn't knowingly send us out on anything dangerous, unlike other clients I've had, who couldn't care less. It's not their mugs looking down the barrel of a gun."

I didn't point out that most of Gunz's jobs came with a certain amount of trouble. "I'm moving forward, looking into the property, but I don't want my snatching it out from under his big behind to bring hard feelings back on you." I stared out the window, realizing Fab had never answered the *Where are we going?* question.

"It could turn out the other way around—him besting you. Then what?"

"If you're asking if I'm going to hold it against you, the answer is unequivocally no. And judging by your smirk, you knew that."

Fab turned off the highway, and I knew right where we were. What did she have up her sleeve? She slowed at the gates of Travis West's mansion and checked out what she could see of the property, which wasn't much. The house was barely visible from the street.

"I was thinking…" She tapped the steering wheel with her finger as she continued down the street, checking out the neighborhood as though we hadn't done it more than a few times when we were attempting to motivate West into buying the neighboring property. There was no sign that there'd ever been a fire on the lot where the Taco Wagon used to sit, and the parking lot had been removed and grass planted.

"Before you start concocting what surely will be a felony, here's a heads up—it's broad daylight." I ignored her snort at the obvious. "You pull up and park, and the neighbors are going to be craning their necks out the window. The ones that can see his property anyway." I twisted in my seat and counted two, maybe three, houses that could monitor comings and goings.

"We need to get inside." Fab U-turned and

crawled down the street again. "We'll have to come back at night or early morning."

"Are you tired of having sex?"

"Okay, smarty, you come up with something to get the husbands on board." Fab snapped her fingers. "And make it that fast."

"I say that we—"

Fab waved me off. "There is no we; it's all you." She powered down the window and snapped a couple of pictures, then cruised out of the neighborhood and turned towards home.

I checked the clock on the dashboard and called Creole. "Hey, hon," I said when he answered. Dead silence. Sometimes, it wasn't an upside for your husband to know every trick in your arsenal. And I swore he had mind-reading skills. "You got dinner planned?"

"I'm still at the office." Creole's tone told me he was waiting for me to get to the good part. That would come later.

"Amazing wife that I am, tacos are on the way. So you and Didier might want to pokey your… Just pokey, and we'll see you at home." I blew a kiss through the phone and hung up.

"You know he's already complaining to Didier that we're up to something."

I called Jake's, the bar I owned in the middle of town. Just so happened that we served the best Mexican food around and had awards decorating the walls to show for it. I placed an order with Cook for one of his taco platter extravaganzas. It wasn't on the menu, but it was understood that he'd make sure there was enough to feed an army and would include everything we liked. One of his kin would make the delivery.

"Let's see if I'm understanding this plan of yours... Feed and liquor them up. Then what?"

"We..." At Fab's raised eyebrows, I amended. "I... Happy now?" I didn't wait for an answer. "I'm going to take the straightforward approach. Toss in a bit of guilt." I flashed her a big phony smile.

"If it works, I'll take credit. If not, you're on your own."

"That's a sucky plan. If you're going to take credit, then you're in it all the way. If the plan collapses, oh well. Maybe next time."

Fab exited the highway onto an unassuming street that cut through a forest of trees and appeared to go nowhere, which was the way we liked it. She hit a button on the visor, and the security gates to what we affectionately called the compound rolled back. Creole and I had originally lived at one end of the street before buying one of the three other residences dotted along the other end. This was after Fab had eyed the house at the far end of the block when house hunting; at which point, her papa had swept in, bought up the block, and installed fencing.

My phone started to ring as Fab pulled into my driveway, and I wasn't surprised to see Mac's face. "Good news?" I asked when I answered. "Putting you on speaker."

"Cruz wasn't happy when his private line started blowing up every six seconds, and after the first two calls, he told Susie to deal with it. She used my idea, and Crum now has an attorney for the bail hearing." From the excitement in Mac's voice, she was happy. "And not to worry, he's a good one—I asked and then had Xander run a check. Susie got a bonus for making it so Cruz didn't have to listen to any more complaints. He told her he only half-believed the stories of his relatives' belongings being tossed in the street and was convinced that you'd bribed them. Which Susie claims impressed Cruz, but he would never admit it."

"You're the best."

"There's more," Mac said breathlessly. "Kevin called in a favor and got me a jail visit for tomorrow, so I can update Crum in person."

"That was nice of Deputy Cory. I'll remember to have more patience the next time I see him."

I had history with the sheriff's deputy. First, his sister dated my brother. Then his neighbor had a cooking accident when the meth he was stirring caught fire and burned the building down. And my do-gooder brother (runs in the family) moved him into The Cottages when my back was turned. You'd think that would have made us besties. Hardly. Too many times when law enforcement got a call for something Fab or I, or both of us, were involved in, he drew the short straw.

"Don't worry, I got Kevin covered. Food is the best way to get on his good side."

"Men. They're so easy."

We laughed and hung up.

Fab and I got out of the SUV and went into the house.

I dropped my purse on the entry bench and headed straight to the kitchen. "I'm going to set the table outside. Why waste what's going to be a beautiful sunset?"

The two of us managed to set everything up and toss down a drink before the guys rolled in, food in hand—they'd met the delivery man in the driveway.

"Isn't this fun—all of us together for morning coffee and now dinner?" I smiled sweetly.

Didier dropped a kiss on his wife's cheek and said, "Can't wait to hear how your day went, since we didn't get a call."

We had a rule that sometimes got ignored: anything happens, whether it could be construed as good or bad—call.

"It's not like we shot anyone. Or did we?" I winked at Fab, who shook her head. "Seriously, it was quite the day. You might want to wait for an update until you have a full stomach."

We filled our plates and tabled all serious talk until we finished our food. It was an amazing evening to sit outside; there was a stray breeze, and the water gently lapped the shore.

Finally, Fab updated the husbands on the day. She told them that Crum now had representation for his bail hearing and how it'd happened, then moved on to the property that Gunz wanted to acquire.

Creole turned to me. "Let me guess—you want to add to our real estate portfolio?"

"If it's a good deal, why not? Part of me doesn't feel the least bit bad about irking Gunz, but truthfully, I don't think I'd feel any differently if it were someone else. I know everyone on the block. Not *know* know, but I could pick them out in a lineup."

Creole smirked. "You check it out, and any decision you make is fine with me. You need muscle, I'm your man."

"Funny you should say that..."

"New job today," Fab announced. She was saving her breaking-and-entering idea for last, as she went on to relate the details of the call from Raul and Dickie.

"Who steals off dead people?" Didier asked, clearly not sure he believed the story. "If one of these women has it, how are you going to get her to hand it over?"

"Madison came up with a good con." Fab grinned at me. "It would probably get us in the door, though that might be a long shot, cuz who invites a stranger in for a chat?"

"Can't wait to hear." Didier turned his ice-blue eyes on me.

"Poochy, my cat, is missing." I wiped the corner of my eyes and sniffed. "I'll hand them a flyer. No need for them to know it's one I've recycled a few times."

Creole laughed.

"I thought you banned eye-rolling at your house," I said to Didier in response to his and got an exasperated frown in return. "Or we could wait for them to leave the house and then go in and toss it."

"I vote that your funeral friends call these women in one at a time and negotiate a payoff to the thief in exchange for the ring's return," Creole said.

"Is that your non-confrontational way of saying that my Poochy plan sucks?" I eyed him.

"How many times have you gone looking for this cat you can't seem to keep an eye on, sold bogus school candy, or other con jobs?" Didier asked. "And how well have they turned out?"

"Help me here." I nudged Creole. He shook his head. "Unfortunately, I don't keep stats on these jobs of your *wife's*."

"Eee," Fab squealed. "Injuries over here."

"We can compare tire marks later." I met her stare. "That brings us to our final adventure of the day."

"I'm certain we haven't settled all the outstanding issues," Creole said.

"Sure we have." I maintained eye contact and managed not to laugh when I caught Fab's smirk.

"Where was I?" I squinted at Creole. "Oh yes…we detoured by the West mansion, and you'll be happy to know that, while we slowed to a crawl for a look, we didn't get out." I ignored both men's groans. "Since my tenant is charged with his murder, I'd like to have a look around the crime scene."

"No." Didier slapped his hand on the table.

"Illegal," Creole stopped short of snapping.

"That's why…" I tapped my temple. "Thinking again." The smirk was a good sign; Creole wasn't too mad. "I know an ex-cop, and I bet he has plenty of shifty skills he hasn't used in a while. He could get us in and out without ending up in cuffs. He should thank me for looking out for him, not wanting his skills to get rusty."

"My wife is not going," Didier said adamantly.

"Don't get your shorts in a bunch, Frenchie." He laughed—much to his disgust, I was certain. "Look, you two. You're always telling us that anytime we need you, you're there for us. You failed to mention legalities, so that's on you two. I'm being upfront, pitching the plan, and your answer is just no?"

"You're inside, then what?" Creole asked.

"Do a walk-through, take pictures." I looked to Fab for confirmation. She nodded.

"How is that going to be helpful to Crum's case?" Creole asked.

"It might be a total waste of time… Or it might tell us a little more about West and lead us in the right direction to locate another suspect." I glared at Fab. "Jump in anytime."

Creole nodded at Didier. "What's your verdict?"

"Are you going to do this no matter what we say?" Didier asked Fab.

"Probably," I answered for her. "I recall running into you a time or two, poking around people's houses," I said to Creole.

"As the member of law enforcement you spoke of earlier, I had a legal right to be there. It's called a court order."

"That's why you're the best man for the job. To lead the team."

Both Creole and Didier shook their heads, then conversed in guy shorthand.

"We'll do it," Didier said finally. "As long you agree to do what you're told."

"Probably going to regret agreeing to that provision, but okay," I said. Fab nodded.

"Tomorrow night, then," Creole said. "That will give me a day to do a drive-by. I already think this is a bad idea. If after checking out the property, I think it's not doable, then we're agreed that it's not happening."

Fab and I stared at him. He must have noticed that neither of us responded, but he didn't call us out on it.

"Back to your cat scam," Didier said. "When's

that going to happen?"

"Here's hoping you've got time to come up with a better name than Poochy." The twitch of Creole's lips let me know he thought he was amusing.

"Told you," Fab said.

Now she speaks up.

"I'm thinking tomorrow's going to be busy," Fab added. "We'll take care of the job in the morning. The funeral guys are freaked out that the woman, Troopie or something, might call in the cops."

Chapter Five

Fab and I decided, before she dragged her disgruntled husband home, that we'd get an early start on our hunt for the missing ring.

"I appreciate the good job you did on trying to guilt Didier and me into saying yes to your scheme," Creole said.

"Some would say that's a half-assed compliment."

Creole's blues bored into me. "I'd appreciate it even more if after you've cooked up one of these schemes and realized that there's a chance, they might get you arrested, you'd forget about it. Jail visits don't appeal to me."

"How about instead of promising I'll never do it again, I super swear to tell you about it *ahead* of time?"

"As long as we're agreed on before and not after."

We shook on it and then kissed.

The next morning, Fab sent a text that she was on the way over. I picked up my purse and briefcase and gave myself a second glance in the mirror, checking out the full skirt that I'd paired with a tee top to cover the Glock holstered at the small of my back. I slid into my tennis shoes and stuffed flip-flops in my bag. The guys had left earlier. Fab strolled in through the patio doors as I walked into the kitchen. She turned and locked them behind her.

I checked her over, decked out in a pencil skirt, button-down, and a pair of sensible heels that I'd have never thought she'd own. "What's up?"

"Forget the cat business. I've got a better idea." She scrutinized me from head to toe. "I'll explain on the way to the first stop."

"As long as the first stop is coffee. I need it if you want me to be my usual perky self."

"You're on."

We hopped into the Hummer, and Fab roared out of the compound and over to the coffee drive-thru, ordered our favorite drinks, and slid into a parking space.

I flipped off the lid, appreciative that she'd had the foresight to add extra whipped cream to mine, and took a long drink, inwardly sighing in appreciation. "I come up with these great plans that you ixnay for...exactly what have you concocted?"

"Here's a new one—the truth. Sort of, anyway. Bang the door down, trot out the professional no-nonsense tone, and announce we're investigating the missing ring." Barely a breath—she was on a roll. "Not giving them the opportunity to speak, we launch into the consequences of not returning said ring—jail, fines, public humiliation. I won't be accusatory in a direct way; I'll work up a vague alternative before we get there."

"No wonder you needed a triple shot of espresso—all that planning." I almost laughed as her smirk slipped. "You're not worried about getting kicked off the stoop and them calling the cops?"

"I'll let my badge do the talking. That way, they'll think they're already talking to law enforcement without me having to say anything. I can't help what people believe."

"The PI badge that looks cop-like if you squint?" I ignored her intense stare. "As your partner, trainee, whatever this week, I'll stand by your side, befuddled look on my face, obviously in over my head."

Fab backed out, rolled down the window, and recycled the cups before hitting the highway. "First stop, Mrs. Porter's house. She was a close friend of Mabel Griffin—you know, the deceased. According to Raul, all the guests were either close friends or family."

"We're going on the word of Mabel's daughter, who may or may not know what she's talking about. More and more, I like Creole's idea."

"What? Sit home and do nothing?" She waved me off. "I don't want to know."

Fab, the human road map, rolled up to a small stucco house that had been around for at least seventy years and wasn't in bad shape. She parked at the curb, and we got out and strolled up the walkway. Seconds later, loud screams came from inside the house, sounding like a female in extreme distress. We both drew our weapons and ran to the door. Fab tried the knob, which turned. On the floor was an older woman, attempting to cover her face while a cat, an oversized tabby the size of a mini elephant, stood on her chest.

"Help me," the woman screamed, flailing around on the floor.

Throwing open the door had startled the cat, which took a flying leap, landing in the entry, then leapt to freedom. I stepped around the back of the door, where I'd taken cover, closed it, and reholstered my weapon.

The woman cried and whimpered, covering her face, blood trickling through her fingers. Fab helped her to her feet and into a chair while I called 911.

"Such a pretty cat," the woman whimpered. "I thought he was hungry, coaxed him inside and fed him, and then the bounder turned on me. I just know he was going to eat me."

The enormous feet on the "cat" would've been a good first clue that he wouldn't make a good house pet, his overall size another.

At Fab's gesture, I ran to the kitchen and grabbed a glass of water and a roll of paper towels. I handed the woman the water and shoved the roll into Fab's hand. Not wanting to go outside, in case the cat hadn't gone far, I peered out the blinds and was relieved to see the ambulance roll up. "Paramedics are here." Not waiting for a response, I ran outside and met them on the walkway, telling them what we'd seen as they hustled into the house.

Fab came out and joined me. "I can't believe you left me in there."

"You're better with blood than me."

We turned as a cop car pulled up behind the ambulance and parked.

Kevin Cory got out and strolled up. "I'm absolutely shocked to see the two of you here."

"Didn't your mother give you the sarcasm talk?" I almost pointed my finger, but at the last minute shoved it behind my back.

"There was no need because I was a perfect child."

I chuckled at that one.

Fab had perfected her poker face.

The paramedics were back, having loaded Mrs. Porter on the stretcher, and rolled her down the walkway.

"Could you ask her if there's anyone she wants us to call?" I asked one of them.

"She's hysterical. Keeps asking for her daughter."

"I'll figure it out and make sure she gets a call. Taking her to Tarpon Cove hospital?" She nodded, and they loaded her into the ambulance.

"We should make sure the door's locked."

"What happened here?" Kevin asked.

Fab told him what we'd seen.

Kevin groaned. "My guess, it was that lynx—we've had several sightings. A couple of folks had the same hands-on experience and are lucky to still have their hands. He starts out friendly, then gets aggressive. Animal Control thinks that someone thought it would make a great pet and when it got too much to handle, let it go." His tone let us know what a stupid idea he thought that was. "Would've been nice if they'd called Animal Control, who would've informed them that the pet idea was a bad one. If they had, it would already have been taken to a nearby zoo until they figured out what to do next. They can't relocate it to a natural habitat around here, as there isn't one."

"I just hope someone doesn't end up shooting it," I said.

"What are you two doing here? Friends of Mrs. Porter?" Kevin asked.

"Just checking on her," I said. "A good friend of hers died last week, and we wanted to see how she was doing."

Kevin nodded. "You two are lucky—if it was the lynx, and it probably was—that it didn't turn on you."

"If that had happened, you wouldn't have to worry about looking for it," Fab said. "If I'd thought I was in danger, I wouldn't have hesitated to shoot. Especially after one look at Mrs. Porter's face covered in blood."

I shuddered.

"Nice of you to arrange Crum's bail and line up an attorney." Kevin nodded his approval. "Be interesting to see if the district attorney has the evidence to back up the murder charge."

"Tank's his attorney," I told him, even though I knew that Mac kept him updated. "If you could point to any exculpatory evidence, that would be beyond cool of you. Keeping in mind that the old guy is a friend of yours."

Kevin ignored me and headed up the walkway. "I'm going to check out the inside and make sure it gets locked up."

Once Fab and I were in the car, I said, "You need to call Raul. He can track down Mrs. Porter's family through Mabel's daughter."

Fab got on the phone and relayed what went down. Raul assured her that he'd get on it and make the call. They hung up. "Next on the list," she said, a little too cheerfully.

I groaned. "I don't want to go."

Chapter Six

Fab pulled up in front of a shotgun-style shack. The yellow-and-lime green house, although tired and a bit bug-eaten, held a certain charm. It was one in a row on this street, and all the surrounding houses had charming wide porches, plenty of seating, and not a person in sight.

"I'm going to sit this one out."

Fab jerked on the steering wheel, turning towards me. "You get out of this car or I'll make you."

"Whatever substance was added to your coffee, I'm sure it's illegal," I said with a smile I didn't bother to disguise, which had her shaking her head.

"Before you ask, we're winging it. You try to make a run for it, and I'll put a bullet in your butt cheek. Ouchie." Fab accented that with an unidentifiable noise.

"There have to be exceptions to that edict. The first wild animal, and I'm out. If I think of any more before we get to the door, I'll be adding to the list."

We walked up the steps and onto the porch. The floor-to-ceiling windows were shuttered. Fab opened the wood screen door and knocked. The door opened almost immediately, and a grey-haired woman filled the entry, looking us over.

"Mrs. Brian?" Fab said.

So that was her name; I'd forgotten to ask. I couldn't hear the brief exchange, but Fab crab-walked the woman back inside her house. I followed and let the screen door bang shut, not sure what was happening.

"You get out of here now, or I'm calling the police," the woman croaked.

"That's a great idea." Fab flashed her badge, which had the woman snapping her mouth closed. "While they're here, they can arrest you for felony theft." She jerked up the woman's hand, and both women stared at the large ring on her wrinkled finger.

"I didn't steal this," Mrs. Brian blurted, totally flustered. "I mean, no one said that I couldn't take it. It's not as though my sister-in-law would know. She's dead."

"Do you know the kind of jail time you could get for purloining personal items, or anything else, off dead bodies?" Fab asked.

Mrs. Brian backed away from her and plunked down in her easy chair. "Who's going to press charges? You? I don't even know you. My word against yours."

"Troopie Griffin is pressing charges, and once you've done your time, she'll be taking you to court for damages."

I wasn't getting involved. I sat on the arm of a faded overstuffed shabby chic chair and smiled at the woman, whose raised eyebrows let me know I was nervy.

"That sounds like Troopie—always stirring up trouble in the family, setting us against each other and sitting back to enjoy the show. She'll be salivating if she finds out it's me, and all over a ring that isn't worth five bucks." She spit on the stone and wiped it with her finger. "Years back, Mabel and I got our drunk on, and she confided that it wasn't real. She loved that when folks got an eyeful, they had no clue it was phony."

Fab stepped back and sat on the arm of a different chair. "You stole it off a corpse, so the fact that it's fake isn't going to get you brownie points with a judge."

Mrs. Brian flinched. "Not sure why it has to go that far. But knowing Troopie, she would probably drive me to jail and gloat all the way." She covered her face with her hands and unleashed a sob.

Fab telegraphed, *Your turn.*

"You're in luck today." I stood but stayed back. "We both have a fondness for older folks, and we don't like to see them hauled off to jail. So we have an alternate plan for you."

Fab shook her head.

What did she want? More drama? "You give us back the ring, and we'll return it to the funeral home. The owners are friends of ours and..." I thought for a moment. "They'll tell Troopie that the ring was dropped off anonymously—no note or anything—and they surmised that whoever took it must have felt bad about their actions. We won't out you to our friends or anyone else."

"You'd do that?" Mrs. Brian wiped her nose on the back of her hand.

"As long as you raise your right hand." I almost laughed at how fast her hand shot in the air. "Super swear that you won't be stealing at another funeral ever again. In general would be better, but I don't know your habits."

"I swear, I swear," she said in a pitiful, hopeful tone.

"Go buy yourself another cheap ring at a discount store." I smiled lamely. "Between you and me, you can get a better selection at the flea market."

Fab rolled her eyes.

I faux glared at her—after all, I didn't do that to her. Sometimes anyway.

"You super swear not to mention my name?" Mrs. Brian attempted to twist the ring off her finger.

I raised my hand. "It so happens that I have the authorization to swear for both of us." I flicked my finger between Fab and me.

"Before you rip the skin on your finger, I suggest you go into the kitchen or bathroom and use a little soap and water, and it'll come right off," Fab said.

Mrs. Brian stood unsteadily, holding onto the arm of the chair, then ambled toward the kitchen.

"You think she's going to make a run for it?" Fab asked me.

"If she does, my money's on you to run her down, truss her up, and drag her back."

She shook her head. "A simple no would've been faster. Good idea you had for resolving this situation."

Mrs. Brian came back, ring in hand, and handed it to Fab, then threw herself back in her chair. Fab, who had her phone out, compared the ring with the photo, then stuck it in her pocket.

"Out of curiosity, how did you manage to relieve the corpse of her jewelry without being caught?" I asked.

Mrs. Brian flinched. "Before and after the service, we got to file by the coffin and pay our respects. On the last trip by, I was the last in line. It caught my eye, and I thought she wouldn't be needing it anymore."

Fab looked down, and I'd bet on her swallowing a laugh.

"A little more free advice for you," I said. "Next time someone knocks on your door, at the very least ask 'Who's there?' Peeking through your shutters would be a better idea. If the screen door locks, you should keep it that way."

"My sons have told me that more than once, but I got the message this time. Thank you for not hauling me in and, most of all, for not outing me to the family. I'd never be invited to any get-together ever again."

Fab had stood and was already at the door.

"You going to be okay?" I asked Mrs. Brian.

She nodded.

I followed and checked out the screen door. No lock. I double-checked that the front door was locked.

"Wonder if Troopie thinks she's getting back a pricey heirloom," I said when we got back in the SUV.

"Then she's in for a surprise," Fab said. "I'm thinking the less we tell our digger friends, the better. They're not good at anything deceitful."

"I'll follow your lead."

"Let's take care of this now." Fab revved the engine, a "hurry up" to the cat waddling across the street, who I swear turned and glared.

She zipped around traffic, and it didn't take long to get to Tropical Slumber.

Both of us groaned as she turned into the parking lot, which was full of cars.

"I'm not crashing a funeral," I said adamantly.

"Me neither." Fab pulled around back to the guys' front door—handy having your abode attached to where you worked. It was a large apartment with several bedrooms that they'd tricked out. She whipped out her phone and sent a text. Her phone dinged a minute later. "Raul's on his way." She got out.

I powered down the window. "I can give you

moral support from here."

Raul came out of their door, and Fab handed over the ring. They had a brief chat, then hugged. I waved.

"Raul was happy with the story you worked up, as he doesn't want to be in the middle of any drama caused by fingering someone, and he knows Dickie feels the same," Fab said as she slid behind the wheel.

"We need to make a quick stop at the office, and then you can take me to lunch."

"A stiff drink sounds good."

Chapter Seven

Fab cruised past the security gate that ran across the front of the unassuming three-story warehouse building that Creole and I owned, along with the two next to it, which housed a boat dealer. We owned more property farther down the block, as did Fab.

The Boardwalk offices were on the first floor; Creole's old boss, the Chief, had bought into a securities firm after he retired and moved his offices to the second floor; and Fab and I took over the third floor.

We got out of the SUV, and Arlo bounded out from under the roll-up doors and skidded to a stop for a sniff. We apparently passed muster, and he ran off to look for bugs, or whatever Golden Retrievers went on the prowl for.

Lark—a leggy woman wearing a billowing sundress with her long brown hair tied up in a ponytail—came out to check on her dog. I may have had a reservation or two when I hired her to run the office for the guys, but she'd worked out spectacularly. "It's boring around here today," she announced as she walked up.

"As soon as you say that, all hell breaks

loose." I smiled at her.

"The guys are at a meeting, the Chief's playing golf, and that leaves me and Xander," Lark updated me before the office phone had her running back inside with a wave.

Fab and I rode the elevator to the third floor and found Xander on the couch, laptop in his lap. As soon as he saw us, he sat up and said, "Good news, partially anyway. Crum's bail hearing isn't until tomorrow, but the attorney checked out. He's no slouch. I called Spoon, sure he'd have a referral to someone who wouldn't screw you on the rate, but his man has retired. He warned that it wouldn't be cheap to get Crum out, not with pending murder charges. I'm working on finding another bondsman."

I nodded and made a mental note to call and thank Spoon. My mother had waited a long time after my father died to finally meet a man that made her happy, and the two were quite compatible. It was fun to see how much he doted on her. Spoon rarely said no to any of my requests, much to Mother's chagrin, so I didn't ask unless it was important.

I sat opposite Xander, and Fab slid behind her desk. "Were you able to find out what evidence they have against Crum?"

"There was paperwork spread out on his desk that showed he was either blackmailing Crum or in the process of." Xander tapped on his screen.

I wondered if it said what West was trying to

blackmail Crum over, then decided I really didn't want to know. "Crum would never cave to blackmail." I knew he wouldn't shoot the man either. "You uncover anything interesting about West?" I was really hoping for another suspect since a blackmailer rarely stops at one victim.

Xander's fingers raced across the keys. "So far, West's boring. I've been digging into his business, trying to uncover a few of his clients. He had an office in Miami, which I found interesting. It's a long haul if you're driving it every day. Also going through court records to see if anyone filed suit against him or he was party to a suit of his own."

"Text Fab the address in Miami." I turned to her. "It would be interesting to check out where he conducted business."

Fab nodded, taking out her phone.

"I'll run a check on the address this afternoon and get back to you before you make the drive, so you'll know what to expect."

"Were you able to get me info on the property I'm interested in?" I asked.

"You've got an eight am meeting with Mr. Eugene at that coffee place where Lark lives. He didn't want to meet in town, not wanting anyone to see him talking to you since he's afraid of Gunz, who made it clear to Mr. Eugene that if he wants to sell, no one will give him a better offer. Talked to Mr. Eugene myself. He detailed the repairs the property would need. I included everything we talked about in the report I just sent you."

"Why does he want to sell, besides something about his retirement?" Fab asked.

"He owned a number of properties throughout South Florida, and he's been slowly getting rid of them. This one has been a hard-sell, since it's filled with small-time criminals—his words, not mine." Xander half-laughed. "Mr. Eugene says they get to drinking, then take it out to the street and oftentimes start fighting, and that's when the cops get called. As soon as sirens are heard, everyone scatters."

"Why not evict them?" I asked.

"Fear." Xander took a layout of the house out of a folder and handed it to me. "A friend who lives on the street thinks they get tipped off that the cops on their way, and that's how they manage to clear out in time. He also passed along a rumor—if it's illegal, it can be bought at that address for the right price."

I perused the layout. "It shows here that there's five bedrooms. A rooming house?"

Xander nodded. "An illegal one."

"You'd think the cops would get tired of being called repeatedly to the same address, only to find that everyone's run off," I said. "As for the illegal rooming house, you'd think they might sic the code department on them—more money for the county."

"That address hasn't been high priority, since

the cops have only received nuisance calls," Xander answered. "It's my guess that they don't know about the illegal activity as yet…or they don't have enough to get a warrant."

"So I'm meeting this Mr. Eugene in the morning? Should be interesting." I pulled out my phone and sent myself a message.

"You're only getting this sit-down because Mac knows Mr. Eugene and vouched for you. So be on your best behavior." Xander smirked. "He also knows a couple of your tenants in the apartment building, and they said good stuff about you. I think if you make a good offer, Mr. Eugene will take it."

"It sounds like if you do make an offer, you're buying a house full of trouble," Fab said.

"That's easily remedied." Although depending on how savvy they were, it might not be an easy fix. "I'll offer them a deal to hit the road. If they don't take it, I've got the muscle to set them out on the curb *and* have them racing out of town if they're smart. These folks sound like what I had at The Cottages when I first took over, and I'm smarter now, having learned a trick or two."

"Florida living: You either get smart or it buries you," Fab said.

I nodded.

"Do you have a valuation report on the property?" I asked Xander. "After the drive-by, I'll know what kind of offer we're talking about. I pretty much know the real estate values in the neighborhood. If they've run off other buyers, I can't imagine that they're going to treat me any different, but if I opt not to do a walk-through, that would be a wild card."

"I just emailed it," he said. It didn't surprise me he already had the report ready.

"A cash deal always sweetens the pot," Fab suggested. "The guys have plenty of sources of money."

"Have you thought about what you're going to tell Gunz if you make this deal happen?" Xander looked worried. "'By the way, I snatched this property out from under you'?"

"I didn't know you were interested in the property," I said in an overly sweet tone. "Someone, I don't remember who, casually mentioned that the house was up for sale…blah, blah."

"Keep it short," Fab said. "It's a good idea not to mention names unless it's someone more badass than he is."

"What's your story going to be?" I asked Fab. "You know Gunz is going to burn up your phone. Probably demand a sit-down and include the edict: don't bring your friend."

"I'm going with the same level of ignorance you just laid out." Fab smiled at her idea. "One better: I'll place the blame on him for sneaking around. I'll make it clear that if he'd told me, I would've told you—friends and all…"

"As we all know, Gunz has a tendency to stop by the office when he gets a wild hair…or he would if he had hair. When you're here by yourself, keep the door locked and don't feel compelled to answer if someone beats their meaty fist on it," I told Xander.

"Got it. I was shamed into signing up for a self-defense class, the person—who shall remain nameless—telling me it was stupid not to know how to defend myself, considering my friends." Xander grimaced.

"I can think of a couple of people that would put it just that way. Just know that if they didn't care what happened to you, they wouldn't have bothered," I said.

"I've started already, and so far, I'm enjoying it. It didn't take me long to figure out it was good advice."

"Anything else?" I stood. Xander shook his head. "I'll let you know how it goes with Mr. Eugene, since you set up the meeting. When we leave, I'm going to get my driver to go by the house." I winked at Fab.

"Don't go knocking on the door, thinking you're going to be able to check it out," Xander warned. "Keep it quiet until it's a done deal."

"Good advice." I smiled at him.

Chapter Eight

Creole and Didier were waiting for us when we got home. Creole started by reminding us he had the final word on whether or not we went to check out the West Mansion. When Fab sputtered, about to argue the point, he cut her off. "Who's got the most experience?" Then he went on to tell us that he and Didier had driven by the property and checked it out, finding the front gate unlocked. "I found that odd, considering the large security sign." They left without trying the door, not wanting to attract unwanted attention.

Before we piled into the truck, Creole mic'd us up. He and Fab rode in the front, going over the logistics of what would go down once we arrived and they were inside.

I turned to Didier. "How do you feel about sitting in the truck, looking pretty?"

He and Creole chuckled.

"Remind me what you're hoping to get out of this late-night visit," Creole said as he roared out of the compound.

"From everything Xander has dug up—what

little there was—it would appear on the face of it that West didn't have any enemies. Except someone killed him." If Creole knew about the blackmail, he might put a stop to their breaking in, thinking it too dangerous.

Creole turned into the neighborhood. "You two need to keep an eye out," he directed at Didier and me. "If anything smacks of trouble, give us a heads up so Fab and I can get out of there. She assures me that if we need to go on the run through the neighborhood, she can get us out without getting arrested."

Fab turned and said, "At that point, I'll call, and you can pick us up."

"Reminds me of old times."

"I'm afraid to ask how many times you two have done this kind of job," Didier said.

"A few, and look, we're here to do another. You're in good hands." To change the subject, I told the guys about my meeting with Mr. Eugene in the morning.

Creole cruised to the corner and parked—a good spot, since there wasn't a direct view of it from the nearby houses—then tested all our mics.

"Be careful," I said as he and Fab got out.

The two turned the corner and cut across to the West mansion while Didier and I climbed into the front. I didn't know if Didier could drive like a madman and hoped we didn't have to find out.

"Do you think the cops left the gate unlocked when they were finished processing the crime scene?" we heard Fab ask Creole over the headset, accompanied by the click of the gate opening.

"That's not something they'd normally do. They'd want to discourage people from poking around." His tone told me he wished he hadn't agreed to this trip.

"We're going inside," Fab said. The plan was that once they got in, she'd use her skills to override the security system before it sent off an alert.

Didier and I heard the door being opened and their footsteps in the entry.

"Someone beat us here," Creole said in a low tone.

I was tired of sitting in the truck not knowing what was going on, especially since neither Creole nor Fab were being particularly wordy. "I'll be back," I said to Didier and slipped out of the truck before he could react.

He opened his door and hissed through the night air, "What do you think you're doing?"

I ignored him and ran across the street. The gate had been left slightly ajar, and I slipped through, leaving it like I found it, and hurried to the front entrance, holding the door for Didier, who was hot on my heels.

"Someone wanted something awfully bad," I said, surveying the scattered cushions and emptied drawers.

Creole turned to me. "I thought you were... Never mind." He nodded to Didier.

I caught a glimpse of Fab in the hallway and took off after her.

"Don't touch anything," Creole called after me.

As though I didn't know. I passed a couple of rooms, a quick glance telling me that they were in the same condition as the living room. The office where I found Fab was in the worst shape of all—papers everywhere, drawers overturned, books ripped out of the bookcase. Drawing on past experience, I prowled the room, checking out every corner, looking for anything that stood out. The desk where West died had been cleared of paperwork, but there were several dark stains in the wood.

Fab flashed her light around, focusing on a file full of paperwork, which she flicked through. "We need to come back when we can see what we're doing."

"Good luck with that plan."

I followed her to the master bedroom. Surprised me to see that the sheets had been stripped off the king-size bed and left in a ball on the floor. Wonder what whoever broke in was looking for. I stood in the doorway as Fab prowled the corners, then followed as she continued through the rest of the house. No room had been left unscathed. We met up with

Creole and Didier in the kitchen.

"What's your professional opinion?" I asked Creole.

"An amateur, who was in a hurry and got increasingly frustrated as they went room to room. My guess is that they didn't find what they were looking for."

"Now we know that West had something someone else desperately wanted," Fab mused.

"Let's get out of here," Creole said.

"I'm going to check out the property and meet you back at the truck." Fab slipped out the back door before anyone could say anything.

Didier groaned as his wife disappeared from sight. "I knew this wasn't going to be a simple in-and-out."

"Pick us both up." Creole nodded to Didier, then was hot on Fab's trail.

As Didier and I made our way back to the truck, I kept an eye peeled, but the neighborhood had stayed quiet—no lights on in any of the nearby homes. Not so much as an animal wandering the streets.

"I was hoping for a smoking gun, and that didn't happen," I said as we got in the truck. "What we do know is that Crum wasn't tossing the house, since he's in jail. So who did and what were they looking for?"

"Tank's a good lawyer; you should let him do his job. If we'd been caught tonight, it could've gone badly for Crum...not to mention the charges we would be facing." Didier shook his head.

"I'll update Tank—tell him what we did tonight without mentioning you or Creole." I took out my phone and sent myself a reminder to find out the time of West's funeral, since Fab's guy had to put off the security camera installation a couple of days. And made a mental note to choose something tasteful and black and show up early to get a good seat. In the back.

"I hope this means you're going to take my advice," Didier said in a hopeful tone.

"For the most part." I ignored his snort. "I can promise that I won't involve Fab should I latch onto a new hare-brained idea." I could guarantee that Fab wouldn't like that promise, should she find out...and she would.

Didier sighed. "Creole or I should be keeping a list of all these promises, for whatever good that would do. I don't suppose you remember the one about telling us your plans *ahead* of time." He pointed out the windshield to where Fab and Creole were climbing up an incline on the adjoining property—the one that West had purchased to keep Crum from becoming his neighbor. "How did they find that path?"

"Your wife is a human compass."

Fab and Creole got in.

"That was an interesting trek," Creole said.

Chapter Nine

The four of us headed off in different directions early the next morning, but only after Fab and I got an admonition to call if anything went haywire.

"Yeah, yeah," I responded and got a double stink eye.

"Happy it wasn't me they were growling at," Fab said, waiting until after she closed the car door in case one or both of our husbands had bionic hearing.

"Howl's." I flicked my finger at the windshield as she cut out to the highway. "You know where it is."

"What? No reprimand for me to be on the lookout for people who don't look where they're walking, which is most everyone in town?"

"Since you brought it up…keep an eye out for animals running wild, and I mean the four-legged ones." I knew that Fab was only pretending to ignore me. "I put out the word that I'll pay for any reliable information that would help Crum's case. I won't be involving you, so as not to get you in trouble with your honey."

"I win." Fab rubbed her hands together. "Didier and I had this conversation, and I put money on you going all Nancy Drew. Don't think so. If you even try to go it alone, I'll find out and track you down."

"Good news for me—that means no griping about being my date for a funeral." I took my phone out of my pocket and called the Digger Dudes. Raul answered, which didn't surprise me, since he was the front man. "Calling for a favor. And you're on speaker."

"Good morning, Fab," Raul cooed. "The answer is always yes to any request."

"What time is Travis West's sendoff into the afterlife?"

"They changed their minds." Raul's irked tone clearly conveyed what he thought about that. "No heads up to us either. Our coroner friend called when another funeral home picked up the body, knowing that we'd been contacted first."

"Wonder why?" I mused. "You've got the best reputation around."

"It's never happened before," Raul said on a frustrated sigh. "I read about the murder online. Knowing Crum, it's hard to believe he'd pull the trigger.

"Can you find out where the shindig is happening and the time? Me and my date here would like to attend."

Raul laughed. "A couple of calls is all it should take. If it's a private funeral, I'll have your names added. That way, you won't have any problem getting in."

"Was Troopie sufficiently grateful to get her mother's ring back?" Fab asked.

"You pretty much called it when you said she'd be mad we didn't have the name of the culprit to hand over. Dickie and I went to her house together, and I used the story you suggested. I don't think she believed me and didn't care. The only thing on my mind was getting out of there." Raul chuckled. "The upside is that Troopie stopped burning up my phone." He ended the call, saying he'd get back to us.

I texted Xander to ask that same coroner for any information about the West case. He'd made the connection through Raul and Dickie, and I'd authorized a food-and-drink bribe so the man would take his calls.

"What are you going to do if the funeral's already been held?" Fab asked.

"Get you to wiggle in and bribe someone for the guest list. Which we may have to do even if we're able to attend, since we won't know who's who."

"That sounds fun."

Fab's sarcasm was expected and didn't deter me. "Listen up, because you won't want to miss this good tip. Choose someone introverted like Dickie and charm the heck out of him."

Fab veered off the highway and up to a small cement building at the entrance to Howl's, an all-service RV park, campground, and storage lot for boats and whatever else—they accommodated it all. The nude male mannequin was still holding court next to the walk-up window. The only change was he'd ditched his welcome sign and had one arm in the air, a demented grin on his face. A stack of folding chairs had been tossed on the ground, a "help yourself" sign off to one side with an arrow. In the center of the gravel picnic area, a white-haired gentleman in wrinkled khaki shorts and a tropical shirt sat at one of the tables.

"Look who else is here." I pointed at Mac, who walked out of the hut, drink tray in hand, and sat down next to the man, handing off one of the cups.

"What was his name again?" Fab stared at the man.

"Parker Eugene, and he goes by his last name. Be friendly. Dust off some charm—it's good practice for the funeral."

We got out and walked over. Mac made the introductions. "I got you something to drink." She pointed to the cups sitting on the table. "Don't look so worried; I know what you like."

Just the same, I'd take a small first sip to be sure and bet that Fab was thinking the same thing. "Nice to meet you." I picked up my cup and toasted the man.

"Mac-y speaks highly of you. Insists that you're no greasy con-artist," Eugene said in a raspy tone.

"Been called lots of things but missed getting put on that list."

Eugene attempted a laugh, which turned into a cough. Mac slapped his back. "I'm going to lay it all on the line, let the chips tumble. Not going to bull you in any way."

"Good to know. I'd hate to have to shoot you." Fab trotted out crazy-girl smile.

Eugene grinned.

"Don't listen to her; she doesn't do it very often," I assured him.

Eugene cackled, his laughter sounding rusty. "Been in real estate all my life. Now, in my twilight years, I'm liquidating my holdings, so I can enjoy my retirement with friends up north. I'm sure you're aware that when it comes to the house I own on the block where you own property, simply listing it for sale isn't going to work. No one's going to want to buy without seeing the inside—an investor, maybe, but I don't want to price it as a fire sale." He took a long swig of his coffee and coughed some more. "If I tried to show the property, the current tenants would put on a show to discourage anyone interested. I know what you're thinking…" He waved his hand. "Evict them. Tried that already. I couldn't get the papers served and had them posted. The next day, my car was damn near run off the road. Barely escaped a ditch."

"Sorry to hear that. If I'd known, I could've

arranged a private eviction service that would've given them the heave-ho right into the street." No need to mention that all it would take is a thug or three showing up at the door and encouraging them to pack their bags—pronto.

"Mac's been such a great friend that I didn't want to get her involved." Eugene patted her hand. "But after the car accident... She came by to check on me, and I spilled everything."

"The more we know, the better. That way, we can handle any situation that might come up." I nudged Fab under the table to turn on the charm. She ignored me. "But only if you want to share."

"The driver didn't leave the scene, but he placed the blame on me, telling the cop I was driving erratically. I called BS, but in the end, it wasn't clear—to me, anyway—who the cop thought was at fault. Neither of us got a ticket." Eugene unleashed a long sigh. "Two days later, two greasy boys showed up at my door. The bald one stood back, dark glasses covering half his face. I pegged him as the one interested in the property, as I'd seen him around a time or two. The other man, who wore his hair in a bun, did all the talking—made a low-ball offer. I laughed, which angered him, and I told myself not to do that again. He rambled on about how I wouldn't be losing any money, as he knew what I'd paid for the property. I told him to beat it, shut the door in his face, and double-locked it, knowing it wouldn't keep them out if they wanted in. That's when I knew I had to speed up my plan to leave town."

"Have you seen either man around since?" Fab asked.

Eugene shook his head. "Bun head yelled through the door: 'Best offer you're going to get,' and tucked his card in the door jamb. Also heard him grumble, 'I'll be in touch.' Been looking over my shoulder ever since."

Fab ran her finger across the screen of her phone and held it out to Eugene. "Is this one of the men that showed up?"

Eugene took it from her and studied it for several seconds, his face showing him to be reluctant to answer.

Mac batted the phone away. "I already showed Eugene a picture of Gunz, and he made a positive ID."

I was surprised that both women had pictures of Gunz on their phone. I'd also bet a healthy sum that he didn't know they'd snapped them. I'd ask later and see if I got a straight answer.

"Since I said I'd be upfront—know that if you buy the property, you and whoever you get to represent you will have problems with the brick outhouse as well as the tenants," Eugene said. "Not a one of them is familiar with the word no."

"You don't need to worry about us," I told him. "The outhouse knows that threatening either of us would be bad for his health. He's smart enough to have relayed that to his friend."

An old convertible rust bucket cruised into the parking lot. That description was kind for what had once been a sought-after sportscar. The paint on the white exterior was peeling, and based on looks alone, it was surprising that it ran.

"That used to be a nice Corvette." Fab nodded at it. The women knew cars.

A tall, lanky man unfolded himself from behind the steering wheel. He slapped at his dark brown hair to make it stay put, and it cooperated. Sort of.

Eugene waved him over and pointed to the chair next to him.

The man scratched at his scruffy beard, flashing perfect white teeth as he ambled over. Trouble on a stick took a seat. Fab nodded in response to his insincere smile. It was hard to tell if they knew each other.

"I'd like you ladies to meet a business associate of mine—Frack." Eugene introduced us. "I'm assuming you're both real estate investors, and he's a good man to know." He patted the other man's knee. "He's a good boy. My cousin's son-in-law. Used to be anyway. Sometimes in a divorce, you end up picking sides, and not always the logical choice."

"How's your friend, Frick?" I couldn't resist.

His dark stare turned to me. "You know how many times I've heard that joke? It's old."

"You've crashed the wrong party if you're not into juvenile humor."

Fab coughed to cover up her grin.

Frack handed me his business card. Typical Floridian—one name. Hard-money lender, bail bondsman. Hence the flashing neon "Trouble" sign when he walked up.

"These two think they're funny, and sometimes they are." Mac flashed Frack a flirty smile. "I was thinking…"

I swallowed my groan.

"I've been trying to get with Cruz's bail bondsman, but he's been ducking my calls." Mac straightened and thrust out her good-sized chest, both men's eyes following. "Sooo… Frack here is the solution to my problem and, more importantly, Crum's."

"Since a reliable bondsman is always a good thing to have on speed dial, I'm happy to talk terms." I returned the flinty stare Frack was leveling at me.

"Hate to break up this party," Eugene grouched, although clearly not. "Can't sit out here all day, as it's getting stinkin' hot."

Florida was synonymous with hot, but I kept that to myself. "What's your price for the property?"

Eugene reached behind his back, pulled out a sheaf of rolled-up papers, and handed them to me.

Surprised that he came prepared with a contract for the property, I scanned for the price, and it was less than I'd come prepared to offer.

"My lawyer will need to look this over. I can have it back to you by the end of the day. I'll also want my title company to research any property issues." I scanned the terms, and everything appeared to be standard. However, I'd had firsthand experience with shysters and didn't want to take the chance. "If it all checks out, we can close in ten days."

"I thought this would be a waste of my time. Guess not," Eugene said. "The older you get, the more time-suckers make you gripey."

"Why didn't you use your kin here with regards to your other problem?" None of my business, but that didn't stop me.

"I might have if I'd wanted to keep the property." Eugene turned to Frack and gave the man the briefest of explanations. Clearly, it was the first the man was hearing of the problem.

"Last to know?" Frack's brows shot up. "Don't like it one bit, and you can bet we'll be having a chat about this later."

Eugene ignored him and what'd sounded like a threat. "I invited Frack to this party because he's a handy man to have in your arsenal."

"That would depend on his rates… 'Screw you' doesn't work for me, and knowing that upfront prevents mutual time-sucking," I said. "If we can come to terms, I'd have a use for your services, but that said, I wouldn't be a regular customer."

"You might want to talk about Crum's case,"

Mac interjected, as if we hadn't all heard her the first time. "Considering the problems I've been having getting a bondsman, knowing the person would be a leg up." *Don't you think?* in her tone.

"I'm disclosing that I know Crum," Eugene said. "Interesting guy. Thinks he's smarter than everyone else, but I disabused him of that notion when I showed the geezer that I could keep up. Taught him a few tricks—mostly how to cheat at cards—and that cemented the friendship."

I leveled a stare at the man. "That's a good way to get your old butt kicked."

Frack nudged his shoulder. "I thought you'd stopped with the card tricks after our talk."

"Calm your shorts; it was just a little fun amongst friends." Eugene sniffed. "Let's go, girlie." He held out his hand to Mac and helped her to her feet, then extended his hand to me.

Fab intercepted, sticking her hand in his. "She's a germy chick."

"I wouldn't put it that way." I assumed the meeting wasn't over, since Frack had stayed seated. "I'll be in touch with you later today, Mr. Eugene." I pointed at Mac, indicating, *You too.*

Mac grabbed Eugene's arm and held him upright as the two hobbled across the gravel. Frack didn't take his eyes off her backside in the Miami football jersey that, knowing her, she'd altered to fit tightly over her curves. She assisted Eugene into her pickup, revved the engine, and they blew out of the parking lot.

"I happen to know that contract has a ten-day, cash-close clause." Frack pointed to the paperwork in my hand. "You got the money lined up?"

One thing about the man, he knew how to get to the point. "All I have to do is make a call."

"No need, since I'm sitting right here."

His smile was a tad hair-raising, but I'd seen worse.

"It would be a good start to our new business relationship," he went on. "We'd know in short order if we're both going to live up to our word. If not, it's better to cut our loses and no hard feelings."

After we discussed terms, I said, "If the contract is as straightforward as it appears, I'll be moving forward. I'd be happy to do business with you."

"I've done some digging on Crum's case. Don't be surprised if it's high—murder could be upwards of a million. You need a bondsman, give me a call." Frack stood. "One thing, which I tell all my clients—don't think you'll get away with screwing me over."

I pulled out my phone and called the number on his card. "Now you have my number. I don't take kindly to getting screwed over either and am not without associates who can take care of any pesky issues without leaving a trace."

"We're in agreement." Frack nodded and walked back to his car.

"You want to follow him?" Fab bubbled with excitement.

"Calm down." I laughed. "Like Frack wouldn't notice. Then the chase would be on, and who knows where the two of you would end up." I watched as he started up the Vette. The engine roared, and he took the same route as Mac. "These people with their single names think they're so clever. Xander will need to figure out who he is and get a background run on him."

"Do you really need the aggravation of another property? More crazy people to deal with?"

"Probably not. But…" I ignored her groan.

Chapter Ten

Since Tank wasn't available, I had Fab drive to the office so I could have Brad look over the contract. My brother was the one that scrutinized legal docs for the Boardwalk before they were sent on to the lawyer.

As we walked under the roll-up door, Fab's phone rang, and she headed straight to Didier's desk and sat next to him while she took the call.

Emerson and Brad were talking at the conference table and waved me over. The two had dated before she left town to handle her grandmother's estate. She returned a couple months ago, and from the way they were looking at each other, maybe she'd be staying.

I scanned the room for Lark and Arlo, who were nowhere in sight. Come to think of it, I hadn't seen her car in the parking lot. "Good news, I hope." I sat down.

"I just got back from Logan's grandparents' property, and they've moved." Emerson made a face.

She was a family law attorney and had come back to help Brad with this case. He'd been dating a woman who'd left town, leaving her supposed son with him along with a power of attorney. But it'd turned out that her son, Logan, was actually her nephew. The boy's parents had died in a car accident, and no one in the family that we'd talked to thus far wanted custody.

"Please tell me you didn't go out to the Everglades by yourself." Fab and I had made that drive. It was in an isolated area, and the grandparents were, in all likelihood, doing something illegal and might kill anyone who stopped by uninvited.

"I took Brad with me, since he wanted to check out the place for himself. He was under strict orders not to get out of the car. Ultimately, it didn't matter that I'd wrangled that promise out of him, as we didn't get past the front gate. Rang the bell and, when a man's voice came over the speaker, told him I wanted to see the Winters. 'They moved.' I asked for a forwarding. 'Don't have one.' He may or may not have cut the connection; it was hard to tell."

"There's one way to know if he was telling the truth, and I'd bet not—have Xander check the records. If the man wasn't a total liar, then Xander might possibly find a forwarding."

"I asked him already. Hope you don't mind." Emerson's cheeks pinkened.

"I'm happy to help Brad and Logan in any way I can." I smiled at my brother. "What's happening with Logan's case?" Getting custody of a non-family member was difficult at best, and under these circumstances...

"Luckily for Brad and Logan, I've got a couple of administrator friends in Social Services. If I didn't, Logan would be in foster care already. Brad's filled out the paperwork, been assigned a caseworker, and passed the first home visit." Emerson smiled at him.

I slid my contract across the table to Brad. "Before I sign, I just need your more-experienced eye to look at this and see if I missed anything. Then I'll drive it over to the title company."

"I know you won't listen to me, but this newest acquisition of yours isn't going to be worth the headache," Brad said.

"That's the general consensus," I said. My phone dinged with a message from Jake's: *Opening later than usual. Got everything under control.* What did *everything* mean? Dead body? I squirmed, my imagination running rampant with ideas about what would take a few hours to clean up.

Fab was back and brought Xander with her, both sitting at the table.

"An old client called," Fab announced. "He wants me tail his wife and get pictures of her cheating on him."

I groaned. "The last job you had like that, the husband—or wife, I don't remember—ended up dead. At the risk of suggesting something you've already given thought to, how about sluffing the case off on your right-hand man?" Toady was a crusty old fellow who had a giant crush on Fab. Whenever a job came up, he never said no and—another trait that made him ideal for these jobs—he wasn't afraid of anything.

Creole and Didier came out of their office and sat down at the table.

"I'm only going to do a drive-by—so I know what I'm talking about when I talk to the client—and then, as you said, sluff it off on Toady."

"I'm in." I gave her a toothy smile. "If we're doing this today, Jake's first. There's an issue I need to check out."

"What kind of problem?" Creole asked in a testy tone.

"I solemnly swear—" I held up my right hand. "—if I knew, I'd have started with that tidbit. I did rule out a dead body." My reasoning: a picture would've been attached to the text.

Didier laughed.

Creole shook his head.

"We need to hit the road." Fab stood.

Emerson raised her hand. "Since this isn't a good time, maybe we could speak later?" she said to me.

"I'm making time now. It's the least I can do for one of my favorite people." I stayed seated and winked at Brad, who shook his head at me, conveying, *Stay out of my love life*. As long as he didn't hook up with some crazy chick, I'd at least make an attempt.

"I'm tired of hotel life, and I'd like to rent your

and Creole's beach house. Brad offered the apartment next door to his, but we didn't want to confuse the kids. Besides, if you rent to me, *my* house will be more fun." Emerson winked at Brad.

"That would mean we could put up a no-vacancy sign at the front gate." No one found my idea amusing. It also meant that, for the first time, all the houses in the compound would be occupied. "Casio, his kids, and Larry the Australian Shepherd will be your closest neighbors."

"Casio's brood came to dinner, and we had a great time. They brought Larry, who was well-behaved." Emerson chuckled. "Mila has since dropped a million 'let's get a dog' hints."

My little niece had a one-track mind when it came to getting what she wanted. I glanced at Creole, a *Well*? look on my face.

"Good idea." Creole nodded. "You'll make a great neighbor."

Both Fab and Didier nodded their agreement.

"Now that it's settled, I'll get a cleaning crew over to spit on it, top to bottom," I said.

Brad made a face. "That sounds disgusting."

"As soon as you move in, we'll have a block party down on the beach." I smiled at Emerson.

"Let's go." Fab motioned.

Chapter Eleven

Fab took the back way to Jake's, cut across the highway, and cruised into the parking lot of the short block I owned. Fab's vacant lighthouse was on the right. That it was vacant was a bugsome issue between the two of us. I thought it should pull its weight and attract customers. Not her. Across the drive was Junkers, an old gas station that had been converted into a garden antiques store. Although it had posted hours, it was rarely open. It wouldn't surprise me if it was a front for something, but I hadn't asked since the cops had never shown up.

Jake's, my popular dive bar, sat at the back of the property, a big tire with a "Not Open" sign blocking the entrance. There was a paper taped underneath the sign. Couldn't wait to read what it said.

"Park in the front for a change. No one expects us to come through the main entrance." We almost always used the kitchen door, where we could come and go without attracting attention.

Fab and I got out. She beat me to the sign and read the scribble on the torn piece of paper aloud: "Have patience. Big mess inside. We're hurrying."

I squinted over Fab's shoulder. "That's Kelpie's writing. She might've been expecting a slow day and staged a stunt." I jerked open the front door. Music was blaring from the jukebox. "This better be good," I yelled to the room at large.

Doodad, the manager, was busy power washing the cement floor while Bouff—the night bartender, always accommodating when it came to showing up at the last minute—was hiking down the hall, a case of liquor in hand.

Fab and I claimed seats at the bar and watched as Kelpie—who'd changed her purple hair back to pink, pronouncing, "I'm over that snit"—gyrated to an unidentifiable song.

Enough of this. I slid off my stool, took a few steps, and turned off the jukebox.

Doodad caught sight of me and shut off his machine. "It's not my fault; I had nothing to do with this. Nothing."

That wasn't an answer to my unspoken question: *What the heck is going on*? "How about I ask the manager? Is he in?"

Bouff laughed and set the box on the bar top.

"Your best bet would be to ask Cook." Noting my annoyance, Doodad added, "I'd hate to give you a half-assed answer."

"I'll tell her," Kelpie said with a note of glee, dancing around, hands over her head. She'd pinned tassels to her shirt, and they moved with her. She came to an abrupt stop. "Cook got this great deal on a fresh meat order."

"And?" *Hurry it up.*

"He was planning this huge menu special—" Kelpie threw her arms wide. "—to attract new customers. But..." She frowned. "When the order got delivered, it didn't quite go as planned."

Fab shook her head with a laugh. "Could you be more vague?"

Kelpie leaned across the bar. "You got the high points; what more do you need?" she asked in a huff.

"As much as I don't want to ask, I feel compelled. What kind of animal was Cook going to cook up this time?" I directed the question to Bouff, knowing he hadn't picked up the evasive techniques of the other two. Yet, anyway. Hopefully, he'd give me a straight answer.

"Iguana."

I tried not to squirm and squeezed my eyes shut to stay calm. "I specifically remember banning that from the menu." At least I thought so. With Cook, one had to be specific. If he saw a loophole to exploit, he was through it before you could blink.

"You know Cook's always on the lookout for a great deal," Bouff hedged. So he had picked up a few tricks. "He didn't feel like he could pass this up."

I swiveled around and stared at Doodad.

"Where were you when this executive decision was being made?"

"You know diddly damn well that I don't have control over anything that goes on in the kitchen," Doodad grouched. "No one does. Not even you."

He had a point there.

"You three are being so evasive, my head aches." Fab rubbed her temples for effect. "What does a good deal on lizards have to do with not opening on time?"

"They got loose and started running all over the joint," Doodad announced.

I jerked my feet up and checked out the floor.

"No worries. Most of them escaped out the deck door and went over the side."

I craned my neck to look outside.

"The rest went out the front. So if you're worried about them being underfoot, don't." Doodad gave the floors a quick scan.

Kelpie had stayed uncharacteristically silent, although she grinned throughout the entire conversation.

"You've got to feel bad for Cook," Bouff said.

"Why?" I demanded, continuing to eye the floor.

"A few of the bars are turning on the tricks to bring in the customers, and Cook wants to maintain his number-one rating." Kelpie sent her tassels in a whirl.

"His mistake was buying from a shady

purveyor," Bouff said. "He thought the shipment he signed for was frozen, but when he and his son opened the crates, the buggers ran out."

Fab started laughing, and everyone stared at her.

"Whoever packed the shipment didn't know what they were doing," Bouff continued. "You've got to keep them on ice. Once they warm up, the chase is on. So to speak."

I grimaced. I didn't poke my nose into what went on in the kitchen, but lizards run amuck?

"The reason we're opening late is that we had to clean up every trace of them." Doodad wrinkled his nose. "It got a little messy."

I glared at Fab, who hadn't made an attempt to control her laughing, and slid off my stool. "As owner, my word is law; try to remember that. I was never here. If Cook asks, not a one of you was willing to step up and tell me anything."

"Cook's not here now," Doodad said. "But since there's no secrets in this joint, he'll find out. Speaking of…who told you?"

I ignored the question, covering for Kelpie. "It has always been bar policy to call the owner—first and not next month. But in this case, ignorance is fine with me." I returned Doodad's even stare. "I'm delegating this problem to you as manager, and I don't want any more live animal incidents in the future." I ignored his snort and hustled to catch up to Fab, who'd beat it to the door. I turned and waved. "Later."

Fab jumped behind the wheel, and we hadn't even gotten the doors closed before she burst out laughing. Again.

I turned toward the window and unleashed a long sigh. "How far is it to this boring drive-by?"

"Not far."

I groaned.

Chapter Twelve

I should've known our destination would be Miami. By any sane person's estimation, that would never be considered "not far." The only thing that could be said about the drive was that it was a beautiful day and the traffic was light.

Fab turned into a quiet neighborhood and circled the block a few times before parking across the street from a house with a well-maintained yard.

"What's the story?" I asked.

"My client, Mr. Huntly, wants his wife, Trixie, tailed. He needs proof that she's cheating so he can nullify the pre-nup. His words: 'I don't want to pay her a damn dime.'"

"How is showing up here in the middle of the day helpful?"

"Mr. Huntly claims that, according to the tracker he put on her phone, she returns home every day around this time."

"Wait until two certain someones find out that you knew all along that this jaunt was more than a drive-by. One of them might make you sleep on the couch."

Fab snorted. "As if. I told the truth," she

huffed. "Kind of, anyway."

I laughed.

"It's not like I plan on confronting the woman. I'm here to take a few pics to show the client that the job is a priority before turning it over to Toady, who's finishing up another job and can start tomorrow." Fab opened the door, one leg out.

"Hold on, sister." I grabbed the back of her shirt and tugged. "Where do you think you're going? Get back in here."

She squirmed away and stuck her head back through the door. "I'm looking for my cat." *Duh* in her tone. "Rolling your eyes isn't very nice. If you can use that tired old excuse, then so can I."

"You're telling me that you're going to trot over there, yell 'Here, Pussy' a couple of times, take a few pictures, and then hustle your backside back to the car?"

"Yes Mother, and you can sit right here and keep an eye on me." She shut the door before I could call baloney and turned with a smirk before running across the street.

"Don't think I won't be reminding you that your plan needed work before you hopped out," I mumbled, my eyes locked on the windshield. I couldn't help thinking I should go after her, but two people creeping around a stranger's yard would certainly attract attention.

Fab skulked across one end of the property, snapping pictures, then disappeared around the side. Out of sight wasn't working for me—she had one minute to reappear before I went looking for her. I made a mental reminder to ask more questions about her client when she got back to the car, since this was the first I was hearing his name. Another red flag in my book.

A hefty woman with a mop of curly brown hair that had a mind of its own sidled around from the opposite side of the house.

I snapped forward when she brandished a gun that had been previously tucked away by her side. I jumped out of the car and bolted across the street as Fab came back around the corner. Surprise registered on her face, and she skidded to a halt, caught off guard by the woman pointing a gun at her.

I stepped up on the curb, then stayed put, not wanting to give the woman a reason to overreact.

Fab slowly raised her hands in the air, one holding her phone.

"Is there a problem here?" My Glock was in easy reach, but now wasn't the time to add another firearm to this get-together.

"None of your business," the woman barked with barely a glance my way. "Move along."

"I'm calling the cops," I said and pulled out my phone.

"Give me a minute to explain," Fab said. "I'm certain we can clear this up. I thought I'd run over a cat and got out to check on it, but it ran off, so it must be okay."

"You shouldn't be trespassing for any reason," the woman said with a sneer. She stuck her gun down the front of her pants and approached Fab with her hand out.

Still wary, Fab pocketed her phone. At the same moment, the woman swept her foot out, and Fab launched herself out of the way, hitting the ground hard. The woman stepped forward, and Fab rolled to the side.

"One more step, and I'll shoot you," I bellowed.

The woman turned and was clearly surprised to be staring down the barrel of a gun.

A second or two later, sirens could be heard in the distance, getting closer.

Since none of us had made the call, that left a neighbor peering out their window.

The woman turned and barreled back around the far side of the house.

I reholstered my Glock and went to help Fab, who was getting to her feet.

"Let's get the heck out of here, in case the cops are after us," Fab said and hobbled back to the car. She slid behind the wheel as I ran around to the passenger side. She was just pulling away from the curb as the cops came around the corner from the opposite direction. The woman hadn't reappeared.

"Are we risking arrest for leaving a crime scene?" I flipped down the visor and used the mirror on it to watch behind us.

"I hope we don't find out this is one of those fine lines that ends with us in jail."

"You okay?"

"My side and hip are killing me; I'd be surprised if I'm not sporting bruises. I crash-landed on the concrete in a place where the pieces were jagged and uneven."

"Was that the wife?" I asked.

"I've got no clue who that was, and I'm not even certain I got a picture." Fab sighed and handed me her phone. "Check for me. I moved my finger over the screen, hoping for the best…and that she wouldn't notice and pull the trigger. She held the gun with confidence, so she wasn't a newbie. If she'd shot me, she couldn't claim ignorance. Or self-defense."

"Probably a stupid question, since you're a human map book, but is there a chance you had the wrong address?"

"Hardly."

I flicked through the pictures she'd taken. "You've got a partial of the woman. I'm thinking anyone who knows her could easily make an identification."

Fab glared at the road as she turned south toward home. She hadn't uttered one word about any detours, so that made me happy.

"Please tell me this Mr. Huntly wasn't one of your clients from the old days."

"I'd done a couple of minor jobs for him back when, and everything went okay." Fab took her phone back from me and made a call. "Voicemail," she said in a disgusted tone. "This is Fab Merceau. I have an update on your case. Please call me back as soon as possible." She threw it in the cup holder. "When we get back to the Cove, I'll track down Toady and tell him that the case is on hold until Mr. Huntly calls back. If it's not the wrong address, he'll have to find someone else. I'm not going to risk Toady getting shot, no matter that he'd reassure me it's unlikely to play out that way."

"I thought she was going to shake your hand and be done with it."

"Same here. She got this smarmy smile on her face and made her move to get me to the ground. Who knows what she'd have done after that if you hadn't caught her by surprise."

"The approaching sirens cut into her fun. Since she didn't hesitate to take off, my guess is that she had something to hide…maybe?" It surprised me when Fab exited the highway and rolled into a gas station.

She pulled off to the side and parked. "You can drive." She got out and rounded the front of the SUV.

I met her midway. "Lift your top." I stood where I was blocking the view of anyone turning into the parking lot. Her right side showed signs of significant bruising. I barely touched it, and she winced. I walked with her to the passenger side and held the door while she got in, then went back around and slid behind the wheel. I called Mac, and when she answered, I asked, "You at the office?"

"Yep-o. What's up?"

"Can you get Blunt on the phone and tell him to hightail it over?"

Fab knocked me in the shoulder and shook her head.

"He loves being at our beck and call. Says no call has been a dead bore."

I laughed. "If he's busy, book him for later. Now would be better, though, and I'm happy to pay any increased fee."

"I'll get on it. But before I hang up, who's in need?"

"It'll be a surprise. Won't that be fun?"

Mac snorted and hung up.

"I don't need a doctor," Fab insisted.

"You're going to be agreeable to calm my nerves. Another good reason is that when Didier gets an eyeful, you can reassure him that you're fine. I bet Blunt would even give you a doctor's note."

"Didier's going to kill me," Fab lamented.

"Probably. But I'm willing to bet that he'll wait until your bruises heal up."

Fab leaned back against the seat and closed her eyes, something she never did, even when complaining on the few times I got to drive.

Chapter Thirteen

I'd tease Fab later that I'd gotten us to The Cottages in one piece. I parked in front of the office next to a beat-up older model Mercedes that I recognized as belonging to Blunt. I went around, prepared to offer her assistance, but she was already halfway out of the car.

"This is a waste of time," she grumped.

"Humor me." I attempted to take her arm, which she shrugged off.

The door to the office flew open, Mac filling the doorway, but as we approached, she moved out of the way.

Blunt waved from one end of the couch. He was wearing his typical work uniform of wrinkled shorts, a tropical shirt, and flip-flops, his grey hair sticking up on end and his doctor bag on the floor at his feet.

I pointed at Fab, who glared, over to the couch and turned to Blunt. "Fab fell. Check her out, no matter what she says. Mac and I will be outside. If she gives you any trouble, holler, and I'll come back in and hold her down." I shot Fab the stink eye.

As soon as the door closed behind us, Mac

blurted, "Fab fell? That's hard to believe."

I stopped at the SUV and grabbed cash out of my wallet, sticking it in my pocket. We crossed the driveway and took a seat in the barbecue area.

"The truth is a bit more involved."

Mac huffed. "Is that your evasive way of saying none of my business?"

I sighed and told her what happened.

"The other woman is damn lucky she caught Fab off guard. Otherwise, she'd be nursing a bullet hole. And the two of you would still be enduring questioning from the cops."

I'd left out the part where we'd lit out barely one step ahead of the law. "Fab and I have had this discussion before, but she needs to stick to Gunz's jobs and not answer when an old client calls."

"Once Gunz finds out that you one upped him—and he will find out—he probably won't be burning up the phone either."

"I don't want to damage their friendship, but I don't want him as a neighbor either. Anyway..." I raised an eyebrow at her. "Did you get Mr. Eugene home okay?"

"You should be happy that I know everyone on the block." Mac preened. "I'm disclosing here and now that I'm buying the duplex next to me. They have it on a vacation rental site and are tired of it."

"All my resources are available to you, and

I'm more than happy to put in a good word with anyone you need."

"Frack's going to walk me through the process." Mac glowed.

Note to self: get a background check done on the man and now. "Don't let anyone talk you into anything other than a standard loan on a long-term investment. Our bank is set up not to dawdle on approving loans," I told her, knowing that we used the same one.

"One of Frack's friends is a loan officer at a different bank, and I have my application in already. I told him I was using your title company, and turns out he knows the owner and assured me they have a good reputation." Mac leaned back and stretched her legs out for some sun. "I probably should've called, but you're here now." She grinned.

Now what?

"Called Cruz's bondsman and left a message that I wouldn't be needing his services. Guess he didn't care about the commission, since I didn't hear back from him."

"That's so weird—you'd think they wouldn't take a pass on a client who could pay."

"Frack's got a different approach. He got a jail visit with Crum today. Surprised me, since it was short notice, but he confided that he had a friend who worked at the visitation center."

"That man's got one good connection after another."

The office door banged open. "Ladies," Blunt yelled and waved us over.

Mac and I got up and joined him, and the three of us went inside.

"Fab here needs an x-ray or two. Judging by her spitting responses, she has no intention of taking any of my advice. Sooo...rest and suck it up, because bruised ribs—if that's all it is—are going to hurt. If it gets so bad it's hard to breathe, then maybe she'll trot on over to the hospital. Ice may help. Aspirin or some such can sometimes make a dent. Not sure she was listening to that either."

"I don't like my personal business being shouted out." Fab grunted and winced.

"Well then, missy, if there's a next time, make that clear up front." Blunt stared her down.

"Thank you for coming." I stepped between the two. "No matter how gripey the patient, I appreciate that you make house calls." I took the money out of my pocket and put it in his hand.

He stared down at it and attempted to hand some back. "This is too much."

I waved him off. "I'm not making change, so you'll just have to suck it up."

Blunt hooted and threw the door open. "Fine with me, girlie." He turned to Fab before leaving. "If you forget anything I said, give me a call." He was gone.

"If you're ready, your driver is here to take you home." I pointed to myself. "Me getting to drive twice in one day—that'll be fun." Guess not, judging by her scowl.

It took a hiss or two for Fab to get to her feet, and then we made our way out to the SUV. A hair's breadth from a getaway, Toady's truck blasted into the driveway and took the space Blunt had vacated.

He and a woman got out, and he hooked his arm in hers. Since I'd only heard about Fuchsia and never met her, I assumed this was her based on her bright purplish-red hair. There was a slight resemblance to the color. The two joined us, and he made the introductions. He hung his arm around her shoulders.

"Saw your car and wanted to tell you I finished up the job for my client and I'm good to start yours tomorrow," Toady informed Fab.

She leaned against the side of the SUV and told him about earlier events and that she hadn't been able to get ahold of the client.

"Wonder what the hell you stumbled into there," he growled. "If you hear back and the job's still on, text me. You already forwarded me the info I'll need."

Standing in the middle of the driveway, Toady and Fab talked about a couple of his other cases. It was the first I was hearing that she had a new repo account and would be forwarding all the contracts to him. I was happy to hear we wouldn't be boosting cars—great way to get the heck beat out of you, or worse.

It was hard to eavesdrop and make small talk with Fuchsia at the same time. I finally turned my full attention to the woman. "You Toady's backup?"

She growled out a laugh; I'd guess she was a heavy smoker. "Instant attraction. We found out that we have a lot in common and have been side by side since day one." She came off as being able to handle herself, which was just what Toady needed.

Fab and Toady joined us, and we said our goodbyes. However, before we could get to our cars, three cop cars pulled into the driveway. They got out, guns drawn. "Hands in the air," one ordered.

Fab and I exchanged a wide-eyed look. The Miami woman must've copied down my license plate number, and the cops had tracked us down. Who knew what she'd told them? And we looked guilty, leaving the property.

"Jola Bren, on the ground," another cop barked. "The rest of you step back."

Who? Since it wasn't my name he'd belted out, I did as I was told. To my shock, after a long pause, Fuchsia dropped to the ground.

Cop number two holstered his gun, stepped up, and cuffed her, helping her to her feet. She didn't say a word as he read her her rights and stayed silent as he led her to his car. He pulled out shortly after.

Toady waved to one of the officers and threw

his hands up. "What the heck's going on?" The officer motioned him over to the barbecue area. Toady was well acquainted with local law enforcement, claiming to have several friends on the force; maybe this was one of them.

Another officer stepped up to Fab, and me and asked, "How do you know Ms. Bren?"

I introduced us. "I'm the owner of this property, and Fab and I just met Jola for the first time a few minutes ago. But not by that name—she introduced herself as Fuchsia." Fab nodded.

I didn't know when Mac came out of the office, but there she was, standing next to me. "I met her a couple of times, but as Fuchsia," she told the officer. "Toady introduced her as his girlfriend."

He took down contact information and joined his partner and Toady in the barbecue area.

Since my SUV was blocked in by the patrol cars, the three of us went back in the office, not a one of us wanting to be in the middle of whatever was going down. I claimed one of the chairs while Fab eased down on the couch and stretched out.

Mac stood guard at the door and peeked out the blinds. "What do you suppose Fuchsia, or whatever her name is, did? Must be something big to bring three officers out."

"I noticed that she didn't put up one word in her defense," I said. "If I was innocent, I'd have at least said you've got the wrong person."

"How did the cops know she was here?" Mac asked.

"They had to have been following her and decided now was the best time—the neighborhood is quiet, no one lurking around," Fab said.

"Toady's not going to be happy." I got up, moved to Mac's chair, and turned on the computer.

"The other two officers are still talking to Toady, and they're doing all the talking. Toady's listening and not interrupting," Mac reported.

"You know what I thought?" I made a face at Fab.

"Same thing as me—that they were here for us." Fab shook her head. "I did wonder why it would take three officers to bring us in but didn't have to wait long for the answer."

"Anyone remember the name the officer yelled out?" Guess not, since neither answered.

Mac wasn't giving up her post, and Fab had closed her eyes.

I put my head in my hands and drew in a breath for patience, trying to remember Jola's last name.

"You could call Creole and Didier," Fab suggested.

"Yeah, sure. If that was unclear—not a chance. I'm going to use one of your tricks and tell Creole when we're in bed." Fab made some kind of noise but smiled. "Let's not have dinner together, in case Didier finds out you're bruised up and ignored doctor's orders and all hell breaks loose."

"Maybe I can tell him—"

I cut Fab off. "The truth. It's going to come out sooner or later, and it would be better if it's not after a pack of lies, or even one or two."

"Here comes Toady." Mac opened the door.

He stormed inside, throwing himself down in a chair. Mac closed the door and took a seat. All eyes were on the man, and no one said a word. "I suppose I should be counting my lucky stars, but I liked Fuchsia." He unleashed an irritated sigh and huffed out a couple more breaths. "Not going to forget her anytime soon. The upside is I'm still breathing and have all my parts, and they're where they're supposed to be."

Who was going to ask? It wasn't going to be me.

"We know this is a bad time for you." Mac reached over and patted his back. "If you want to confide in us, that's what we're here for."

"Well…if the cops are right—and they say they have the evidence—I've been shacked up with a double-murderer. They say she offed her husband first and a boyfriend after that. I asked if she had a motive, and they didn't have anything definitive, just that she was ready to move on." Toady buried his face in his hands.

"Two. She should've thought through her options a little better." Mac stood and grabbed a cold water out of the refrigerator, then tapped his shoulder. He looked up, took it, and nodded his thanks.

"I take it Xander didn't run a background check?" Though that probably wouldn't have done any good, since he didn't know her real name.

Toady shook his head.

Fab hissed, "Madison," and shook her head. "What happens now?"

"She'll always be Fuchsia to me. Anyway, she sits in jail until she's extradited to Gainesville." Toady had clearly been thrown off his game. "I need to get out of here; I need a stiff drink or six."

"You need a ride, you call me," Mac offered.

He waved and flew out the door.

"I don't know about you two, but that's about all the excitement I can stand for one day." I stood and snapped my fingers at Fab.

Fab eased herself up and shuffled to the door, which I held open.

"You're not going to be able to hide your pain for five seconds," I said as I followed her to the car, then turned back to Mac. "Try to hold off any new excitement until tomorrow."

Mac waved as I backed out.

Chapter Fourteen

It had been three days since I'd last seen Fab. Creole assured me that she was alive and well, but that Didier wasn't happy, to put it mildly. He didn't take no for an answer when telling his wife that she would get x-rays. I don't imagine she went kicking and screaming, but she was definitely attitudinal. Lucky for her, the bruises were the worst of her injuries and she hadn't broken anything. I didn't have the nerve to go visit, knowing her guard husband hadn't left the house.

I'd been spending the days with my husband—riding in together and hanging out at the office, where I'd shuffled around a lot of paperwork and got caught up on everything. This morning, however, the pattern changed.

Mac called while Creole and I were drinking coffee. "Crum's being sprung from jail, and I'm on the way to pick him up," she shouted over traffic noise. I was tempted to tell her to roll up her window. "A million bucks."

"Were you in court?"

"You betcha. Cruz went before the judge and

argued that Crum wasn't a flight risk and some other stuff, and I found out afterwards that he and the district attorney had already agreed on the bail amount."

"Cruz Campion?" Who else? But I'd thought there wasn't a chance in hell.

"The original lawyer bailed at the last second. Good excuse, though—his wife had gone into labor with their first child, and he beat it to the hospital."

"I'm thinking Cruz wouldn't appreciate a thank-you note from me."

Mac's laugh was cut short by her laying on the horn. "Hey buddy!" she yelled. "Gotta go."

I looked at the screen, and sure enough, she'd disconnected.

"I'm afraid to ask… What now?" Creole held up the coffee pot. I shook my head. He refilled his cup and slid onto a stool at the island.

I relayed my conversation with Mac.

"That's kind of amazing, considering how adamant Cruz was about not touching the case."

"I'm just happy that Crum is out. Or soon to be anyway."

"Are you coming to the office with me today?" Creole asked.

"I'm headed to The Cottages, but you're certainly welcome to join me. I'm throwing a mini-bash for Cruz's relatives, who helped pull this off." I ignored Creole's smirk. "Then ask that they call him and gush with effusive thanks, giving him all the credit for the added perks they've received." I deciphered his eyeroll as "Not interested."

"As much fun as that sounds, maybe next time." He leaned across the counter and kissed me.

"You behave yourself."

"Goes double for you." One last kiss, and he was out the door.

* * *

When Mac texted me, *We're back*, I grabbed my purse and lit out the door. I didn't bother with shortcuts, since traffic was light, and took a cruise through the neighborhood before parking in front of the office.

I got out and scanned the front porches of every cottage, and surprisingly, all were empty. I'd expected one or two tenants to be catching a quick nap, since it was a little early for any of them to be passed out. I turned and followed voices to the pool area. Several guests shouted my name and waved as I came around the corner. I waved back.

Crum's door flew open, and he stepped out in his signature attire…sort of, a dish towel tucked into the front of his underwear.

"Happy to see you," I said, coming face to face with the man, and stopped short of saying, *And not behind bars.*

"I didn't kill that man," Crum stammered, not his usual blustery self.

"I already know that and knew it from the beginning."

"Thank you..." He scuffed his toes on the pavement. "I'd still be sitting in jail if not for you and Mac."

"Mostly Mac." I smiled at the woman, who stood guard at the pool gate.

"You know me...speaking my mind." Crum winced. "It didn't help that I told that one bondsman he was a dimwit."

So that was why the man went MIA. One would think, in his business, he'd have heard it all. The women congregated around the pool had all stood and began to gyrate in circles, chanting, "Crum."

"They missed you." I nodded over my shoulder.

It surprised me to see Tank headed to the pool. Built like his moniker, he was decked out in professional attire—shorts and a tropical shirt. He waved and stopped to say something to Mac that made her laugh. The two took a seat at the tiki bar.

"Tell Tank I'll be over as soon as Rude gets here and takes over," Crum said.

"That will give me time to ask a few questions of my own." The two of us went into the pool area, then headed in different directions. I acknowledged everyone with a wave and sat across from Tank and Mac. "I planned to call you later, and look, here you are. Does that last dollar I gave you still cover me on client confidentiality?"

Tank nodded with a smirk. "Kind of afraid to ask what you've been up to. Are we talking murder or crime in general?"

I filled him in about the trip to West's mansion and let him read between the lines about who I'd been with. I was certain he figured it out instantly. "I had an extensive background check done on West, and a copy is being forwarded to you."

"West's house having been tossed is interesting. Wonder what they were looking for and if they found it," Tank mused. "The DA's theory is that West was blackmailing Crum over the previous altercation and Crum offed him instead of paying."

"Crum wouldn't succumb to blackmail—he wouldn't part with the cash, especially not when West was the one who blacked his eye. West wasn't hurt himself." I shook my head, remembering how out of control West had been when I showed up. Thankfully, it didn't take much to defuse the situation. "Even without Crum's ability to squeeze a nickel, the cops have a stupid case, as it's difficult to blackmail someone over something a couple dozen people saw happen *and* for which the cops got called. And even if the cops are right about the blackmail but wrong about what West had on Crum, I've known the man a few years now and can't imagine anything he'd have done that would give rise to blackmail."

"I think the prosecutor has a weak case at best, and it comes down to what they can prove," Tank said. "Cruz's assistant emailed over a file, along with a note saying, 'Keep him away from your female relatives.' I asked Crum about it when I talked to him for two minutes on the phone this morning. He grumbled, 'The woman was hot for me.' I didn't want to hear any more."

"I wouldn't have called Cruz if you hadn't been out of town. So next time trouble blows in, try to arrange your schedule accordingly."

Tank saluted.

"Once Fab is off home confinement, we're going to hit the highway for a trip to Miami to check out West's high-profile business address." I told him what had happened on our last trip to Miami and how Fab had ended up bruised.

"I'll bet there's a messy backstory that Fab's client didn't bother to divulge. I've got a friend who's a divorce lawyer, and the stories he tells make criminal law seem like a cakewalk. Almost." Tank chuckled. "Back to West. I checked around with my sources and got nothing—no one has had dealings with the man, which is kind of unusual. I'll be interested to hear how your trip goes."

"Did you hear about the arrest that went

down out in the driveway the other day?" I asked.

"I'm representing Toady, so I can't talk about the case. I can say that's it not a crime to date someone who's homicidal and I don't expect any charges against the man. Toady may be worn around the edges, but his background is impeccable. Better than most that live down here."

"Surely there's a way for me to wiggle in a couple of questions you can answer without violating client confidentiality." I ignored his raised eyebrows. "Fuchsia—what's happening with her?"

"Jola Bren is being held without bail and awaiting transfer to Gainesville, which shouldn't take too long, as she's not fighting it. The court appointed her an attorney, and word at the courthouse is that she's kept her mouth shut." Tank shook his head. "It's my understanding that the cops have amassed a lot of evidence against her. The best any lawyer may be able to do is to keep her from frying."

I made a face. In Florida, you had that option—not sure why anyone would choose it. "If you need anything investigated on Crum's case, give me a call. Xander's also on loan to ferret out any information you'll need. I know he wants to help, as he and Crum are friends."

Rude came bursting through the gate decked out in skin-tight yoga pants that left little to the imagination and, when she turned, showed a man's smiling face emblazoned across her butt. "Sorry I'm late," she yelled, "but we're going to have fun." The slight, grey-haired woman threw her hands in the air.

Tank's brows shot up. "That one's too cheerful for me."

"And she doesn't drink caffeine." Mac grinned.

The ladies gave Crum a round of applause as he came over and sat down.

"Either of you need anything…" I waved my phone at them and stood, motioning to Mac, then waited until the pool gate closed to say, "I'm thinking a thank-you gift for Cruz is in order, since he showed up in court when he could've put off the hearing."

"Got it covered." Mac grinned. "At Susie's suggestion, I sent him a bottle of his favorite wine. Spendy, by the way."

"Totally worth it." And better than anything I could've come up with, not knowing the man's tastes. "Do me a favor and keep an eye on the neighborhood. I'm closing on the property down the street in a couple of days."

"Don't you worry your red curls. If anything happens, I'll know about it."

A car bounced into the driveway and slowed, rolling down the window. "Bet you this is our new guest—a first-timer." Mac went over and directed them into a parking space.

I waved and hopped back in the SUV, pulled out my phone, and called Fab. When she answered, I asked, "You still on house arrest?"

"I was allowed out to come to the office," Fab huffed in a low tone. "Gunz called and wanted a meeting, so Didier and I came in together."

"I'm on my way over. Use the time to come up with a good reason for the two of us to sneak away. I want to go check out West's office. It will give you something to think about while you're half-listening to Gunz."

"I'm bored with this good-girl act, so you can bet I'll come up with a good story that won't have Didier growling at me again."

Chapter Fifteen

I cruised to the office and parked, noting that Gunz had beat me. It was hard to miss his Escalade with the blacked-out windows. Arlo was waiting when I opened the door, Frisbee in his mouth. I threw it a few times, until something else caught his attention. When I walked under the roll-up doors, Lark pointed her thumb to the ceiling—her way of telling me that Fab and Gunz had gone upstairs. I'd wait down here for them to be finished.

"Everyone behaving?" I asked.

Lark laughed. "Sort of."

I walked into the office the three partners shared. Didier and Creole were at the conference table, my brother nowhere in sight. I bent down and brushed a kiss on Creole's cheek, then sat down. "Once Fab has finished her meeting, I'm stealing her away for a ride to Miami." I went on to tell them my idea, which got a lukewarm reception. Fab would have to save whatever excuse she'd come up with for next time.

"Not sure why you have to get involved," Didier said. "A man did end up dead."

"I have no reason to think that today's jaunt

won't be safe. It's a high-rise office building in the middle of a fancy business district. I thought I'd ride up to his office and ask whoever's there if they can refer me to another lawyer. So sad about West." I frowned.

Creole shook his head.

"Fab's not a hundred percent; she's still quite sore," Didier said.

I couldn't fault him. Creole would be acting the same way. "I'll make the drive myself then." Neither man was happy with that declaration. "Are you really that worried about what could happen?" I asked Creole.

"If you wait until Friday, I can go. We can have lunch, and you can pick the waterfront restaurant."

I knew that bit was added for incentive and turned to Didier. "You have to know that Gunz is upstairs pitching a job to your wife, and you'd better work up a good reason for her to say no or plan on going with her." I heard voices and, concluding that the meeting was over, headed for the main room, coming to a screeching halt in the doorway. Gunz had his big behind bent over Lark's desk and was about to lock lips with the woman…or already had; it was hard to tell.

"How's fatherhood, Gunz?" I asked loudly as I stomped into the middle of the room. "I never did hear what you named the baby."

"You're a new father?" Lark asked in surprise.

Gunz straightened and turned, more

annoyance on his face than I'd ever seen.

"How is… What was her name again…? Oh yes… Tracy, wasn't it? How's she doing?" I somehow managed a patient smile, ignoring the daggers Gunz was shooting my way.

"If it's any of your business, Tracy's doing fine. She and the baby are living with my sisters," he snapped.

"Is it safe to leave her out there?" In the weeds? With those two nutjobs—certifiably crazy, the both of them? But I didn't have the nerve to ask.

"Congratulations," Fab cut in smoothly, before Gunz and I came to blows and I was left in a puddle in the middle of the floor.

I skirted around closer to Lark's desk. "Tracy also has a young son. Does he call you Daddy yet?" I'd guess not by the snarl he unleashed.

Fab linked her arm in Gunz's and had a difficult time getting him to move toward the door. "I'll get right on what we talked about," she said in a placating tone.

Creole and Didier were standing in the office doorway. Creole looked about ready to laugh, Didier not so much.

I leaned down and said to Lark in a low tone, "I blurted all that out to alert you that there's a lot you probably don't know about the oversized cretin. The last thing I want is for you to get hurt. Then I'd have to shoot him, and that would mean jail time."

Lark jumped out of her seat and hugged me. "So sweet of you, but there's no need to worry. A couple of others, who wish to remain unnamed, already had the 'no banging bones with that man' talk with me."

"If you're interested in finding your true love, my mother lives to matchmake. To be honest, she sometimes sucks at it, so you'd have to be very specific. Or if you have your eye on someone in particular, she's nervy enough to set that up."

"I love that idea," Lark enthused. "Even a few sucky dates would be good practice, since it's been a while."

I pulled my phone out of my pocket and called Mother, and when she answered, whispered, "Can you sneak away?" I'd just come up with another good idea. Or so I thought.

"You bet I can," Mother said eagerly. "I'm doing housewifey things that annoy Spoon, who always grouches he can't find anything when I'm done." She giggled. "Then I get in so much trouble."

"I'll be right over. I've got two items on my agenda, so don't let me forget."

"If you see me out on the street with my thumb out, you'll know I got impatient."

"See you in a few." I was laughing when I hung up. "Mother will be calling," I whispered to Lark, then waved to Creole and Didier. "See you—I've got a date with Mother." I turned back to Lark. "One more thing. Stay away from

Gunz's relations—the Q sisters, Kettle and Watusi. Neither is normal. Watusi maybe a little bit, but not the older one. If you think I'm being too hard on them, ask Fab."

Once again, Fab appeared out of nowhere. "They live out in the boonies, so there's a miniscule chance of ever running into them."

"I think Tracy living with those two is criminal."

Fab stepped in front of me. So much for my quick getaway. "Hold up, I need your help on Gunz's case. It's a simple welfare check."

That had trouble written all over it. Maybe if it was one of his older relatives…still trouble. "I'm sorry," I said, not sounding it one bit. "You'll have to get permission from your husband, and good luck with that. Besides, Mother's waiting on me to hustle over."

"I know you're up to something," Fab said.

"I am, and I'm going to enjoy every minute."

Fab stepped in front of me again and nudged me back, lowering her voice. "Give me two minutes." She raced over to Didier. "Young girl…knock and go. I'll make Madison do it."

Creole came over, hooked his arm around me, and walked me to the car. "What are you up to?"

"I don't know for sure, except I'm picking up Mother. And waiting to see if Didier's going to let Fab out of his sight." I hooked my arms around Creole's neck and gave him a big kiss.

"Nice try. I can be distracted, but not before

telling you to be careful." Creole kissed me again.

"I'll call as soon as we're done, so you know it went well." I flashed him a perky smile.

Creole's eyebrows went up. "So you know…if anything happens to you, I'm killing you."

"That's too mean."

Didier walked Fab out to the car and helped her into the passenger seat. I wondered what crock she'd sold him.

One last kiss for Creole, and I slid behind the wheel, hit the gas, and squealed out of the parking lot. I didn't bother to look in the rearview mirror.

"If my phone rings, you're answering it." Fab dropped her phone in the cup holder.

"How are you feeling?" I slowed once I turned onto the road.

"The pain's controllable with aspirin. I didn't divulge everything Gunz told me, which didn't seem so bad, but if I had, Didier would've put me on lockdown again."

"Hold off on the details until we pick up Mother. Since I don't know what's going on, you need to concoct a plan that covers every contingency."

"That would be some plan," Fab grouched. "We have a lot to catch up on, since you stayed in lousy touch."

"Now that you're not on lockdown, it will be easier." I stopped short of smirking. "Not much happened, except that Crum is out of jail. What's happening with your Miami case? Any word on the identity of the woman?"

"I never could get ahold of my client. Toady insisted that he'd check out the address and track down the woman who attacked me, and if it's not the wife, then find out the woman's identity." Fab sighed, sounding relieved not to be the one doing it.

"Then what? It's not like he's going to beat the heck out of her."

"I told Toady to let it go, but he wasn't listening. He's found out something and wants to meet in person to tell me what he learned. Surprised me he got answers so quickly."

"Wow. Happy I wasn't there for that showdown."

"I couldn't bring myself to ask what mayhem he'd committed and on whom. I got out a burner and called my client, and his number had been disconnected. Just as well, since I didn't know what I was going to say if he answered."

I hit my hand on the steering wheel, which made me wince. "Listen up. These old clients of yours are all trouble. You either stop taking their calls or change your number."

"I only said yes because I didn't have anything going on at the moment, so I thought, why not?"

I rounded the corner to Mother's condo and scanned the street. "If you see a woman—blond bob, dressed cute—it's probably Mother, since she thought it would be fun to stand out on the curb with her thumb out."

"She would flip if you did that."

I pulled up to the security panel and entered the code.

As the gates opened, Fab pointed. "Madeline and Spoon are standing out in front. It's probably as far as her over-protective husband would let her go." The fierce-looking man in his fifties, with brown hair and a hard edge to him, had his arm looped around her.

"You feel up to driving?" I asked.

"It was hard not to get into the driver's seat, but doing it in front of Didier..." Fab drew her finger across her neck. "But I don't want to sit here and do nothing—been doing that for days. Hopefully, he'll understand if I tell him before he finds out."

I parked, and we got out. "Hello, you two." I hugged and kissed Mother, then looped my arm in hers and walked her around to the passenger side while Fab slid behind the wheel.

"You try to stay out of trouble," I said to Spoon.

"You can keep an eye on me and see for yourself." He slid into the back seat from the opposite side.

Fab turned. "What are you up to?" she asked Spoon.

"Knowing my wife as well as I do..."

Mother giggled and turned in her seat. She lived to have her husband go into protective mode, enjoying every minute.

"I didn't get the whole story about Madeline's outing with her daughter. Something about maybe lunch and maybe shopping and a couple of 'I don't knows.' So I thought I'd come along and see for myself what you actually end up doing, since my spidey senses are telling me that it isn't any of the things she mentioned."

"Lunch and shopping probably aren't happening today." I smirked at Mother's wink. "But we'll definitely be taking a rain check on both of those fun outings. Mother's offered on dozens of occasions to be backup, and I'm taking her up on the offer, though I might not have spelled it out in the conversation. But she never says no, and here we are."

"Now would be the time to hop out," Fab said to Spoon. "Once I hit the road, it will be a while before I stop, and then you'll have a long walk back."

Spoon crossed his arms and leaned back. "I'm comfortable back here."

"This is going to be fun," Mother cooed.

"I would wait for the details." I tapped Fab's shoulder. "Plans changed between when I called and now. I've got a general idea of what we're doing; Fab can fill us in."

"We're doing a welfare check on one of my client's relatives," Fab said.

"Gunz," I whispered loudly, and all eyes turned to Fab.

"I think that young man can be delightful," Mother said. "But he's trouble."

I looked at Spoon and rolled my eyes. He chuckled. "Really, Mother. What were your first ten clues?"

"Why not send the cops?" Spoon asked. "They're prepared if something goes wrong."

"Gunz wants me to take a low-key approach," Fab said, irritation in her tone. "The woman just turned twenty and has moved out on her own. Gunz says she's shy."

"You should tell everyone why you're staying in the car," I said to her.

Fab reluctantly told them about our trek to Miami, but left off the latest update.

"Here's the plan. Maybe. I'll go knock and politely say whatever you want me to." I hoped this wasn't one of my worst ideas. "Then tell the young woman to call Gunz…or someone else? Or we all go together and pretend we're selling something."

"Hate to be the one to tell you, but neither of those are a good idea." Spoon rolled his eyes.

"If you're going to be one of the girls for the day, you need to lighten up," I told him. Mother laughed. "Remind me to get a couple of pictures, since no one will believe the big guy came along as our chaperone."

Fab pulled into a neighborhood of older homes and stopped in front of a peach-colored single-story.

The four of us got out of the car. Fab had apparently decided that since this was her case, she'd take charge. She beelined for the front porch, then came to an abrupt stop. I came up behind her and saw that the wooden landing had collapsed in on itself. The front door was off limits.

"Gunz needs to send someone to fix this," I said. "Since he's taken care of these issues for other relations."

Fab had her phone out, taking pictures.

"I'll check and see if there's a side door." Spoon walked around the side of the house, maneuvering around a white panel van. He was back in a minute. "The only entrance is around the back. But you've got bigger problems. I looked in the window, and there's a girl inside—twenties, I'd say, stringy brown hair—with her arms tied to a chair. She's slumped to one side, eyes closed, and a guy about the same age is on the couch, asleep or dead. Probably the former. This is where you call the cops."

"Gunz would prefer that I handle the job myself." Fab took a couple of steps.

"How?" Spoon snapped.

"I'll knock on the door and shoot him." Fab lifted her shirt, showing her Walther.

"That's a ticket to jail," I said.

Fab attempted to walk around Spoon, and he grabbed her arm. "Your husband would kill me if I stood here and did nothing."

She sighed. "Since he's tired of all the drama, it would be me he'd kill."

"I agree with Spoon," I said. "Call the cops. Or Gunz—he has friends on the force. Let them come out and take care of it."

Mother grabbed Fab's arm, and tugged her further away from the house while they talked. Then Fab pulled out her phone, and I guessed she called Gunz, judging by the animated conversation. She hung up and said, "He's making the call now."

A scruffy twenty-something came around the corner of the house. He'd somehow gotten his eyes open after a bender, but just barely. He had a gun in his shaking hands and pointed it in our direction, moving from side to side, as though not sure which of us should be his first target.

Mother yelped. Fab jumped in front of her with a wince.

The guy turned his weapon toward Fab and Mother. Spoon cleared the distance between them without hesitation and kicked his butt to the ground. The guy dropped the gun and, hand out, attempted to crawl forward, reaching for it. Spoon planted his shoe in his backside and sent him airborne, then took a step and kicked the gun into the bushes. "Go ahead, get up; then see what happens."

I shot Spoon a thumbs up.

Not much of a listener, the guy struggled to sit up. Spitting weeds out of his mouth, he rolled on his side and wiped his face on his shirt. "You're trespassing, and all of you are going to jail."

"You can tell it to the cops, since they're on the way," Spoon barked.

And here they came, rumbling around the corner and parking in the front. Kevin got out of the first car. Gunz's police friends must have all been busy. I knew for a fact that Kevin thought Gunz was a criminal, despite the fact that he denied it.

Kevin walked over. "The whole family's in trouble this time." I heard the smirk in his tone, but then, I knew him.

Spoon growled, "You're not funny." He closed the distance and explained what had happened.

The second cop, who'd heard everything, cuffed the guy on the ground. Despite his attempts, he hadn't made it to his feet and now shouted, "You're taking their word, and this is private property!" Whatever the cop said, he calmed down, but it didn't diminish his militant scowl.

Kevin went around the side of the house. The other cop talked to Spoon, who pointed to the area where he'd kicked the gun. Mother and Fab got back in the car, and I went over and stood next to the passenger side. Mother rolled the window down, and when the second cop finished with Spoon, he came over and questioned me, then Mother and Fab.

It took a while, but an ambulance finally rolled

up. The medics hopped out with their bags and a stretcher, and the cop pointed them around the house. Kevin came back and had a short conversation with the other cop, who loaded the guy into the back of his car. Then Kevin questioned Spoon again.

The EMTs rolled a woman strapped to a gurney around the corner. She'd apparently been awoken from a stupor and was yelling "Petey" over and over. They loaded her in the back of the ambulance and, with a wave to Kevin, drove off.

Another cop rolled up in an unmarked car, got out, and strode over to Kevin. The two motioned to Spoon; it appeared that they had a few more questions. It wasn't long before Spoon made his way back to the SUV. He held the door while he and I slid into the back.

Fab didn't waste time getting out of the neighborhood.

"You appeared to get more information out of Kevin then we ever get," I said to Spoon.

Mother turned in her seat. "Before you get started, Brad called and wants to have a family dinner, and I told him we'd meet him later at the Crab Shack."

I laughed. "Are you certain that's what Brad wants?" Mother flashed me her secretive smile, and I knew she was up to something.

"You should call our husbands and issue the same edict. We'll meet you at the restaurant," Fab said.

Mother took out her phone and made the call. I could only hear bits and pieces but could tell that she'd called Creole and asked to be put on speaker. She didn't order the two men to be there, but close. "Love you both." She hung up.

I covered my mouth and laughed.

Spoon nudged me with a wink.

"Now, what did Kev-o tell you?" Fab asked Spoon. "Madison's name for him, by the way."

"Petey and Anne are apparently drug users and, according to Anne, like to get high and get their kink on. The problem is that when she asked to be untied, well… Petey wasn't going for it. Anne was extremely worried about Petey when she woke up and noticed that he was gone and didn't so much as flinch at Kevin standing there. She's not pressing charges for being restrained, but they'll both be hit with charges for the assortment of drugs found on the table. And depending on the ownership of the gun, possible weapons charges. Just a guess, but I'll bet Petey bought it off someone on the corner or stole it." Spoon was struggling to control his anger. "This is the kind of job Gunz sends you on?"

That last part hurt my ears, and I was happy the question wasn't directed at me.

"Gunz had no idea," Fab said in a tone conveying that she believed him. "When I called and reported the little I knew, he wavered between being mad and worried. Anne's mother had contacted Gunz when she couldn't get ahold of her daughter, as she lives out of state. Not a word to him about what a hot mess her daughter's life is."

"It's highly likely that her mother had no clue." I snuck a peek at Mother, who was shaking her head.

"I suppose it's your job to call Anne's mother and let her know that she's in the hospital?" Spoon asked in a disgusted tone.

"Gunz is making the call; I called him as soon as they loaded Anne in the ambulance." For once, Fab ignored the driver that just cut her off. No speeding or shortcuts, she headed back to Mother's condo.

Before Spoon could get out, I leaned sideways and pecked his cheek. "You rock, dude."

He growled, then got out, opened Mother's door, and helped her out. He stuck his head back inside. "Dinner should be interesting. We need to catch up on what kind of jobs the two of you go out on."

Fab groaned but stayed silent.

Spoon looped his arm through Mother's, and they went inside the building.

"You know I'm available to drive," I said before moving to the front seat.

"Just get in." Fab motioned. "Not that you're a terrible driver; I just like being behind the wheel."

"Was Gunz yelling by the time you two hung up?"

"He's not much of a yeller, but when he's angry, it comes through the phone loud and clear." Fab shuddered. "At first, he didn't believe me, since he was under the impression that Anne was a goody two-shoes. The third cop that showed up was a friend of his. I remember him showing up at another job. I wouldn't want to be Petey when Gunz finds out about him."

"I'm thinking that once you update your husband on how the afternoon went, I won't be seeing you tonight. I'll make your excuses," I teased. "I'll come up with something good."

"We'll be there. Didier and Creole have a weakness for Madeline's antics and would never hurt her feelings by being a no-show." Fab laughed. "Heads up: Emerson is coming to dinner."

"Happy to hear." And I meant it. "I've got my fingers crossed that she and Brad hook up again. Mother would also love that. They were great together before, and she likes the kids. I overheard Mila telling her, 'You're cool.'"

Chapter Sixteen

The guys knew when they'd been out-maneuvered, and they took it well, laughing and joking on the way to the restaurant.

The Crab Shack was a family favorite and served the best seafood around. Overlooking the blue waters of the Atlantic Ocean and decorated with fake palm trees, fish mounted on the walls, and rope lights strung all around, it had a low-key atmosphere. Mother and Spoon had already arrived and gotten a table inside with an unobstructed view of the water.

I sidled up to Fab on the way in the door and whispered, "Pitcher?"

She nodded enthusiastically. "How are you going to pull it off? You know everyone gets antsy when we're getting our drunk on, which is what will happen before we get to the bottom of said pitchers."

"What are you two whispering about?" Creole confronted us with a squinty look, as though he could ferret out our thoughts.

Good luck. "I'll meet you at the table; I'm going to the ladies' room." I veered off before he could say anything. Knowing I'd be caught stopping at the bar, I waited and waylaid the server to place the order. This day deserved a good stiff one. I went back to the table and kissed cheeks. Brad and Emerson sat next to Mother, who was at the end of the table with Spoon. I slid into a chair next to Creole and winked at Fab. Didier caught me, and I smiled and turned away.

"Where are the kids?" I asked.

"Their nanny said she could stay late tonight. As much as they like her, I still had to use cookie bribery to get out the door." Brad grinned at Mother—that was a trick he'd learned from her. "The kids aren't used to me going out at night."

It surprised me when Toady strolled in, waltzing up to Mother and kissing her cheek. He whispered something that had her giggling.

Spoon cleared his throat.

Toady smiled broadly at everyone, his gold tooth front and center. Decked out in a silk shirt and shorts and his signature cowboy boots, he took a seat on the other side of Fab. She'd coached him in his wardrobe, and the first thing she did was ixnay the wife beaters.

"Why is that I think you're up to something?" I tapped my cheek and stared at Mother. "More than usual, that it is."

"Good question," Brad mumbled.

Two servers arrived, one with our pitchers. I pointed where they went, and he set them down and poured us each a drink, then took orders from those that didn't have a drink yet. Fab waved an olive at me in thanks for remembering to request a pick of olives and cherries, and Mother groaned from the other end of the table, clearly thinking that Fab and I getting our sauce on wasn't a good sign.

"You know you find it hard to behave when you've tossed down a couple," Creole whispered in my ear.

"I'll drink slow." I leaned in and kissed him.

It didn't take long for the server to return with the rest of our drinks.

"To family and friends," Mother toasted. "As you all know, it's unsettling to me to be the last to know, hence this dinner. You can each update me on the goings-on in this family."

I waved at Mother, at the same time sucking down half my drink. "I'll go first." Mother didn't roll her eyes—because "ladies don't do that"—but came close. "I told Lark that you'd be calling her about your matchmaking services. Won't that be fun?" From the looks on their faces, those who'd been on the receiving end of Mother's matchmaking attempts thought I'd lost my mind. "I did assure her that you would take her criteria for a honey-bunny seriously and not go off half-cocked."

"I never..." She faltered.

Spoon laughed and laid his arm across her shoulders.

Mother sent me one of her *behave* glares. "I'm

going to call Lark and suggest lunch. That'll be fun."

I winked at her. "You can get her to tell you what it's like to work for these guys."

"Just don't scare her off, Mother. Not now that we're in agreement that Lark's a perfect fit," Brad said. "That would mean Madison would end up running the office, and you know how she can be."

All eyes turned to me, and everyone laughed. I toasted and took a healthy sip of my margarita.

"When Lark showed up with her own office decorations, a bow and arrows, and her dog, it was off-putting," Didier admitted. "I thought that Madison was pranking us, which is the kind of thing she'd do."

Most smirked at me, knowing it was true.

"But Lark showed right away that she can hold her own with the pushiest of clients," Didier added. "We were adamant that she not take any nonsense off anyone, and she doesn't."

"Arlo turned out to be a good addition too. He's always up for a game of catch," Creole said.

"The only one Arlo hasn't cozied up to is Gunz." When a dog doesn't like you, what does that say? I didn't ask the question.

"Speaking of..." Mother smiled at Fab. "Although I did relish my role as backup today, you can imagine my surprise and shock at finding out that Fabiana had been hurt and I hadn't heard about it. If I had, I'd have come over every day to make sure she had everything she needed."

Hovered is what she'd have done and driven Fab crazy. "She had her own personal nurse," I said. "Hot, sexy French guy...heard he wasn't half-bad."

Fab snuggled closer to Didier. She said something in French, and the two laughed.

"Spoon was the star of the day; we'll let him tell the story," I said and flourished my hand at the man. "Make us proud."

"How is it you were recruited?" Creole asked.

"I'm thinking I've got a free afternoon, look up and my wife is strapping on a thigh holster, and wondered why she needed that if she was going shopping as she said. Except when she goes out with those two, she likes to gun up. Wonder where she got that idea." Spoon sent a faux glare my way. "I got the bright idea, why not go along? I knew hinting at an invite wouldn't get me anywhere, so I waited until I was in the car to inform the ladies." He went on to tell everyone how the job played out. It was the first Creole and Didier were hearing it, and they weren't happy.

"In my defense..." Fab waved her martini glass. "Like Spoon, I'd have looked in the window and called Gunz right away, then waited for one of his cop friends to show up and handle it."

"His jobs are getting dicey," Toady grumbled. "You should toss more my way and bill him double."

I was sure that if a vote were taken about that, it would have been unanimous.

The server was back. Mother motioned him over and spoke quietly. After he left, she said, "I already placed a special order with the chef, and I don't think you'll be disappointed. I've got everyone's favorites covered."

"I eavesdropped on the call," Spoon said. "Madeline ordered enough for an army."

"An abundance of food can always be counted on at family gatherings," I said.

"We have time for one more update before the food gets here," Mother said. "We'll let Toady have the honor."

He leaned over and whispered to Fab, who nodded reluctantly, then downed her martini and poured another one.

You're a good sport, I projected, hoping she got the message, and sent her a smile.

"As you know, Fab got injured on one of her jobs. She originally assigned it to me, and it had been her intention only to drive by and scope out the property, then forward me the information," Toady relayed. "Turns out that Huntly, the husband, knew there was a really good chance that his wife, Trixie, would go off on Fab when she caught her snooping around the property. He even sent Fab a grainy picture, setting it up, so they'd be sure to get into it. Huntly had it figured that she'd shoot his soon-to-be ex or, worse case, Trixie would shoot Fab. Either way, dead or in jail, he wouldn't have to pay alimony."

Not very smart, since he also risked going to prison.

"How did you find all this out?" Mother asked.

Didier appeared about to explode. "Good question."

"I generally like the direct approach. I confronted Trixie, telling her I was there to investigate the incident the other day." He flashed his gold tooth around the table. "I'm quite the charmer when I want to be." More than a few eyebrows went up. "Turns out, you weren't the first person the old bastard had sent to tail his ex, although you being a woman threw Trixie off, which is why she didn't shoot you on sight. Trixie had warned Huntly that she'd shoot the next person he sent snooping around."

"I'm going to pay this Huntly character a visit," Didier growled.

"I'll come with you," Creole said.

"No need, I handled it. I paid Huntly a visit, introduced myself, and then rearranged his nose. I stood over him and threatened to relieve him of several body parts, after which, he was more than eager to admit to using Fab. As his blood dripped on the floor, I told him he got off easy and if he ever contacted Fab again, he wouldn't get lucky a second time. Said I'd better never hear his name again." Toady pulled an envelope out of his shirt pocket and handed it to Fab. "Told him to triple the agreed-on rate. He wrote a check, which I threatened better not bounce, and to be sure, I cashed it immediately."

"No wonder his phone has been disconnected." Fab smiled at Toady.

Several large platters of seafood arrived and were set down in the middle of the table. Mother tabled all intense talk until we'd eaten. The food exceeded the restaurant's already high standards. I wanted to call dibs on leftovers, but it had all been inhaled.

Once everything had been cleared away, I asked Mother, "Who are you going to put on the spot next?"

"You, actually." Mother smiled. *Gotcha.* "Heard you bought a new property."

I glared at Brad, who shook his head. "I didn't tell her. I don't think this latest acquisition is so swell, but I get why you did it, even if I don't like it."

I told everyone about the house and that it was set to close in a couple of days.

"Oh Madison," Mother groaned. "Another property full of crazy people. You have two already."

"You'll be happy to know that I'm politely asking the current residents to get out, then turning it into a vacation rental for people who need room for a passel of relatives or friends that want to hang out under the same roof and risk a good fight."

"I like the rental idea." Creole smiled at me. "There's a couple of websites Xander can list it on, and it will probably get a good response, being so close to the beach."

"I'm happy to serve the eviction notices." Toady cracked his knuckles.

Mother's eyebrows went up, but I knew she was happy that I wouldn't be doing it. "Everything will be done by the book," I assured her, "since they're known troublemakers. I'm hoping that they pack up and leave quietly."

"Don't be surprised if they burn up your phone with all kinds of excuses for why they can't move," Spoon said.

"Xander set up a burner phone for just that reason. If they want to talk to me, they'll have to leave a message, and I'll get back to them at my convenience."

"Send all those calls to me. Better yet, give me the phone; I'll see to each one personally." Toady grinned. "To hand over the notices, I'll leash up one of my alligators and take him for a walk to the property. I'll have to tie up his mouth, which he won't like, but I'll make it up to him by feeding him something special."

I was waiting for someone to ask him to define "special," but it didn't happen.

"As long as Frisco doesn't eat anyone, it

shouldn't be a problem."

Aww…he named his alligator.

Emerson, who'd been quiet all night, laughed. "Never dull a moment. I've missed these get-togethers."

"If you're going to be friendly with my brother…" I tapped my index fingers together, which made her laugh again. "Am I going to need to update your background check?" I'd had her checked out when she signed on to be Brad's lawyer for the custody case regarding his daughter, Mila, and she'd checked out. No crazy in her background.

"I'm sorry it was a boring report." Emerson continued to smile.

"Don't apologize; you're hardly boring." I winked.

Brad rolled his eyes. "If Emerson didn't already know you, she'd run out of here."

The server was back with dessert menus.

"I say each end of the table order several desserts. I've got mine whittle down to three, and that way we can share," I said, mentally licking my lips.

"This is the last opportunity to call someone out," Fab said.

Brad raised his hand. "Don't want to be left out, even though it doesn't have anything to do with me directly."

Emerson shook her head at him to be quiet. "Later," she whispered.

That didn't deter him. "Emerson has a dilemma, and I know two women that could help out. Doing so would help pave the way for me to get permanent custody of Logan. Unless a family member shows up, and I've come to the conclusion that's not going to happen."

My opinion was that the family was knee-deep in illegal, and I knew Fab shared the sentiment.

"Seriously, we can do this another time." Emerson's cheeks pinkened.

"As you already know, this is one nosey family, so you might as well do it while we're all together," I told Emerson. "We're happy to help with whatever you need."

"Brad's caseworker, Gail, needs help locating her sister, Allison, but working for Social Services puts her in an awkward position. She doesn't want to involve the police because she's afraid that it will spook her sister into running off again."

"And you'll make sure that Brad gets all the credit for getting us involved?" I asked.

"Of course. But feel free to say no, as Brad's already gotten glowing reports." Emerson patted his hand. "Custody would've gone to a family member if they could've found one interested, but so far, nothing. Not a one of them is returning calls."

The server delivered the desserts on two platters and handed out forks.

Fab leaned forward. "You want us to find the sister?" Emerson nodded. "What can you tell us about her? Or should we wait to talk to your friend?"

"You'll definitely need to have a meeting with Gail to go over specifics. She can also provide you with photos. The last known address is just north of the Cove. What I know is that Allison was happily married, and they had three children. Then the husband was killed in an auto accident. She went off the deep end and hasn't been able to get her act together. Her kids have suffered greatly, and when Allison got wind that her sister was going to take custody until she straightened out her life, she took off with the kids and began to move around. Gail knows the situation has gotten dire, as the son, who's twelve, was picked up for being homeless. He told his aunt where his mother was living, but when Gail got there, Allison and her two daughters were gone."

"The boy is living with his aunt now?" I asked, and Emerson nodded. "Call your friend and set it up for Fab and me to talk to her."

"Once you find Allison, you won't have to confront her—call Gail, and she'll do it. Ideally, she'd like to get her sister help so she can become a good mother again."

"Anything Gail can tell us about her sister would be helpful—phone number, past addresses. We'll have Xander run a check on everything, and hopefully, it'll turn up a lead to her current location," Fab said. "We'll also go to any old addresses and talk to the neighbors; maybe whatever information they have will lead us to her. We might luck out and one will know something definitive."

"Anything you can do to help locate Allison would be greatly appreciated. The son's stories are frightening."

"It's surprising that the boy was able to go off on his own," I said.

"He ran away." Emerson grimaced. "He's lucky he got picked up right away and was able to give the police his aunt's number."

"We volunteer." Fab flicked her finger between her and me.

"I'm also available for anything you need," Mother announced. "I expect you not to hesitate to call. Ignore Brad's groaning; I can be very useful."

Emerson laughed. "If I can be of any help, I also volunteer."

The desserts disappeared the same as the food. One requirement to get into this family—you had to have a sweet tooth.

"When are we going to do the job we were supposed to do today?" Mother asked.

All conversation stopped. The men turned to stare at me.

I tipped my glass to them, tipsy enough to make eye contact with each one and laugh…just enough to irritate them. "I'll be picking you up early; be sure to gun up." I shot up the room with one hand, my drink in the other. "We're going to Miami to check out West's office and then to lunch. Dress casual chic and we'll fit right in. Maybe ixnay on the gun. Unless you want the security guard to feel you up." I winked at her. I didn't know whether the building had that amenity, but it sounded good.

"Why are you poking your nose in Crum's legal case? Doesn't he have a lawyer?" Spoon grouched.

"I damn well agree," Creole said.

"Mother, he said a bad word," I said in a whiny tone, pointing at Creole. That garnered laughter from the table.

Creole leaned over and whispered, "I'm so paying you back."

I winked at him and turned back to the table. "I feel a bit responsible, as I hired Crum to irritate West's last nerve in the hopes he'd snap up the neighboring property. I didn't think it would spark raised fists. Or that it would lead to a murder charge. I know that Crum didn't murder West and don't want him ending up in the big house."

"We'll pick you up in the morning," Fab told Mother. "Before we head out, we'll hit up our favorite coffee place."

I pumped my fist. "That means I'm not driving, and with Fab behind the wheel, she can leave her barf bag at home."

"Madison Westin," Mother said in a horrified tone.

Fab grinned.

"Don't 'Madison Westin' me—Fab's the one who claims my driving makes her sick."

Chapter Seventeen

Mother arrived early the next morning, her arms loaded down with pink bakery boxes. I texted a heads up to Fab to bring Didier and hustle over for yummy food while Creole broke out the extra coffee pot and brewed up everyone's favorites.

After getting the "don't look for trouble" lecture, we lit out of the house and hit the road. No need to stop at the coffee joint; we were stuffed and coffeed up.

Fab flew up the highway to Brickell, Miami's financial center, where West's office was located. The ritzy area catered to the banking and business crowd.

"Xander easily located the address of West's office but couldn't find anything beyond that," I said. "His office is at the top of one of the tower buildings. Translation: his lease costs him plenty."

"He certainly chose an address to impress his clients," Fab said.

"Won't the receptionist think it's weird that you're showing up?" Mother asked. "Since you don't have an appointment. Or maybe they're closed altogether, since he's…no longer with us."

"I called a couple of days ago, and a woman answered, identifying it as his office. When I asked to speak with him, she was evasive, saying that he wouldn't be in for a while. I assumed she didn't want to get into a 'he was murdered' conversation. I tried a second time, attempting to disguise my voice." I mimicked the voice I used, which got a groan from Fab. "I admitted to knowing of his demise, offered condolences, and asked if they had an attorney to whom they were referring his clients. She told me to leave my name and someone would get back to me, and they never did."

"Don't you think you're going to hit the same dead end showing up in person?" Mother asked.

"What I'm hoping for is someone bribable, who'll answer my questions for a few bucks."

"The younger the person, the better," Fab said.

"That's where you come in." I tapped her shoulder. "You take the lead—wiggle your way in and name-drop ad nauseum. That trick has worked on more than one occasion for scoring information."

"What am I going to do?" Mother demanded. "Don't tell me to stay out of trouble. I hear that enough."

"Don't be grouchy. If there's no on-street parking and the only alternative is the parking structure, you can slide behind the wheel and be the getaway driver." I smiled at her.

"No," Mother said adamantly. "Done that before. Don't think you're going to ditch me in the red zone or send me driving around in circles. You run the risk of me getting lost and you two having to walk home. Better idea: I'll be backup and you be the driver."

"I'd like to see you explaining ditching us to our husbands. Don't think that your husband can protect you from their wrath." I returned her stare-down.

Fab circled the block and, rather than trying to conjure up a parking space when they were limited, drove into the garage. She rolled down the window and flirted with the attendant, who let her have one of the five-minute spaces.

We got out of the car, and Fab corralled us. "Both of you listen up. This shouldn't take longer than ten minutes, so no wandering off and getting lost." She gave a flinty glare to Mother, who wasn't the least bit affected.

We strolled past the guard, who barely gave us a glance; he was too busy laughing with someone on the phone. We rode the elevator not quite to the top, as the two top floors were locked off, and the doors opened into a large reception area. The young brunette sitting behind the large desk looked up and smiled.

"You're up," I whispered to Fab.

Fab walked up to the desk, a briefcase in her hand that I hadn't noticed before. "We had an appointment with Mr. West." She introduced herself. "I understand he's deceased and hoped that another lawyer had taken over the file. So sad about what happened."

"Mr. West was a one-man office." The woman shrugged, looking embarrassed. Her phone started ringing. She apologized to Fab, then checked the phone display before answering the call. Then another call. Each time identifying herself as a different business. She took messages for both.

A man in a suit got off the elevator lugging a giganto briefcase. "My usual office?" he asked the woman, who nodded. He barely slowed. "Give me five before you send my client back."

Mother had wandered over to the roster of people listed on the wall. Mimicking Fab, she pulled out her phone and took a discreet picture.

I walked up behind her. "What are you doing?"

"How many offices are on this floor? There's a lot of names listed here."

"We're going to stay out of the way and let Fab work her magic." Mother and I glanced over, and Fab and the woman were laughing.

Good to her word, Fab motioned to us not even five minutes later, and we met at the elevator, not saying a word until the door closed.

"This entire floor is comprised of upscale office space. Some can be rented by the hour, which Carrie, under threat of losing her job, is not to divulge to anyone," Fab said as we rode down to the lobby. "It's set up to look like a large firm occupies the floor, but there's rarely anyone around on a regular basis. It's all about wanting an address to impress clients. Carrie forwards all the calls, sorts the mail, and signs for packages."

The doors opened into the lobby, and we got out. As we were about to step onto the escalator to the garage, Mother stopped us in our tracks, saying, "Pick me up out front."

I grabbed her arm, and she jerked out of my hold. "Where do you think you're going, young lady?"

"You'll see. Now behave and do what you're told."

Fab chuckled as I joined her. "What's your mother up to?"

As we got on the escalator, we noticed that Mother had approached the security guard.

"I'll go back and get her," I said.

"And she'll kill you. Just let her do whatever, and if she ends up in jail, we'll bail her out."

"You're not funny." I got in the car while Fab over-tipped the attendant. "West renting hourly office space suggests that he didn't have any clients, or not many anyway," I said as Fab got behind the wheel. "How did he afford a mansion on the beach?"

"Something doesn't add up…unless he comes from money." Fab pulled out of the garage and scanned the sidewalk. No sign of Mother. She merged into traffic for a scenic cruise around the block. "I'd planned to go back to his house for another look around, sans husbands. Then I got sidelined. It's still on my to-do list. There were files strewn all over the floor; maybe a closer look would tell us something about the man."

"You plan on pulling this little trek off in the middle of the day, so as to avoid the watchful eyes of your husband and mine?"

Fab circled the block and came up in front of the building, coasting slowly in the red. "Where's your mother?" she growled.

"I'm sending a text: *Fab's irked at having to wait, see you at home.* Done, you can go now."

"It wasn't funny when it was your mother's idea, and it hasn't gotten any funnier," Fab grouched.

I made a pouty face. "You were supposed to laugh."

"I've been feeling off my game since that woman blindsided me. I've been over the incident numerous times, and I'm disgusted I didn't see it coming."

"I've been over it as well, and you protected yourself and held your own, considering you were caught off guard. If she'd had her way, you'd have left the scene in an ambulance."

Fab cruised around the block once again, and this time, Mother stepped off the curb and waved.

"Be sure you ask her what she was up to. Use the same demanding tone you use with me." Fab pulled over, and Mother slid into the passenger seat.

"According to the security guard, West hasn't been around in a couple of months," Mother relayed, full of excitement. "He remembers because West was rude and looked down his nose at him."

I remembered that look from when I talked to the man.

"Clark, the security guard, was friendly. I made up a story about having an appointment and said no one in the office would tell me a thing. All I wanted to know was if his cases had been referred to someone else. Clark commiserated and said that no one ever mentions his name and you'd think his murder would be hot gossip. I tried to pay him, but he wouldn't take the money."

I moved forward and stuck my head between the seats. "And when Spoon hears about 'Clark'—" I made air quotes that she slapped down. "—good luck getting out of the house."

Mother laughed. "I'm not worried."

"This wasn't a total waste of time, but close. That husband of yours have a small power boat I can borrow?" Fab asked Mother. "One that you could sneak me the keys for?"

Interesting subject change. "Why not borrow the bigger version? We know he has one of those. Do you know how to drive either one? Don't say that you can drive anything. I could say the same thing, and we know how that would turn out. It's okay to say you don't know how to do something."

Fab snorted.

Mother punched her arm. "Stop that; you don't want big nostrils. That would be so unappealing."

I laughed and leaned back against the seat. "Brad and I figured out when we were kids that that's one of those Mom-isms you made up."

Mother turned and said with a smirk, "You'll find out that I know a thing or two when your nose holes blow out."

I continued to laugh, lightly tracing my nose.

"What do you need the boat for, honey?" Mother asked Fab.

"Criminal activity," I yelled.

"Do you have to be so dramatic?" Fab sighed.

"Now girls. There's a small fishing boat that the guys use on occasion, but Spooner is going to demand an explanation and will subject you to questioning. Good luck blowing him off; it never works for me. Half-truths won't get you anywhere either."

I scooted forward again and tapped Fab's shoulder. "What are you up to?"

Fab humphed. "It's still in the planning stages."

"That swanky mall's not far from here." Mother pointed in the opposite direction of home.

Chapter Eighteen

The house down the street from The Cottages closed a day earlier than scheduled. Eugene had already signed his part of the paperwork, and Mac whispered that he'd packed up and beat it out of town with Frack's help, relocating north. Frack had advised the man to leave no forwarding, which had me wondering how bad the chaos Eugene was leaving behind was and hoping it didn't either follow him or land on my doorstep.

Toady had talked to a couple of the neighbors and found out that there was a woman living in the house, Vicky Prell, who claimed to own the property and ran it as a boarding house. I took Toady up on his offer to serve the eviction notices. As it turned out, I was left unsupervised that morning—Creole at the office and Fab and Didier off doing something secret—so I lay in wait at The Cottages, ready when Toady parked his truck, and surprised him when he got out. I scanned the back for Frisco and was happy to see that the alligator had been left at home.

"You need to stand back for your own safety," Toady grouched. "I'll be the front man, inform the tenants that the property is now under new ownership and that due to non-payment of rent, they need to move, pointing out that they've been given more time than most landlords would extend. As for you, no introduction is necessary." He leveled a hard stare at me. "My best advice—which you're paying for, by the way—anyone who asks, let them think I'm the owner. You blend into the sidewalk."

"I'm only tagging along to find out who's who, in case I run into one of them on the street. I want to know who I'm dealing with and not get caught off guard." I practically had to skip to keep up with Toady's long-legged stride as he hustled down the sidewalk, paperwork in hand. I caught a glimpse of several guys standing out in front of the house; they were a ragged and transitory-looking bunch. "This will make you happy—I'm going to wait across the street."

Toady nodded, having spotted the same group. "I'm not expecting any trouble, but you never know, and if...then you duck and cover. Got it?"

The only thing missing was him jabbing his finger at me. "Calm your shorts. I'm just here to observe the master at work." His lips quirked. "Here's *my* advice: Watch your back."

"Cross the street here, and I'll distract them as I walk up. You won't attract attention, other than possibly being written off as a nosy neighbor." Toady walked up to the guys, and whatever he said, they pointed to the house. He disappeared behind a hedgerow on his way to the front door.

I moved farther down the sidewalk so I could watch events unfold. I saw the door open and had a good view of Toady's back. A minute later, he was standing on the sidewalk, sans paperwork. He stopped to talk to the men, who hadn't taken their eyes off him.

A forty-something woman came running down the walk waving the paperwork, screeching, "You hold up." Strands of her dark brown hair coming out of the bun at the nape of her neck, she rushed him and took a swing. He stepped back, and she came up short, which infuriated her all the more.

I'd put money on that being Vicky Prell. Apparently, the sale of the property had caught her off guard.

"I'm not taking these," she screamed, shoving the papers against his chest. They fell to the ground. "Listen up. No one is telling me when I'm going to move."

Two more men came down the driveway, and judging by the glares they sent Toady's way, they were ready for a fight.

Despite Toady's admonition, I had my hand on the butt of my Glock, holstered at the small of my back.

The woman launched herself at Toady again,

and he turned, easily avoiding her. "You..." She unleashed a litany of foul words disparaging his parentage.

Toady never took his eyes off the last two to show up. One stuck his hand down the front of his pants, and Toady pulled his gun. "The first of you punks ready to be dispatched to the afterlife, step up. Then I'll pick you off one by one."

A car backfired, shattering the silence, and they all turned and stared. It was enough of a diversion that the first three scattered; the late arrivers didn't move.

I ducked behind a car and watched as the men squared off. The two left didn't appear eager to move against Toady.

It didn't take long before sirens could be heard getting closer. The woman, who'd been ready to provoke a fight earlier, ran back to the house, her feet slapping the concrete, and slammed the door hard enough to be heard in the next block. The two remaining men split up and went in opposite directions, both cutting through neighbors' yards.

Toady clapped his hands together and crossed the street. "Scattered like cockroaches."

"Just so you know, if one of them had shot you, I'd have returned the favor."

"No doubt." Toady grinned.

"Was that Vicky Prell?" I asked, and he nodded. "She's going to be a problem."

"It's one I'm going to enjoy taking care of."

Toady nodded, glancing over his shoulder.

Two cop cars rolled around the corner, Kevin the first on the scene.

"I'm going to continue to maintain my low profile over here. I'm not totally ditching you; if you need a witness, I'll be right here."

"Don't you worry, girlie; I've got this." Toady crossed the street and waited for Kevin to get out, the second cop about two steps from joining them.

The neighbors, having decided the coast was clear, rolled out of their houses and clustered in groups to trade stories about who saw what…which would be nothing. I suspected a few would make something up.

Both cops questioned Toady. Kevin looked my way but didn't acknowledge me.

The second cop went to the door and unleashed a loud knock. No answer.

It wouldn't surprise me if Vicky had gone out the back.

Kevin and the other cop went over to the neighboring house.

Toady rejoined me. "I've been excused."

Chapter Nineteen

The guys had barely cleared the compound when Fab picked me up the next morning. She had her sneaky smile in place, clearly up to something, but when asked, wouldn't offer up a single hint. I didn't tell her about waylaying Toady, though I had fessed up to Creole. I timed my confession for when he was almost asleep, which went well until he woke up remembering and I got my ears lectured off. It didn't escape my notice that in between, he wanted to know every detail.

I didn't need my neck hairs to tell me that turning into West's neighborhood spelled trouble. "What are you up to now? If it's escaped your notice, it's broad daylight." The one good thing was that all appeared to be quiet, and no one was lurking about, but that didn't mean someone wouldn't show up out of nowhere.

"Calm your frizz. Just taking a quick turn around the neighborhood."

"You stole that line from Rude, or maybe Mac. Wait until they hear; they'll be more enamored of you than usual." She hadn't factored in me ratting her out—good. "You're looking for trouble, and I'm hoping you don't find it."

"We're leaving. Happy now?" She'd circled the block twice, then cut back out to the main highway.

"I'd be happier if I knew what you're up to. I promised Creole that I'd stay out of trouble for a couple of days and would like to keep that promise."

"You can always blame me."

Her big smile told me she was proud of the idea. News flash: Done that and it doesn't work.

She turned off the highway and wound down to the water and into a bike and boat rental place.

I twisted and stared out the window to double-check the sign, then crossed my arms. "I'm not setting one foot out of this car until you tell me what's going on."

"Just get out. It will ruin the surprise."

"You know how much I love surprises," I grumbled and got out.

Fab linked her arm in mine and tugged me down to the dock. The young man on duty pointed to one of the power boats and gave her quick instructions.

I shook my head, knowing exactly what she was up to.

Fab came over, jiggling the keys. "Don't make me go by myself. I need you as backup. You'd feel awful if something bad happened to me."

"Stop with the guilt." I followed her, climbed onto the boat, and took the seat opposite her. "Good luck explaining this outing to Didier."

Fab ignored me and fired up the engine, cruising off over the water, which was thankfully calm. I was happy she didn't speed off and scare the devil out of me. She cruised along the coast, and it didn't take as long as I'd thought it would before West's mansion came into view. I had a million questions but would wait until the engine was off and Fab could hear me. She cruised up to West's dock and idled alongside.

"Do you know how to tie this boat up so it doesn't float off?" I eyed the weathered cleat attached to the dock. She grumbled something, her eyes glued to the shore. "Now what?" I scanned the beach and then the house, and all appeared quiet. "I'm thinking what we're doing is worse than trespassing, as far as criminal charges go."

"Once I enter the house, it becomes a felony, even if the owner isn't around to press charges." Fab whipped a pair of binoculars out of her bag and checked out the house. "If you're worried that one of us might need bail, you can wait in the boat."

"It's called accessory. That's what I am at the moment, and I'm sure my culpability is about to get worse." Fab knew all this without me having to tell her. "Once you're inside, how am I supposed to back you up if I'm outside? You probably lucked out, as all looks quiet."

Fab hopped over the side of the boat and secured it to the dock, making it obvious this wasn't her first time.

I jumped off the side of the boat onto the dock and followed her up the sand. "What about West's security system?"

"It was off the last time we were here. Not sure if the cops would come back and reset it or leave it to his estate."

We strode up the beach, and I waited on the patio while Fab checked out the driveway. She came back shaking her head: *all clear*.

"Once you're inside, then what?" I had no doubt she'd get inside.

"Just a quick peek around."

As it turned out, getting inside wasn't an issue—the pocket doors hadn't been closed all the way. Fab easily pushed them open, and we went inside. All the cupboards and drawers in the living room, dining room, and kitchen were wide open, the contents strewn across the floor.

Fab whipped out her phone. "I'm positive that this is a worse mess than the first time we were here, and I highly doubt the cops would do this. Whether the cops have been back or someone else broken in…busy place."

"Tell me what you need me to do, and I'll do it."

"Get out your phone and take pictures of whatever you find interesting. Be on the lookout for anything out of place. Though it might be hard to notice in this chaos."

"If the police are satisfied that they arrested

the right person and the case is moving forward, why would they come back and tear the place apart?" I asked.

"It makes more sense to assume that another party is involved. If so, did they find what they were looking for? I'm guessing that they didn't." Fab led the way to West's office and stopped in the doorway. I squeezed in beside her. "This room has definitely been re-searched."

The baseboards had been removed, and the trim tossed aside, nothing but drywall showing through. The vent covers lay on the floor, and the lighting fixtures were hanging by their electrical cords.

Fab circled the room, stepping over mountains of paperwork, surveying every inch. "It's interesting that West didn't have a safe. Not in this room anyway."

I bent down and flicked through the pile of papers scattered about. "It would take forever to go through all this on the off-chance we'd find something interesting. Not to mention that we don't have a clue what we're looking for."

Fab changed course and walked the room from one end to the other, testing every inch of the hardwood floor. She sat down at West's desk and checked out every drawer, though they'd been upended. "Nothing." She let out a frustrated sigh, pulled out a knife, and dropped down on all fours. "The last time I was here, I thought I felt some give, right about…" She knocked on the wood, then easily pried the planks apart where they fit together, loosening several and setting them aside.

I hung over the side of the desk. "How do you figure these things out?"

"No wall safe, and most in his income bracket have them, so it had me thinking: where would he stash valuables? My next stop was going to be his bedroom, which I still want to check out." Fab pulled out a small metal box—locked. She took out her lockpick and lifted the lid. "Look what we have here." She pulled out a portable drive that, judging from its size, had plenty of storage capacity. "Interesting." Then two more, followed by a small firearm and cash. Not enough if one were planning a quick getaway. The last item was a passport, which Fab opened. "Not in his name, but it's his picture."

"Now what?"

"I'm taking a picture of the passport. The drives I'm taking with me and handing over to Xander to go through and see if he can find anything that answers a few questions. The rest I'm putting back in the box." She did that, then shoved a disc in each pocket and handed me one. Next stop, the master bedroom. She gave it the same once-over as the office.

We both heard the front door close and turned in surprise. A man could be heard grumbling down the hall, either talking to himself or someone else. Fab motioned me behind the armoire that sat diagonally across a corner and crossed her lips with her finger. She moved behind the open bedroom door, gun in hand. I drew my gun before easing behind the big piece of furniture.

Seconds later, thuds reverberated from the other room. It sounded like the man had decided to empty the bookcase.

Fab crept over to the slider and pushed it back, then turned and motioned to me, and we both slipped through. She closed it, and we flew down the stairs and crept across the patio, skirted around the pool, and ran. Thankfully, no one stood in our way. We hustled down the dock, and I hopped in the boat while Fab untied it. I turned and caught sight of a man standing on the second-floor balcony waving a firearm, which unnerved me. I controlled my shriek as Fab reversed into open water. I told her what I'd seen, and both of us were surprised he hadn't taken a shot. I stood lookout and could safely say that no one followed us.

"I should've confronted whoever that was while we were still in the house," Fab confided after she returned the rental boat.

"Very happy that you didn't." I grimaced. "I can't imagine the legal ramifications if the three of us were caught inside the house and one or more of us was maimed or dead."

"Thanks for coming, even though you didn't want to." Not one to count her blessings in getting away in one piece, she cruised back to West's mansion after leaving the boat rental.

"You need to stop tempting fate."

West's gate was still closed, the front of the house not visible from the street. All appeared quiet. Maybe the man had also taken off after realizing he had company. Fab rounded the corner and saw a newer model pickup sitting in almost the same spot we'd parked the night we came with the guys. She slowed and rolled down the window, taking several pictures, including one of the license plate.

"The truck might belong to one of the neighbors, but that's easily verifiable." Fab finally turned out of the neighborhood.

I hoped it would be the last time I saw the West mansion. "I don't like to hide things from Creole, but I'm thinking this might be a good one to keep quiet about. Because he will seriously kill me." And she'd meet the same fate from Didier, but she didn't need me to tell her that.

"They're going to ask what we did today. Then what? We need to get our story straight."

"That's why you need to think of something before we get home. Don't get too wordy and intense."

"I'm a private investigator, and client confidentiality comes with the job. Didier's fine with it...sort of, anyway."

"Lose the defensive stance. That's a dead giveaway that we were up to something damn dangerous," I cautioned. "Creole wasn't under any illusions as to what he was getting when he married me—you know, crazy wife—but I'm not going anywhere near that excuse. Unless I can't think of anything else."

We both laughed.

I was happy when we drove up to the house, and no one was home. I sighed, but knew the relief wouldn't last long.

"I'm thinking we just fess up," Fab said. "Here's my reasoning: if the drives we purloined have useful information on them, then what do I say? It was a beautiful sunny day, I stole a dead guy's property and luckily got away before someone else, probably wanting to steal the same, caught up to me. That's not a good story?"

Was that a real question? "Being a supportive friend..." I ignored her dirty look. "While you're talking, I'll slap on a pleasant smile and nod. Unless you motor off with some weedy explanation, and then I won't be able to help myself and have to cut in."

"How about a two-parter? We tell them that we searched the house and save the intruder part for another time." It was clear she liked her plan.

"Not a good idea. Creole can only kill you once, so getting everything off your chest from the get-go will make your flight to the afterlife less bumpy." I'd be next on his hit list.

"You're damn weird."

"We all have our talents." I saw Fab's smirk despite her attempt to turn away.

Chapter Twenty

Fab texted me after she'd gotten home. "We're going to surprise the guys with breakfast out."

I called rather than typing out a response. "What kind of plan is that?" I asked when she answered.

"It's my and Didier's turn to host the weekly breakfast meeting, and surprising them with the change of plans will work to our advantage."

Too bad she couldn't see my eyeroll through the phone. "How do you figure?" I was almost afraid to ask.

"They can't kill us in public."

"I wouldn't bet on it."

Fab and Didier showed up early the next morning, before Creole and I could walk next door. With a smug look, Fab yelled, "Surprise." Looking chagrined, Didier shrugged, clearly having no clue what was going on. "Madison and I decided to surprise the two of you with breakfast at the Bakery Café. We'll meet you there." She hooked her arm in Didier's and didn't quite drag him back to the car, but close.

"What was that all about?" Creole eyed me.

"Oh no." I waved him off and grabbed my purse. "I'm not going to be the one to ruin Fab's surprise." I squeezed past him and headed to his truck. "At least we know the food is great."

We talked about other things on the drive to the restaurant, for which I was thankful, because frankly, I didn't know what Fab had up her sleeve.

The four of us were seated around our favorite table at the end of the sidewalk—a good people-watching spot that made for a quick getaway, since the cars weren't far—and were on our last cup of coffee when Fab's phone pinged, alerting her and the rest of us that she had a text. She perused the message and screwed up her nose.

Now what? I didn't have to ask because Didier, who leaned over and read the screen over her shoulder, launched into a torrent of French. I wished they wouldn't do that; I was the only one not multi-lingual, and it made eavesdropping impossible.

"I knew you were up to something," Creole growled at Fab. "Xander ran a license plate for you, and it came back as stolen?" He turned to me. "What's he talking about?"

"I wouldn't want to guess." Although waffley, it was true.

"Read the rest." Didier nudged Fab.

Fab turned her phone over. "The truck was found ditched on the side of the road. It's currently being housed in impound."

Stolen was convenient. Smart of whoever it was not to use their own car.

Fab's phone pinged again.

"Why don't you read us that message?" Didier told her. "When you're done, you can start at the beginning."

I'd long ago finished my coffee, but my cup was glued to my lips.

Fab picked up her phone, read the message, and shoved it in her pocket. "There have been two calls to 911 about a man lurking around West's neighborhood. Both times, the cops went out there and didn't find anything out of the ordinary."

"I wonder who that might've been?" I managed to keep the sarcasm out of my voice. "Let's hope Crum has an alibi."

"I pulled him aside and told him not to go venturing off without an audience and that it would be a good idea to track his whereabouts in case he was asked, for whatever reason," Fab said. "He didn't blow me off like he would one of his drunk friends."

I laughed, even though Creole and Didier were ready to strangle her.

"The beginning that Didier mentioned…now would be a good time," Creole said, not controlling his irritation very well.

I wanted to scoot my chair away, but if it came to a getaway, Creole could easily run me down.

"Keep an open mind," Fab started.

I groaned inwardly and continued to make eye contact with my coffee cup.

"I want you both to know that this was my brainchild and I'm taking all the responsibility. Yes, Madison came along, but I didn't divulge details until my plan was well underway. Yesterday..." She launched into what had gone down the previous day, downplaying the man's appearance and omitting the part where we were all in the house at the same time.

Creole leaned back in his chair, madder than a hornet. "You thought this was a good idea? Did you tally up all the felonies you were committing?" He turned to me. "And you went along, and this is the first I'm hearing about it?"

Didier had plenty to say, all in French. Judging by Fab's expression, he wasn't happy with anything he'd just learned.

"Where are the drives now?" Creole asked.

"In a bag in the car. I planned to drop them off with Xander," Fab said. "I thought if they were important enough to hide, maybe they'd yield useful information as to why someone would want to kill him."

"Is there anything else you want to share?" Didier asked. "Now would be the time."

"Don't be mad." Fab reached for his hand, which he drew back.

"I guess you want me to say go ahead and do what you want, damn the consequences." Didier shoved his chair back and stood. "I'll take care of the check." He walked off.

"You need to..." I pointed after Didier. "I'll have Creole drop me at the house." Once Fab had left the table, I followed Creole to the truck.

Once inside, he said, "Now let's hear your version."

After I was done, he didn't say anything, so we rode in silence.

Once back in the compound, I asked, "Are you divorcing me?"

Creole snorted. "Hardly. And Didier's not dumping Fab either. But we need to talk about the risks you two are willing to take."

Chapter Twenty-One

I hadn't been home long when the front door opened and banged closed. At the same time, my phone rang, Mac's smiling face popping up. I motioned Fab to a seat across from me at the island.

"Good news, I hope," I said when I answered. "You're on speaker."

"The good news is: no one died." Da-da-dah in Mac's voice.

"You need to get to the real news," Fab said.

"Okay fine. There was another brawl last night at your new property. I'd have called sooner if someone had been carted off in an ambulance."

"I don't want you sticking your neck out in any way, just so you can keep up with what's going on at that end of block." I was beginning to wonder if these fights were staged to demonstrate their unhappiness at having to move out. If so, it was a terrible strategy.

"Gotcha."

"I'm calling an impromptu meeting around the pool and would appreciate it if you'd call and ask Toady to hop on over. Also, make sure we've got plenty of cold drinks."

"How soon?" Mac asked.

"We're on our way." We hung up. "You're still alive, so that's good," I told Fab.

"I'm not out of trouble with Didier just yet. We're having a talk later about knowing my limits. I'm going to have to make some concessions—not sure what they'll be." Fab got up and grabbed a couple of waters out of the refrigerator. "Before we go to The Cottages, I need to stop by the office."

I followed her out to the SUV. "Or I could ask Xander to meet us at The Cottages."

"That's a better idea. I need to give Didier time to get over being mad."

* * *

Fab pulled into The Cottages and parked in front of the office. We got out and, after a quick check of the property, went over to the pool.

Crum was sitting poolside, which didn't surprise me, as it was one of his favorite places. But the man sitting at the table with him, I'd never seen before. Time to introduce myself. When I got within a few steps of the table, I realized that Crum was helping the man with a stack of paperwork. I waved as I approached.

"This is Gary, one of my ex-cellmates." Crum introduced me, and the oversized giant nodded. "Before your shorts get all bunched, Gary's staying with me for a few days. Once he gets a job, he'll be getting his own place."

An ex-con—great. Fab chuckled from behind me. "What were you in for?"

"I was part of a car theft ring. We were doing pretty good until another guy ratted us out so he didn't have to do time on a drug charge. The professor said he'd help me stay out, and surprisingly, he's as good as his word." He shot Crum a toothy grin. "Also promised to show me how to make a legal buck. Thought he was full of it, but here I am."

"Gary says he's good with cars, and by that, I mean fixing them," Crum said.

I nodded. "Here are the rules. Cops come here looking for you and you're out. I don't want to hear any excuses; just go."

"I thought it was two calls," Crum grumped.

"No problem," Gary cut in. "Give you my word, you won't be getting any trouble out of me."

I took a step away and turned back. "One more rule," I said, ignoring Crum's groan. "Underwear only is not proper attire." I squinted at Crum.

Gary laughed. "No worries. I don't care to show off my goods that way."

Toady and Xander came through the open pool gate and kicked it closed.

I hadn't seen Mac arrive, but she was pulling chairs around one of the tables and setting an oval bucket of cold drinks in the center. We all sat down at the same time.

Fab's phone rang, and she jumped up. "Don't speak until I get back." She answered the call and walked to the other side of the pool.

"Just to let you know… I've been to your house a couple of times, and no one answers the door, although there's always cars in the driveway," Toady relayed in an annoyed tone. "I got pictures of all the license plates and gave them to Xander."

"It's a good idea to know who we're dealing with, since I doubt anyone's going to be introducing themselves," I said to Xander. "Fab's also got a job for you and will give you the details."

Xander nodded. "I figured, and I'll email whatever I find out."

I turned my attention back to Toady.

"Vicky Prell called the burner phone a couple of times. Each time I returned her call, she harangued me about her right to stay," Toady said. "Told her that she was being evicted, and whether she showed up for the court hearing or not, she was out. Judges don't tend to side with non-payers. Before she could hang up on me like she'd done the previous times, I also told her that once I got the order in my hand, one way or another, she'd be out on the street."

"Do you know anything about what went down last night?" I asked.

"Staked out the house last night from the porch of the old guy across the street, and all it cost me was a case of beer." Toady reached for a soda. "It wouldn't call it a fight. They were yelling and engaging in horseplay—grown men making asses of themselves, ratcheting up the noise as much as possible before hitting the road, which they did as soon as sirens could be heard approaching. I thought it was a setup to get the cops to show, but why? Thinking you'll change your mind about evicting them? Not a very smart plan, because who wants constant trouble?"

"I'm surprised that they'd run the risk of getting arrested. Bail's not cheap."

"They knew exactly when to scatter, and they didn't hesitate. Earlier, I got a chance to talk to a couple of the neighbors. They all claimed ignorance, as one old man got into a war of words with one of them and they threatened to kick his butt. That scared the rest of the neighbors into minding their own business."

Fab stormed back over and sat down. "I thought you were going to wait for me."

I leaned forward, retrieved a bottle of cold water, and handed it to her. "To sum it up, the people down the street are still being a pain. Basically, nothing new."

"That was Gunz." Fab tapped her phone. "He's got a new job for me—wants me to find out who bought the house. He already knows it's in the name of a corporation but wants to know who the players are."

Mac grimaced. "I knew that call was coming and frankly expected it sooner."

"Wonder why he didn't contact Xander directly, since he's the master at uncovering information."

Xander shook his head furiously. "I'm on vacation."

"While Gunz was going on about losing the property, my first thought was to lie, but I changed my mind," Fab said. "I fessed up to knowing the buyer, and before he could ask who, I reminded him about client confidentiality."

"His reaction must've been fierce." Would he hunt me down? I didn't want to think about it.

"He exploded. Practically took my ear off. I waited for him to take a breath, then cut in and calmed him down, telling him that I'd had no idea he was interested in the property, since he hadn't said a word."

"Well played." Toady clapped.

"Gunz wants me to find out if the buyer would be amenable to selling."

"Why is he so hot for the property?" I asked. "It's not his usual multi-units."

"I asked him that very question, only nicer." Fab smirked at me. "Turns out, he's friends with Vicky's brother. The plan was for Gunz to purchase it and she'd make the payments, since she's got no credit to get a loan in her own name."

"That was a bad idea. When Vicky started dancing him around as to why she couldn't pay, and she would have, that would've strained the friendship with the bro. At some point, Gunz would've had to put one of his oversized feet down to stop the games, and the war would begin."

"I told him he should be thankful he lost out on the deal, with all the trouble going on down there. He didn't like hearing that and let me know it." Fab grimaced. "Don't be surprised when he uncovers your name; he's not going to give it up until he gets the information he wants."

"I had no idea you were interested," I said in an overly sweet tone, fluttering my eyelashes.

The guys laughed.

Fab smirked. "You better work on that performance."

"I'm going to hang out down there for a few hours tonight, and at the first sign of anything, I'm going to tip off a couple of my cop friends," Toady said.

"Listen up." I pointed my finger at him. Xander grinned. "I do not want you to do anything that could get you hurt. Got it?"

Toady flashed his gold tooth. "Gotcha, girlie. But if it's okay with you, I don't want to pass on the opportunity to kick some butt."

"What are you going to do when moving day comes around and they haven't gone anywhere?" Fab asked. "You know that's the likely scenario."

"I'll have to take them to court." I sighed.

"Maybe not," Xander said. "Not all of them will hang around. I ran the plate numbers that Toady gave me, and two of the men have outstanding warrants from other states. Both on drug charges."

"Almost forgot—two of them have moved already," Toady said. "So that leaves two more and Vicky. Not sure if the two Xander mentioned are the ones that already beat it out of town. All bets are that the others will follow. Vicky will be the hard one to get rid of."

"I just want them all out and to get the renovation started." I sighed. "Are we about done here?"

"I need to talk to Xander," Fab said.

Chapter Twenty-Two

Mac shoved her chair back, waving her hand. "Hold up. I'd like to cash in one of my favor cards," she directed at Fab. "As I recall, there's a no-grumbling clause."

"This ought to be good."

I shot Fab the *be nice* stare, which she ignored. "We'd be happy to help you in any way we can." I attempted to kick Fab, which got everyone's attention, and as expected, she scooted back.

"I've got a friend that lives around the corner, Marla Davis. Her Maltese, Coco, was stolen two days ago. The next day, Marla swears that she saw it sitting in the neighbor's living room window. She called the cops, who came out and talked to the two guys that lived there, and no dog. But she insists she saw the dog again later."

"Maybe it's a lookalike," I said.

Mac shook her head.

"Not a chance when the cops go there and no dog at all," Fab said. "If it was just a lookalike, there would've been a dog, and the mistaken identity would've been cleared up. So where did the dog go?"

"Here's some more weirdness," Mac said. "Marla claims to have seen a never-ending parade of dogs on that property since the two men moved in. She's also witnessed the guys rushing the dogs back into the house after they do their business in the yard."

"You know dog-selling rings crop up all the time." Toady looked around squint-eyed, as though we were all involved. "What kinds of dogs has your friend seen?"

"Small ones. The only breed she could identify were the Yorkshire Terriers."

"That particular breed is prime for theft, as they bring lots of money and are easily stolen, being just the right size to scoop up and hide away."

I was surprised at how much Toady knew…and that I hadn't heard a word about it going on in the neighborhood.

"That makes another thing I won't mind getting to the bottom of. Because if that's what's happening, then they need to be put out of business." Toady grumbled.

"That would be sweet of you." Mac patted Toady's hand. He grinned at her. "You know the neighborhood better than any of us, and if you could recover Coco, Marla would be over the moon. That's if they still have the dog."

"It's hard to believe anyone exists that knows the neighborhood better than you," I teased Mac.

"I did a little of my own sleuthing, and the

only thing I found out is that the men aren't well-liked by their neighbors. No one had any use for their unfriendly selves."

Of course she did.

"What do you expect us to do? Knock on the door and demand the dog back? It didn't work for the cops; why would it for us?" Fab demanded.

Mac wasn't put off by Fab's 'tudiness. "I've got a plan all worked out for you." She was bubbling with excitement.

Toady growled out a laugh. He'd clearly already decided to help, no matter what we decided to do.

I sat back, thinking this wasn't going to be good, but I didn't want to be blamed for being the enthusiasm killer.

Not deterred, Mac continued: "One of you knocks on the door." She held up her hand and mimicked the motion. "While the other one is picking the lock at the back and enticing the dog out with a treat." *Da-da-da.*

I nudged Fab's foot.

Mac's phone rang. She pulled it out of her pocket and glanced at the screen, holding up her finger. "Everything okay?" she answered. "You're not to do anything until I get there." She hung up. "That was Marla. Neighbor dudes just left. She's talking about breaking a window and going in herself."

"That would be a fast ticket to jail, and she'd

be facing serious charges," I said. "Even if she found the dog, that wouldn't be a defense, and there would be the issue of identification."

Toady jumped up, as did Mac. "You call your friend and tell her to hang tight." He walked along with Mac as she made the call.

"We're right behind you." Fab motioned to me and pointed at Xander.

The three us crossed the driveway. Toady and Mac got in his truck, and I jumped in the bed and knocked on the back window, motioning for them to wait for Fab, who was telling Xander what she needed and handing him a bag. Then she ran over and hopped in beside me.

"If we pull this off and get the dog back, Marla needs to watch her back. If those men are thieves, they won't be calling the cops, but they will keep her movements under a microscope and get back at her," I said.

Fab nodded. "If this is a legit story and not just some woman wanting a dog, Toady will scare them out of the neighborhood."

"I trust that Mac can see through a con. Since the woman's her friend, she would know. Whereas us...we'd need pictures, paperwork, something."

"I'm thinking that if these men aren't home, I'm in agreement with picking the lock and re-appropriating the dog. Hopefully, it'll be the right one, and we'll be done with it," Fab said as Toady pulled over and parked.

A middle-aged woman dressed in jeans, her grey hair a mess of frizzy curls, was frantically pacing the sidewalk. Mac hopped out, ran over, and hugged her, then steered her back towards her house.

Toady got out and stood back with Fab and me.

"Who's going to do what?" I asked.

"Do either of you know diddly about dogs?" Toady asked with a smug smile. "I'm certain you didn't bring that treat you mentioned." Neither Fab nor I said anything. "You two hit the front door with some cockamamie story while, going on the assumption that they're not home, I'll go in the back. Animals of all sizes like me. Think it's because I've got that animal-friendly smell."

I bit my lip and grabbed Fab's arm. "That cat of ours is on the loose again." At her laugh, I said, "If one or both answer the door, Toady's in trouble, so I'll text yea or nay." I pulled out my phone. "You step up and go all sexy sultry."

"Hate that plan," Fab said, tugging me up the steps. "Put on your used car salesman face." I made a face that had her laughing. "Needs work. There's a slight revision to the story—we're here to visit our aunt, who we haven't seen in a long time, and either she moved or we have the wrong address." She served up her best cop knock, which could wake the dead. Nothing. She did it again.

"You're going to be annoyed if you break your hand."

Fab kicked the door.

"Okay, tough girl, I'm thinking no one's home." I turned and looked into the side yard. "I texted Toady. Let's go loiter on the sidewalk—hang out like we don't know anything about what's going down."

"Now we can add dog stealing to our resume."

"Appropriating sounds better."

Everything happened at once.

Toady came from around the back with a Maltese in his arms.

Marla squealed. Mac had only gotten her as far as her front porch.

Excited to see her owner, Coco started yapping.

A truck squealed to a stop in the driveway. Two grungy thirty-somethings bounded out and across the lawn, yelling obscenities.

Toady closed the space between him and Marla, who was running in his direction, and shoved the dog into her arms. He issued an order and turned Marla around, and she ran back to her house. Then he turned back to the two men, unbuttoned his tropical shirt, and showed off his shoulder holster. They couldn't stop, even if they wanted to, and they clearly didn't.

Both went to tackle Toady. He kicked one man's legs out from under him and pivoted away from the other, who missed him and turned around for a second shot.

"I'd stop if I were you," Fab yelled, getting closer to the fray and brandishing her gun.

The second man put his hands in the air, flushed with anger. "I'm calling the cops."

"Don't move," Toady ordered. The first guy crawled to his knees and attempted to stand, but Toady shoved him back to the ground. "Go ahead and call the cops. It's not illegal to chase down your dog when it's gotten out of the yard."

"You stole it," they said, practically in unison.

"Did I? Prove it." Toady threw up his hands. "I can prove ownership, can you? I already know the answer, and it's no. You want to know what else I know? You even look at the woman next door, and I'll be back to feed you your teeth, one at a time. *Capiche*?" Neither said anything. "Answer me."

"Got it," they snarled.

Fab moved next to Toady and whispered something.

"Another thing—I've got a pretty good idea what you're doing here, and it's illegal. I'm telling you now that you're out of business, and if I get the slightest sniff otherwise, I'll see you in jail." Toady motioned to Fab, and they walked over to Mac and me. Toady didn't take his eye off the two men for a second.

The one man helped his friend to his feet, and they headed into the house, each looking back several times.

"We need to get out of here," I said. "We don't want to become a target if they have guns in the house."

"Don't want to call any attention to my truck, so I'll come back and get it later." Toady motioned for us to follow.

"Let Fab lead the way." I tugged on his arm. "She knows every side path, and if they're watching, they won't know which way we went."

Fab motioned. "This way."

"I offered to let Marla stay at my house, but she wanted to be in her own home. Told her to call me if anything out of the ordinary happens." Mac managed to walk backwards, one eye on the street.

Fab led us down the sidewalk, turned down a walkway that straddled two properties, cut over to another street, down another walkway, and over to The Cottages.

I scoped out both of my properties, and all was quiet. I glanced over at Mac's house and did a double take. "What's that?" I pointed to the male mannequin on her porch, not certain how I'd missed it when we arrived.

"That's Harry," Mac said, as though we'd been previously introduced.

The buff dude stood ramrod straight, with a stick up his...bathing trunks, if you could call them that, since they were the size of a postage stamp. If Crum saw those, he'd be wanting a pair in the same size.

Toady laughed. "Is Harry anatomically correct under those... I guess you could call them shorts?"

I punched his shoulder, and he laughed again.

"Did you boost him from Howl's?" I asked.

"Hardly." Mac took a closer look. "They do look similar."

"The sign he's holding says 'Closed.' For what?" Fab asked.

"No dissing Harry; he's a work of art." Mac gave us a stony stare. "Besides..." She waved at Harry. "He's good to talk to when I'm sitting on the porch."

"Don't get upset when he goes missing," I told her. "My guess is that it will happen sooner than you think."

"I suppose you're right. Maybe I can get help moving him inside? Harry's heavy."

Toady took the hint and flexed his muscles. "At your service." The two crossed the street.

"When we leave, we need to make a quick trip back around the corner; I want to take a picture of those guys' license plate. If they're selling dogs, we can turn the information over to one of our cop friends."

"Instead of Toady retrieving his truck, which is a bad idea, I say we recruit someone else to bring it back. Toady going by himself might attract too much attention."

Mac and Toady each grabbed one end of Harry and hauled him inside her house.

"Given that what they're doing is massively illegal, my guess is that they'll be gone within a day and set up shop in a new neighborhood," Fab said.

"Post their picture online with the tag: 'Don't buy dogs from these two.'"

"People aren't stupid; they know what they're buying and don't care. They pay up and claim ignorance."

Chapter Twenty-Three

My phone pinged several times on the drive home. Xander had sent several files, one of them about the sister of Emerson's friend. He'd tracked down the last two addresses where she lived before her life went off the rails.

"We need to get on this for Emerson. I'd want to do it even if it wasn't going to help my brother's case," I said.

"It would be helpful if we could talk to the boy," Fab said.

"I doubt Gail would allow that to happen, especially since it sounded like she was breaking the rules getting us involved." I flicked through my phone again. "I'm going to peruse the file Xander sent over and make a list of anything that stands out, and we can go on a local road trip tomorrow. Won't that be fun?"

Fab pulled into the compound and parked in my driveway. "After that, let's take a couple of days and do nothing. I wouldn't mind another boat trip, and this time, take our husbands. No worries about me wanting to go back to the West mansion. We got away without injury the last time, and I want to keep it that way."

"We were lucky."

* * *

The next morning, I got in the SUV, addresses in hand, and programmed the GPS. The first stop was just down the highway. Fab pulled out of the compound and roared out to the highway, traveled south, and turned onto a narrow street. She rolled to a stop in front of a two-story stilt home with a man rebuilding a kid's bicycle in the driveway.

"I've got this one," I said, and got out. It didn't surprise me that Fab rolled down the window. I walked over to the man, who'd stopped what he was doing. I waved as I approached. "I'm looking for my friend, Allison Kennedy. This is the last address I had for her, and I wonder if you know where she might've moved to."

"We bought the house from her over a year ago and haven't seen her since."

"I figured it was a long shot, but thought I'd stop and check." I nodded to the bike. "Hope it goes together easy."

"I've got the next stop programmed," Fab said as I slid back inside. "I know Emerson thought we should start with this one. I disagreed, as it didn't make sense, but didn't say anything. We're going to Allison's last verified address now. Emerson had a couple of others, but what are they going to tell us unless she left them a week ago? Nothing."

"I'm happy that Allison stayed local and didn't decide to run all over the state." I checked out the neighborhood on the way to the next stop—a little more run-down than the last. "Let's say we luck out and find Allison, then what?"

"Have you forgotten that Gail expects us to call her and keep an eye on Allison until she arrives?"

"And? We stay out of sight, so as to not risk irking her off, and guaranteed she does something crazy like sneak out the back." I grimaced at that scene unfolding.

"Since when do we plan for contingencies?" Fab's expression reeked of frustration.

"Be that way," I teased her. "If she spots us and has questions, we'll be friendly. Or I will. You call her sister and tell her to hop on it. How does that sound?"

Fab rolled up to an apartment building that, to put it nicely, was in need of repair. It was worn down by age and neglect, the surrounding banana trees out of control and covering a good number of the repair issues.

I pointed. "A vacancy sign with a phone number. I'm guessing there's no manager on site."

"I know you want to jump out and go door to door, so I'll come with you."

I turned and made sure she didn't miss me

rolling my eyes. "I knew all along you were going to come."

Fab laughed and patted my shoulder. "I'm on a roll. Here's my next idea. Forget the upstairs. We cruise the first-floor units, and the first one where we hear a television blaring, knock."

We got out and stared at the building. "I'm going to wait here," I said.

"Nice try." Fab grabbed my arm and tugged me forward.

"You make me fall, and I'm going to tell on you."

"Good luck selling that story."

"I suggest that we start with the old gal sucking on a cigarette," I whispered. "Be sure to sneak into the conversation how dangerous smoking in the shrubbery can be. But be nice."

"You've forgotten that I'm the one with old *man* rapport. You're the one good with old women, so good luck." Now it was Fab's turn to drag her feet.

The blue-haired woman leaned back in a webbed chair, the cotton duster she wore swallowing her slight frame. Her head tilted back, she blew smoke rings into the air, the ashtray next to her bootie slippers overflowing.

"Excuse me," I said, ready with a smile as she jerked herself upright. She bent forward and began coughing, dropping the lit cigarette. I crushed it under my foot, clapping her on the back.

She squinted down at the broken concrete walkway. "Damn, that's a waste of a good cig. Did you have to mangle it?" She pulled a pack out of her pocket, stuck a half-smoked one in her mouth, and let it hang between her lips.

Not sure how to answer, I ignored her question. "We're looking for Allison Kennedy, and this is the last address that we have."

"Lived down at the opposite end. Got the boot for not paying. They don't tolerate that here, and they don't bother with legal stuff either. Get out or get your ass kicked and your stuff thrown in the street." She sucked on the cigarette, then jerked it out of her mouth, staring—she'd forgotten that she hadn't lit it.

"Any idea where Allison moved to?"

"That flop motel on the main highway. Pay by the hour, day, whatever. People come and go there, as the management will work with you. If you can't pay, get out, and when you can, you're welcome to come back. Also, there's no limit on how many people you can stuff in a room."

I struggled not to grimace. Bet the code department hadn't gotten wind of that major violation. I thanked her and left as she re-lit her cigarette. Back at the car, I met Fab, who hadn't wasted time getting back behind the wheel.

"No one would willingly stay at that fleabag out on the highway unless they were out of options." Fab squealed the tires pulling away from the curb.

"At least we know right where it's located and that when we've been there in the past, the office person was easily bribable. Stick the money under their nose and ask away."

It was a short drive, and soon Fab and I were eyeing what appeared to be an abandoned motel as we pulled into the parking lot, not a car in sight. The residents parked around the back, which added to the impression of the building being closed for business. We pulled around the back, parked, and entered through the gate, which leaned up against the fence, secured with rope so it wouldn't fall on anyone.

We skirted past the good-sized fellow kicked back in a chair outside the office, earbuds in, his massive arms crossed. He gave us a once-over.

"Your turn." Before she could object, I reminded her, "We're doing this for Brad," and handed her cash.

Fab went inside, approaching the front desk as the young guy behind it eyed her warily. She skipped all pleasantries, held out the cash, and said, "Looking for Allison Kennedy."

He snatched up the money. "If she's still here, she's in 106. There are several people in that room; if she's out, one of them will know where she went." He lowered his voice. "The one to talk to is Reed, except he's at work. He's the one that collects the money for that room and pays weekly. No need to knock, as they never lock the door. No worries about safety when we've got

Rollo." He indicated the man we'd passed coming inside.

The question about whether to knock or not was easily answered as we walked past the window—the blinds were wide open, and the room appeared empty.

"I guess we're going to have to come back," I said.

"After I have a look around." Fab turned the knob and went inside. "On the way out, I'll bribe Rollo."

"Don't touch anything," I whispered.

Fab scanned the room and checked the bathroom.

I cleared my throat and pointed to the closet, where two young girls were asleep on the floor. We would know in a minute if they were Allison's daughters. Fab pulled out her phone and leaned in for a closer look, then turned and nodded.

"I'll stay here while you find out when Rollo last saw Allison. Don't dawdle." After she left, I scanned the room, which was covered in a layer of filth. I stood rooted to the floor, not that there was anywhere to sit except the king-size bed, which had been stripped, sheets nowhere to be found. It was hard to imagine a large number of people crammed into this room.

I crept over to the girls for a better look, and they were sadly unkempt. I moved to the window and watched as Fab walked back to the room, talking on her phone the whole time. I met her at the door.

"Rollo says that Allison hasn't been around in a couple of days and has issues, which I deciphered to mean that she does drugs and takes off for days at a time. The only reason they didn't call the cops is…there's always someone to look out for the girls and make sure they're fed."

"That's a disgusting story."

"I called Emerson. She got Gail on the phone, and she's on her way. I suggested that if the girls didn't know her very well, she bring the brother. That way, they wouldn't be freaked out by being taken away by a stranger. Family or not, that's what she'd be to them if they haven't seen her in a long time. And who knows what the mother said about her."

"Sounds like you handled it well." I smiled at her.

"This job isn't over; Gail wants her sister found."

"How are we supposed to do that?" I snapped and then took a breath. "Allison could be anywhere, doing anything to pay for her habit."

"Agree with you there. I didn't answer Gail. Emerson must've noticed and, after that, did all the talking." Fab looked around the room with her nose turned up. "Plan whatever number we're on is to incentivize Rollo and the other dude with the promise of more money if they call as soon as Allison shows up."

"She's probably going to freak out when she shows back up and her kids are gone. I suppose motherhood takes a back seat when you have an addiction. Maybe, hearing that they were taken away by a woman, she'll assume it was her sister and get in touch."

Fab wrinkled her nose and moved to the doorway. "I don't want to know what that smell is, so don't expect me to move from this spot until Gail gets here."

"I hope you told her to step on it."

"Didn't use those exact words, but close enough. I did ask if she was bringing the cops, and it surprised me when she said no. I wanted to know why not but didn't feel nervy enough to ask."

"I'll stand guard. You go buy off your new friends. Once Gail gets here and gets the girls in the car, we're out of here." I made a mental note to have Emerson check on the kids later and make sure they were flourishing. I wouldn't be a party to delivering them into a situation no better than this mess and neither would Fab.

It was a long forty minutes before Gail drove up and parked out front. Fab ran to meet her as a boy, whom I assumed to be the brother, jumped out. In shorts and tennis shoes, he looked like any normal kid but stood back and stayed quiet.

Fab led the two of them to the room, where the boy headed straight to the closet, got down on his hands and knees, and gently woke the two girls. They threw themselves into his arms, and the three hugged. He held them as both girls started to cry.

"When the call came in, Scott got teary." Gail wiped tears from her eyes as the three reunited. "I was happy that I asked if he wanted to ride along. Scott prepared me for what kind of conditions to expect on the drive over. Still, it's hard to believe that my sister, Ava, and Ella were living like this."

It didn't take Scott long to calm his sisters down and coax little smiles out of them. He talked to them, pointing to their aunt, and they checked her out, wide-eyed. Scott stood and helped Ava and Ella to their feet, grabbed a ratty backpack, throwing it over his shoulder, then grasped each little hand in his.

"I'm hungry," Ava or Ella said, and the other nodded.

"We're going to get lunch right now. You decide what you want," Gail told them with a reassuring smile. "You want me to take that?" She nodded to the backpack, which Scott handed over.

Fab and I followed the foursome down the steps and watched as Gail helped them all into her SUV. She closed the door and turned to us. "I'll be in touch."

"That went better than I expected," I said as we watched them turn onto the highway.

"Let's get the heck out of here. You'd think, having been here before, I'd be used to its creepiness, but no." Fab steered us back up the steps and waved to Rollo as we cut through the center of the property.

"Did you notice that neither girl asked about their mother?" I asked.

"Let's hope that when Allison returns and finds the kids gone, it's incentive enough to get her act together."

A young girl—pre-teen maybe (hard to tell), thin-skinny, a worldly look in her eyes—barreled around the corner and skidded to a stop. "Where are the sisters going?" She stared warily, showing signs of life having kicked her around more than once.

"To live with their aunt," I said. "You live here?"

"Maybe." Mistrust radiated from her brown eyes.

"How about in exchange for cash, you answer a couple of questions?" I asked.

Fab moved closer, but stayed back. I suspected she didn't want to spook the girl.

"Five bucks?" A glitter of excitement in her eyes.

"How about ten?"

"Not sure I know anything that's worth ten bucks…unless you're wanting something weird, and then I'd have to know what it is upfront."

This one knew too much about the seamy side

of life. "How about I pay in advance with the promise that you won't be expected to refund any of the money?" I reached in my pocket, pulled out a bill, and handed to her.

She looked down and registered surprise. "I don't have change."

"Me neither, so let's call it even. I'm Madison, and this is Fab."

"Keely." She continued to stare at the money in her hand, then stuffed it in her pocket.

"When was the last time you saw Ava and Ella's mother?" I asked.

"Allison comes and goes, like everyone in this place, but she's been gone longer than usual this time."

"Would you give her a message when she does show up?" Keely nodded. "Tell her that her kids are with her sister and she can call anytime."

Keely wrinkled her nose. "That might not be such a hot idea, especially if she's strung out. I'm happy for the girls; they're too young to live in this place. It's nice that they'll have a chance to get over being afraid all the time." I swore I heard her mumble, "Wonder how long that takes?"

"You doing okay?" I asked.

Keely nodded.

"One nosey question and we'll be on our way. Why aren't you in school?" It wasn't any of my business, but that hadn't stopped me in the past.

"It's safer for me to stay here at the property.

Wandering around would attract unwanted attention, and no one gets past Rollo unless he says so." Keely's stomach rumbled loudly. Looking embarrassed, she rubbed it.

"How about we get you some lunch? Not sure what's around here." I knew the nearest anything was several miles down the highway.

"McDonald's is the closest. If I could get a ride…then I can walk back."

"You're on, and lunch is on us," I said.

"I need to tell Rollo, so he doesn't come chasing after us." Keely turned and yelled, "Going to get a burger."

"Sounds good. They giving you a ride?" Rollo yelled back.

Keely nodded.

I opened the door of the SUV for her, and she slid in the back seat.

"Nice ride." Keely ran her hand over the seat.

Fab turned around in the driver's seat and said, "Any restaurant you want. We can hit the drive-thru and bring you back, unless you want to eat inside."

"You're going to a lot of trouble for someone you don't know. You one of them do-goodie people I've heard about?"

"I've been accused of that before, but Fab? Never." I laughed. "It doesn't kill a person to be nice."

Keely nodded as though she wasn't convinced of what I'd just said. "McDonald's drive-thru is good, and I'll take the ride back."

"Roll down the window and order whatever you want." Fab motioned for her to move over behind her.

She pulled into the parking lot and up to the speaker, and Keely slid over and placed her order, then tried to hand me the money I'd given her earlier.

I shook my head. "We've got this." I heard Fab add to the order and include a gift card, so I reached into my purse and grabbed cash.

At the window, Fab grabbed the bags and handed them over the seat.

"There's more food here than I ordered."

"That's because I doubled the order and you forgot to add chocolate chip cookies." Fab handed her the gift card. "This is for the next time you come."

"If you don't want the leftovers, give them to Rollo. My guess, he'll eat anything," I said.

"You bet he will. I've never seen him turn down food." Keely laughed.

I turned in my seat as Fab headed back to the motel. "If you ever need anything…" I handed her our business card. "Leave a message, and we'll call you back."

Fab once again pulled around the back, and Keely opened the door. "Thank you so much." With a wave, she jumped out and headed back inside the courtyard.

"Hats off to Keely for being a tough little

cookie." Fab backed out and headed over to the highway.

"I wanted to ask about her situation, her parents, and a host of other nosey questions, but decided food was the most important thing. Even if I got the answers, some things aren't conducive to a quick fix." I stared out the window in hopes of getting a glimpse of the water, but no such luck. "Today has been emotionally draining, and I can't wait to get home."

"First, call Xander and have him run another check for anything new on Allison. I know Gail's going to be blowing up the phone lines, wanting updates about what we're doing."

"I'll also give Doodad a call to put out the word to his street sources, saying he'll pay for reliable information."

"I'm guessing we're in agreement that cruising the streets is a dead end?"

I nodded.

Chapter Twenty-Four

A week had gone by, and it had been a quiet one—not a single emergency call. My latest plan for the new property was to let Toady handle any problems, as he'd already volunteered. I'd stay out of the antics until I couldn't ignore them anymore.

Fab and I had shared our suspicions about what was going on at the dog-napping house with our neighbor, Casio. An ex-cop who still had lots of friends on the force from the Keys up to Miami, he passed the information along and got back to us that they were already under investigation. A couple of days later, the cops raided the house and hauled the two men out in cuffs; they were in the process of hitting the road, but not fast enough.

The neighbor, Marla, watched it all go down from her porch. One of the cops told her—since dog-stealing was a big business and she had a sought-after breed—not to let her Maltese out of her sight.

It was midnight when my phone rang. Creole grabbed it off the nightstand with a growl. He checked the screen and answered. "No, this isn't

Madison. This better be good."

I curled into him and pointed for him to hit the speaker button, which he ignored.

"Anyone get hurt?" he asked. "We're on our way." Creole rolled out of bed and pulled me with him, setting me on the floor. "If you're ready in under five, you get details on the way to our destination." He slapped me on the butt.

"I will so get even with you," I said, matching his growl. Knowing there was a slight chance that he might leave me behind, I grabbed my favorite go-to outfit for when I had no clue what to wear but knew it wouldn't be good—crop sweats and a t-shirt. I ran a brush through my hair and patted it down. It was dark out; no one would notice it had a mind of its own. I grabbed my purse and raced for the front door.

Creole was a long leg ahead of me. He looped his arm through mine and hustled us out to the truck, a near-run for me, then scooped me off my feet and helped me inside.

"Details." I snapped my fingers once he was behind the wheel. I took a swig of water, happy that he'd grabbed a couple of bottles.

"That bargain you just bought…a couple of fire trucks showed and have about got the flames under control. The damage hasn't been assessed yet."

"I'm assuming Mac reported there were no injuries," I said, having checked my phone to see who made the call.

"According to Mac, the woman who ran the place was the only one home, and she managed to get out. She had the sidewalk to herself when Mac ran up; then she collapsed into tears and wanted to wipe her nose on Mac's shoulder. Who, by the way, expects germ pay."

"I heard that two of the renters moved already. How many actually lived there is a mystery, though Toady seemed to think there were five. I'm sure we're about to find out. The neighbors will have plenty to say." Those that didn't have anything factual to relay could be counted on to make something up.

"This will surprise you—they stayed inside and minded their own business for once. Those that didn't sleep through the sirens hung their heads out the windows."

Since the streets were fairly deserted, Creole made good time to The Cottages, and as he turned the corner, we spotted the fire trucks at the opposite end of the street.

"All the trouble and now a fire," I mused. "There's a well-established record of trouble at that property, which has ratcheted up since I bought the place." Let's hope this didn't turn out to be a criminal act.

Creole pulled into the driveway of The Cottages and parked in front of the office. "Be interesting to see what the fire marshal has to say."

We got out, Creole hooked his arm around

me, and we walked down the block, where we saw Mac coming our way.

"Too much excitement for the neighbors to pass on." I nodded to those that had filtered into the street, wearing what they'd gone to bed in.

"What happened?" Creole asked when we met up with Mac.

"I heard from one of the firefighters that it's not a complete loss," she relayed. "Vicky's putting on an emotional show. I heard her tell one of the cops that she smelled smoke, went downstairs to check it out, and flames were coming through the kitchen door. She ran to the neighbors to call 911."

"It didn't jump to any of the neighboring houses?" I asked. Fab was going to be irritated that she missed all the fun. I knew she'd want to drive by tomorrow, phone in hand, to video the extent of the damage.

Mac shook her head. "The fire department was on it."

Creole leveled a squinty stare at me. "You going to rebuild?"

"As co-owners, that's something we should talk about." I knew he'd been lukewarm about the purchase from the beginning. "It's one way to get rid of bad tenants." I winced. "A lot more expensive than I planned."

"I'll be happy if they don't find a dead body when they go inside."

I leaned my head against Creole's shoulder.

That was all we needed.

"It would have to be someone we don't know about, as all the tenants are accounted for. But I'll ask around." With a wave, Mac cut across the street and stopped to talk to the first group of people she saw.

I led Creole to a rental I knew was empty, and we sat on the porch and watched as the firefighters finished their cleanup.

"I'm going to go ask a couple of questions," he said when they started to roll up their hoses.

"I'm going back to the truck." The excitement had dimmed for the neighbors, and most had gone back inside, including Mac; I had no clue where she'd disappeared to.

I didn't have to sit there long; good thing, because it offered a limited view. Creole opened the door and slid inside. "No bodies. One of the firefighters that I talked to suspects arson—off the record, since it's not his job to say. He did say that there were signs of shoddy interior remodeling."

"What about Vicky? I didn't see her lurking around."

"She was hauled off to the hospital, but not before she was heard saying that she planned to sue the new owners."

"I'll sic Tank on her. I'm sure he'll have a litany of questions for old Vicky." I also had good insurance and knew they wouldn't pay one dime more than they had to.

"Before I forget..."

"I don't need to see your smirk; I can hear it." I scooted closer to him.

"I dropped your name and told them to go to Jake's. Told the guy to tell the person behind the bar that you're besties and he'd get a substantial discount."

"I hope they all troop in on Kelpie's shift; she'll show them a good time."

"I bet." Creole laughed.

Chapter Twenty-Five

The fire had been officially declared arson. The cops questioned Creole and me, and anyone else they thought might know anything. The insurance company wasn't very happy. They sent out an adjuster, who had plenty of questions. It took Vicky Prell about a second to find a scurvy attorney that worked out of the back of his car to represent her. The two remaining tenants, who left, who presumably didn't have outstanding warrants, joined in her lawsuit.

Fab and I were sitting on her patio, enjoying watching a blue-grey Heron explore the dock, looking for food.

"Since we get so many of that kind of bird, I did a little research, and you could be feeding them rodents and other small…things." I tilted my head, trying to picture that scenario playing out.

"It's official; you've lost your mind." Fab leaned forward and refilled my glass with iced tea. "It's clear you need more caffeine."

"What have you heard from Gunz?" I asked. "I'd think he'd be hot on the phone, since he has to know there was a fire at the property he wanted. Must make him happy."

"Gunz's distanced himself since our last conversation. Longest time he's gone without a call about some last-minute emergency." Fab looked over at me. "But he won't stop digging until he finds out who the buyer was."

"Do you think he found out already and is the one behind the fire?"

"It's not his style, and once he finds out it was you, he'll give you a pass because of me."

Would he though?

Fab's attention was diverted when her phone rang. She picked it up off the table and stared at the screen longer than usual before answering and hitting the speaker button.

"Is this Ms. Merceau?" a feminine voice asked.

"How can I help you?"

"This is Tracy. We met in a grocery store parking lot when I was driving a car I wasn't supposed to and you helped me out. I was pregnant at the time."

"Yes, I remember." Fab raised her eyebrows at me. "Congratulations on the baby. Hope all's going well."

"You said if I ever needed anything, I could call." I could hear tears in her voice.

"I'll do whatever I can."

"As you suggested, I had a paternity test done as soon as my son was born. Gunz is the father. We were getting along—he's totally sweet with

Joshua—and then he wanted me to move closer. I should've asked more questions. I thought we were moving in together, and as many times as I've been over the conversation, I'm still not sure how I misunderstood."

I shook my head. Knowing Gunz, this was about to get messy, and Fab was in the middle.

"So you've moved, or you're about to?" Fab asked.

"I've moved all right, out to… I don't know where, as I'm not familiar with this area. I do know from the drive that it's just on the outskirts of town."

I knew that was a bad idea when I first heard about it.

"He moved me in with his sisters—Kettle and Watusi. I'm not sure if you know them."

Fab squeezed her eyes shut. "We've met."

That's an understatement.

"I've asked him—pleaded several times—to get me out of here, but it falls on deaf ears." Tracy sniffed. "It's mean to say that I don't like either of these women, but I know the feeling's mutual. I'd have left already, except I don't have a ride. And when I walk my kids up to the road every day, I haven't seen a single bus, just cars flying in each direction." Her voice continued to rise as she became increasingly frantic.

"When you tell Gunz how you feel, what does he say?" Fab asked.

We both knew he overlooked his sisters'

shortcomings. "Scary" being one of them.

"If I hear the word 'patience' out of him one more time, I'm going to scream. I thought I had him convinced to get me out of here, but Kettle got wind and squashed the idea. He listens to them more than me. I'm starting to feel like a prisoner. Gunz shows up every night, plays with the baby, and then leaves. Since he never sleeps here, he has to live somewhere else…maybe with someone else."

"What is it that you want me to do?" Fab asked.

We were persona non grata on that property, and showing up would set off a showdown.

"Since I go for a walk every day, I can get to the road without attracting attention. I was hoping you could meet me close by and take me to my grandmother's. She lives north of the Cove. Anything is better than living here."

"Your best option would be to wait for a day when one, or preferably both, of the sisters aren't home."

I shook my head. Not saying no. Tracy thought the Q sisters disliked her? They hated Fab. I pointed to myself, letting her know I'd be the one to go. The sisters hated me a little less. Fab flicked her finger between the two of us. We'd go together.

Tracy sighed. "One of them is always here. I'm sure it's because they don't trust me."

"How are you going to get the kids and your

belongings packed and everything out to the road?"

"I'll only be able to take the stroller and pack a few things in the diaper bag. It's fine, as everything we own now smells like some herb they burn to chase the spirits or whatever outside. Thankfully, they moved their dead father to another room. Who brings a corpse home?"

"Is the body still holding its shape?" *Oops, didn't mean to say that out loud.*

I got the *nutjob* look from Fab.

"Once I figured out that it was... Well, you know. He also has an odor, which I mentioned to Gunz, saying it wasn't good for the kids. I'm certain that's the only reason they moved him." Tracy started to cry.

"Calm down. Take a breath." Fab took one of her own. She waited patiently for Tracy to stop crying. "You want to arrange a day and time and have me pick you up out on the road—am I understanding that right?"

"It's my only chance to get away. I go for a walk twice a day to get out of the house, and they don't pay attention since they're used to me leaving. If you say no, could you promise not to tell Gunz? He'd tell his sisters, who'd flip, and they'd never let me out of their sight for a second."

"I know Gunz fairly well. If you disappear, he's going to do what it takes to find you and talk you into coming back. If you don't want that, then you're going to have to stand up to him and tell him what you want."

"Does this mean you're going to help me?" Tracy asked in a hopeful tone.

"You set a day and time, and I'll be waiting for you on the road out of sight of the house. Once you get to the end of the driveway, we'll have to load you and the kids in the car fast and get out of there. I'll arrange to have car seats."

"Day after tomorrow, eleven in the morning. I normally go for a walk right before lunch, so it won't be unusual. If I think they're onto me, which I doubt will happen, I won't walk that day."

The two hung up after coming to an agreement, Tracy effusive in her thanks.

"When Gunz finds out that you were the one to help Tracy escape the crazy house—and he will—he's going to explode. But before that, he'll want to hire you to find her."

"Maybe..." It was clear Fab was thinking fast. "What if I relocate Tracy and the kids, then tell Gunz and urge him to work out an agreement with the woman? I'll also point out that he's lucky she didn't just call the cops when the sisters didn't allow her to leave."

"Then you implore Gunz not to mention your involvement in Tracy's escape when his sisters have a hundred questions. Remind him that they're volatile, which is a nice way to put it."

Fab huffed out a breath. "I wanted to tell Tracy no but just couldn't."

"I'm thinking you want me to come along." Fab nodded. "I'll clear the whole day, since we don't know where Grandma lives. I volunteer to be the one to jump out and get them all in the car, and then you speed off…safely. You know…you could tell Gunz that Tracy called me and I picked them up. I confessed my misdeeds, and you called him right away."

"I don't want to give him a real reason to dislike you."

Rather than tell her I had a bad feeling about how this would play out, I suggested, "When you talk to him, suggest that he relocate Tracy and the kids close to him. What he does about the sisters will probably be nothing, so no suggestions there."

"Wait until Didier hears this one." Fab sighed.

"He's not the only one that's not going to like the situation, but neither he nor Creole is going to suggest that you leave Tracy stranded out there."

Chapter Twenty-Six

Two days later, we set out to pick up Tracy and her kids. The guys understood but weren't happy and demanded that we call if we encountered any kind of problem.

Fab headed south and, on the outskirts of town, veered off the highway onto a side road. It wasn't actually nowhere, but close. Ahead of us a hundred feet or so, Tracy was pushing her stroller and was about at the end of the driveway. The house was set back on the property, and she was already out of sight of anyone peeking out one of the windows.

"You keep the engine running. I'll get Tracy and the kids inside as fast as I can." I jumped out and opened the back. Good as her word, Fab had borrowed two car seats, which were already attached to the back seat.

Once Tracy hit the road, she came running the rest of the way to meet us. She lifted her oldest son, who had a big grin on his face, out of the stroller and strapped him in the back, then threw the diaper bag on the floor, picked up her sleeping son, and handed him to me while she flattened the stroller. I handed back the baby and motioned for her to get in while I loaded the stroller in the back. Then I slammed the door, ran around, and jumped in the front seat.

"Kettle and Watusi are home, and it's a good sign that they're not running down the driveway after me." Tracy breathed a big sigh. Once she finished strapping the baby and herself in, Fab pulled back onto the main highway and headed north.

Tracy handed me her grandmother's address, and I inputted it into GPS. It was just north of Homestead and wouldn't take us long. "You're sure that your grandmother isn't going to have a problem with you showing up?"

"Last night when I went for a walk, I called her and told her that I needed a place to stay. She assured me it wouldn't be a problem, and that she had plenty of room." Tracy pulled a phone out of her pocket. "The sisters gave me this to use for emergencies only. I deleted the number every time I made a call."

"You should remove the battery, in case they have a tracker on the phone," I told her. It surprised me when she rolled down the window and sent the phone flying instead.

The baby stayed asleep, and it didn't take long before her older son nodded off.

"If you or the kids need anything, we'll pull over," I said.

"Once again, I want to thank you both for

helping me." Tracy scooted forward. "Gunz loves his son but isn't interested in being a family, and that's kind of what I thought he wanted. His sisters adore Joshua; they tolerate my oldest, and me not so much." She leaned back and closed her eyes.

Fab, who'd been watching her in the rearview mirror, turned and raised her brows. She stuck to the speed limit, which didn't surprise me since there were two kids in the car. I rested my head against the seat and blocked all images of Gunz going berserk. We'd deal with it when this good deed blew up in our faces. I had my visor down so I could keep an eye on Tracy in the mirror, and the second she woke up, I turned. Question time.

"What's your plan, and by that I mean when it comes to Gunz?" I asked.

"Once I get the kids settled, I'm going to call and explain how I feel and hope that this time, he hears me. I'll make it clear that I won't be living with his sisters again."

"You've got Fab's card. Don't hesitate to call if you need help," I said.

The kids woke up, and Tracy had food for them in her bag. Then she whipped out a tablet and read to them, complete with sound effects. Her oldest laughed and clapped.

Thanks to a couple of traffic snarls, it took more than an hour to get to Cutler Bay. Grandma lived in an older neighborhood in a well-kept house nestled under towering oaks. Fab pulled into the driveway and parked behind a small sedan. I got out and wrestled the stroller out of the back. I was surprised how heavy Tracy's diaper bag was; apparently, one could cram a lot of stuff in one.

An older woman opened the door and came out. She took the baby in her arms and covered her other grandson in kisses. She kissed Tracy's cheek, and they exchanged a few words.

I waited by the car while Fab talked to the two women. I watched as she handed both women her card and Tracy one of the burner phones from the office. Then I waved goodbye to Tracy and got back in the car.

"I warned Tracy that Gunz would come looking for her," Fab said. "I told her to stand her ground. If I didn't have history with those two and know that they're whackjobs, I wouldn't have gotten involved."

"What are you going to do if Tracy doesn't call him right away and Gunz wants to hire you to find her?" I asked.

"Didier was worried about him finding out about my role in all this, and I told him that since nothing ever stays secret, I might as well fess up." Fab grimaced. "If they don't talk it out themselves, I'll offer to broker an agreement between them at no charge."

"Let's hope that they're able to get this resolved without you getting involved. Has

Gunz said anything about how he feels about being a father?"

"He never mentions his son."

"If you know a shortcut..." I laughed—maybe if we were in a boat. "Fingers crossed that the two work it out. I'm all for having no further involvement."

We were almost back to the Cove when Fab's phone rang. She glanced at the screen, groaned, and let it go to voicemail. "Gunz." It rang again. "Was just about to call you back," she answered.

I flinched, hearing Gunz yelling but not able to make out the words.

"Calm down or I'm hanging up on you," Fab said. He barely took a breath before continuing his rant, and she hung up. "Well...he knows that Tracy and the kids left...and blames you because they got in your car."

Swell. "The sisters had to have exterior cameras."

"If they did, then they were in an obscure place, as I didn't notice any. But honestly, I didn't look that hard. It wasn't a neighbor, since there isn't one close enough to see anything. I wanted to ask who installed the cameras but didn't, because why find out if he could yell any louder?" Fab half-laughed.

"Whatever you need me to do..."

Fab's phone rang again. We both knew who it was, so she didn't bother looking at the screen. She answered, and Gunz did all the talking, but quieter this time.

"I get that you're upset, but would you rather have had someone else pick Tracy up? She was determined to leave. Or what if she'd squared off with one of your sisters—how would that have ended?" Fab listened patiently. "What do you want? You, not your sisters. I'm going to give you the same advice I gave Tracy: sit down and talk it out."

Seriously, I wish she'd use the speaker.

"Let me know." She tossed her phone in the cup holder.

"If it's any help, blame this one totally on me," I told her.

"He's not stupid; he knows I was the getaway driver. Better this way, because on top of the real estate deal, he'd flip."

He might anyway, but I kept that one to myself.

Chapter Twenty-Seven

It had been all quiet on the Gunz front for the last couple of days, and no frantic calls from Tracy. We decided to indulge in something yummy for lunch and ended up at the Bakery Café, where our favorite table at the end of the sidewalk was waiting for us. The server was just setting down the iced teas we'd ordered when Fab touched my arm.

"Don't turn around." She stared furtively over my shoulder. "We're being followed."

"I'm not even going to ask if you're certain. How long has this person been our shadow?"

"On the drive over, I spotted the SUV over there several times, speeding up, slowing down." Fab pointed covertly to the Ford Explorer a few spaces away. "Black SUVs are everywhere, and I couldn't make out the license plate, so I decided I was being ridiculous."

"I wondered why you made a couple of unnecessary turns."

"Two minutes after we got here, he pulls up, grabs a table at the opposite end of the walkway, and sits facing this direction. Is he staring? Hard to tell with those dark glasses practically covering his face, but too many coincidences."

"If he is following us, then we need to deal with him here. I don't want to get in a car chase and risk my SUV ending up back in the hospital. How many times can one vehicle get repaired before it gives up?"

Fab shook her head. "I'm serious, and you're being dramatic."

"You'll wish you paid attention to me when I replace the Hummer with a Rambler."

"Patience," she whispered to herself.

"We don't have a lot of options," I pointed out, which brought on more huffing from Fab. "Since there are plenty of people here, which means witnesses, we get in his face and ask what the heck. What's he going to do? Run?"

"With our luck, all hell will break loose and fingers will be pointed at us."

"It appears as though my idea is the only one on the table, unless you're getting ready to share one." I motioned over the server, who'd waited on us before. "We're holding off on ordering lunch…or might not order at all. We'll let you know." I handed him a huge tip, and he nodded and walked off. I turned to Fab. "Time's up."

"Let's go." She stood and grabbed her drink. I did the same, and the two of us converged on the man, not waiting for an invitation to have a seat. "What do you want? Skip 'nothing' and get to it. You've been following us, and I want to know why."

The man snickered. "You two are dumber than…" He flashed a badge.

"I've got one of those," I said.

"One? That's it?" Fab said in disbelief. "I've got half a dozen."

"I'm a licensed PI," he said with a smirk.

"That's impressive," I said, an eyeroll in my tone. "Then why try to pass yourself off as a cop? That's what you were doing…except it didn't work, did it?"

He pulled his phone out of his pants pocket, scrolled through it, and turned the screen around to show us a picture of Fab and me on the beach. Judging from the angle, it was taken from West's deck. "Maybe you'd like to explain why you were trespassing on a dead man's property? That's a crime you know."

"You happen to have a date stamp on that?" Fab asked.

He ignored the question. "You want to tell me what you were doing in the house? Don't bother to deny it."

"We were friends of West's. That could've been taken on any number of visits," Fab said.

"I'm being a nice guy here."

I snorted, which had his face turning red.

"We all know that you snooped through a dead man's house, and that's illegal. You either answer my questions or you leave me no option but to turn the picture over to the cops. You can answer their questions from behind bars."

I leaned across the table. "You're threatening me?"

Fab grabbed my shirt and hauled me back. "Apparently, it slipped your mind that if that scenario is true, you were also breaking the law."

"It would be my civic duty to turn you in," he said smugly.

I grabbed the knife off the table and turned, making eye contact with the large bookend just getting ready to take a seat on the patio, flicking the knife in a "get over here" motion, only nicer.

"If you're planning on attacking me with that," the PI said derisively, "I'll have to defend myself." He made a motion to open his shirt but stopped suddenly.

Spoon stalked up. "What's going on?" Mother skidded up behind him.

"This man just threatened to turn me in to the cops over a picture he has on his phone that may or not show me trespassing," I said.

"That was stupid." Spoon sent the man and his chair flying across the sidewalk. He bounced on the ground; then Spoon's foot connected, and crunching glass could be heard. "If you tell anyone anything about either of these two…" He nodded over his shoulder. "…I'll make sure you end up breathing out your hind end."

The man attempted to crawl away, and Spoon hurried him along by planting his foot in the middle of his butt with a hard shove. He crawled up on his hands and knees, then to his feet, and ran off.

Fab bent down and picked up the remnants of his phone.

"I'm hungry," I said.

Spoon rolled his eyes. "Did you get that guy's license number?"

"I did it while you were kicking butt," Fab said, proud of herself.

I moved to where Mother was standing, smiling at her husband. "He's so sexy," she said as I kissed her cheek.

The manager rushed over, wanting to know if everything was okay.

Spoon reassured the woman, then told us, "You might as well join us for lunch, so we can hear what the heck just went down here."

"Mistaken identity?" I threw out.

Fab and I followed Mother and Spoon back to their table.

"When you get an address off that tag, make sure I get it," Spoon barked. "I'll make certain he doesn't bother you again. And while he and I are talking about staying away from you, I've got a couple of questions he can answer…or else."

"Can't wait to hear what you've been up to," Mother said in a gleeful tone. "Don't pretty it up—just the gritty truth."

Spoon smirked at his wife. "You two are a bad influence on my wife."

The server came over and took our order,

raising his brows at me with a grin.

"I'll let you tell them," I told Fab.

"Where do I start? The beginning, the beginning, or just the beginning?"

Spoon shook his head. "It's a wonder your husbands aren't drunks."

"You know how Crum was arrested for West's murder...?" Fab went on to cover every bit of minutia, enjoying herself. By the time she finished, they were up to date on most of our sneaking around. She did leave out that Creole and Didier had accompanied us to the mansion the first time.

"I'm guessing that you found something while snooping, so what was it?" Spoon asked.

"A handful of high-capacity drives from his safe, which are being gone over as we speak," Fab told him.

"If there's evidence that points to another suspect, how do you hand it over and keep yourself out of trouble?" Spoon grouched.

"I don't want either of you going to jail," Mother said adamantly.

"I'll hand everything over to Crum's lawyer, Tank. He'll know what to do," Fab said.

Our food arrived. I'd ordered light, saving plenty of room for dessert. "I need another favor, but know that you have the option of saying no," I said to Spoon.

"Can't wait to hear what you're about to spring on me."

"Crum befriended some dude in the joint, and he's staying at The Cottages until he gets back on his feet. I'd like that to be sooner rather than later. Turns out he's got mechanic's skills." I knew he wouldn't be the first parolee Spoon had helped.

"What was he in for?" Spoon asked.

"Car theft." I flashed a fake smile. "So you know he's good at getting them started."

"Send him over, but before you do, tell him to only show up if he really wants to start over. If he's running a scam, I'll find out and kick his ass. I'd suggest that if it's the latter, he find an easier mark."

"I'll make sure he gets the message, and I'll tell him to take your warning to heart, that you will follow through," I said.

"Let's hope Crum doesn't do that again." Mother wrinkled her nose. "You don't need to import trouble."

We ordered dessert all around.

"I need to take something home to Creole. Sweeten him up before I tell him about this little incident." I motioned to the server and placed an order. "You get one of our coveted favors for stepping in and giving the boot to that man," I told Spoon.

"I know I've got a stack. Not sure how many; I should be keeping track." Spoon looked thoughtful.

"No need. You ask, we do," I assured him.

"I'm ready for a little adventure," Mother said. "Next job, I want to go along."

"Depends on the job," Spoon grouched.

"Here's the thing—there's no guarantee. Oftentimes, they start out tame, and then we're left wondering what the heck happened."

Fab laughed.

Chapter Twenty-Eight

The front door opened at the same time as my phone rang. Fab waltzed in and waved, pocketing her lockpick. She was lucky that Creole didn't know she did that when he wasn't around. The men had an early morning meeting and had split for the office.

I looked at the screen—Mac—and pushed it across the counter. "You're just in time to answer my phone."

Fab ignored it, grabbing a bottled water and sitting across from me.

I managed to get the phone answered before Mac had to call back…and she would. "Good morning." I poured on the sweetness.

Fab jabbed her finger to put it on speaker.

"You need to get your tuchus over here," Mac told me in a harried tone. "There're issues that need to be dealt with, and I'm low energy today."

Fab snorted.

"I heard that," Mac snapped.

"Low energy. Since when? Never," I answered for her. "Take money out of petty cash and treat yourself to one of Fab's favorites—a triple latte with extra caffeine. Make sure you ask for one of those disgusting Euro blends. It'll not only put hair on your chest, you'll be able to fly home. We'll drive you back to get your truck."

"An overpriced coffee sounds good." Mac smacked her lips. "Not that concoction you just suggested—that one sounds barfy." She treated us to that sound effect.

Fab couldn't stick her fingers in her ears fast enough.

"Do I get a clue as to what's going on?" I asked.

"It would be faster if you wait until you get here. Are you on your way?"

"Who's the boss here?" Fab barked.

"If it were you, there wouldn't be problem one; this place would be a ghost town. While I wait for you, I'm going to go get my coffee and be right back." Mac hung up.

"The only reason she's passing on giving the deets twice is because it's something weird and she's afraid you'll be a no-show," Fab said.

I scrolled through my phone and made another call. "You dressed and ready to go?" I asked Mother when she answered.

"Where are we going?" Her voice bubbled with excitement.

"I'm officially hiring you for a job. We'll be there in ten. Casual is good."

"I'll be ready."

"Nice knowing you. She's going to kill you," Fab said when I'd hung up.

"Mother wants to go along on jobs… Well, some are ick." I got up and grabbed my purse. "And no excuses out of you either."

We jumped in the SUV and cruised by Fab's house so she could grab her purse before we hit the road. When Fab turned the corner onto Mother's street, we both spotted her standing in front of the complex. She saw us and jumped out in the street, sticking out her thumb.

I got out and kissed her cheek. "You're not amusing, young lady—playing in the street." I got in the back.

Fab cruised through the coffee drive-thru; she must've been reading my mind. "I'll have my usual with extra whipped cream."

Mother took her sweet time deciding, until Fab tapped her non-existent watch, which made Mother laugh but also speeded up her order. Then she turned toward me. "Are you going to tell me what this job is about?"

Fab handed me my coffee with a smirk. I hurriedly snapped off the lid and took a drink, needing to stall; we were only a few blocks from The Cottages, and we'd be cruising around the corner in minutes.

"Madison Westin." Not quite a shriek. "I should've known."

"Fine. You want to bail? We'll take you home." I gave her my best sad face.

Mother shook her head and turned to Fab as she pulled into the driveway. "And you…you didn't say a word."

"Sometimes we've got to suck it up and be team players," Fab managed with a straight face.

I had to bite my lip not laugh. "Before you ask, I have no idea why my presence is needed. Mac wasn't forthcoming with details. But you asked to come along on our next adventure, and here we are."

"Am I at least going to get to use this?" She pulled up her skirt to show the handgun strapped to her thigh.

"Not unless you agree to clean up any blood." I gave her a steely stare.

"I think it's sexy." Mother shook her leg.

Fab laughed.

"The rock doesn't fall far from the tree, Mother dear." I winked at her and jumped out. And when Mother got out, I hooked my arm in hers and lowered my voice: "Try to behave yourself."

"Stick with me, and I'll protect you from the crazies, including your daughter," Fab said.

The office door opened, and Mac came pogoing out on an old metal model that had to have been an original.

"You're going to break your neck," Mother warned, shaking her head at Mac.

She grinned. "You want to try it? It's great exercise."

"N. O." I tugged Mother closer in case she got

a wild hair. "Try not to be a bad influence while we're here. Now tell us what's going on." My neck ached from watching Mac bobble up and down, which she did a few more times before she hopped back to the door and parked her stick.

Mac turned and rubbed her hands on her skirt. "Problem uno incoming." She jerked her head. "Not in the mood to be the mean one, so you three…have fun."

I turned as Miss January strolled over with Captain, her only boyfriend that hadn't been arrested or died. She had a dreamy smile on her face and was mooning up at him. She might be on borrowed time according to her docs, but she'd go out a satisfied woman.

"Good to see you two out enjoying the sunshine." I stepped forward, attempting to take Mother with me, but she ducked away and sidled up to Fab.

"We're on our way to get a cat from that man selling them behind the gas station," Captain grouched.

What do you know, the man can put together a sentence. It was the most words I'd ever heard him say. "Where's Kitty?" I turned to Mac, who shrugged, clearly indicating *Leave me out of this.*

"Kitty got herself a boyfriend, and they ran off together." Miss January giggled.

Captain nodded.

Kitty was stuffed and not in any shape to run anywhere. "I'm afraid I have some bad news for you—we have a no-pets policy. I only made an exception for Kitty."

"That's horse...what about that damn goat?" Captain grouched.

Miss January absently patted his arm.

"He was only here five minutes. Then he went off to a rescue farm to frolic with other similar animals." At least I thought there was another goat out there. Captain clearly thought I was a stupe, and the feeling was mutual. "I'm sure we can come up with an alternate plan."

Miss January beamed at me.

I turned and gave the stink eye to the three women behind me, at the same time conveying that they needed to step up. Mac got the message and waylaid Miss January. The other two feigned ignorance.

I motioned Captain out of eavesdropping range. "You and I both know that the last thing Miss January needs is a live cat. And that's entirely aside from the fact that you don't even like them."

"She's been whining for one, and I want her to be happy," Captain whined himself.

"That's swell. So why don't you track down Kitty and insist that she get her butt home?"

"If you'd been upfront and told her that the cat passed on to its cat reward when it happened, this wouldn't be an issue."

"You think that's such a swell idea, you tell her and deal with the tears."

"I already promised." Captain pasted on a militant look.

"What happened to the lookalike that Mac sweated over?" That was a stretch, since she'd farmed it out to someone who knew how to sew animals to resemble your dead pet.

Captain mumbled—more than a few things—then said, "That damn thing. I tripped over it in the dark. Scared the holiness out of myself, and I may have stuck my foot through the midsection. Before my honey could notice the gaping hole, I threw it in the trash. She asked after the cat a couple of times, not realizing that there are two stuffed Kittys." He snorted. "I got the bright idea to tell her that it ran off and found its soul mate." He grinned at his idea, tapping his temple. "I told her that we had to be happy for the cat."

"You sure know how to lay it on." His story deserved an eyeroll, but I managed to contain myself. "I'm certain that you can come up with a way to divert her attention from wanting another animal. Unless you're going to promise to take good care of it and not let it run out in the street and get hit by a car."

"I'll tell her I'm allergic."

"Miss January is very happy with you; I'm certain you can keep her thoughts elsewhere."

Captain grunted. "Can I go now?"

Yes, petulant child. I nodded, and he didn't waste time collecting his woman and hoofing it down the street. My guess was to the liquor store.

I joined the three women, refusing to acknowledge their smirks. "All done here?"

"Not quite," Mother said with a grin.

"Go ahead and tell me, Mother, since you're dying to."

"Crum has a court appearance tomorrow, and he needs help getting dressed."

I stepped back. "You want me…" I pointed to myself. "To do that? You've lost your mind."

She laughed.

I glared at Mac. "What's going on?"

"What your mother meant to say was that he needs help choosing something appropriate." Mac gummed a phony smile, conveying, *Isn't that better?* "Crum went on an early morning dumpster run and scored some mismatched, ill-fitting clothes he's calling a suit. I pointed out that they smelled, and he threw them in the washing machine. Now they're… Well, the jacket was black and is now a faded grey; the pants…just faded out. Both are wrinkled so badly, an iron wouldn't help. When I gently suggested that he up his game to make a good impression, he ignored me."

"Isn't it the job of his lawyer to have the 'what to wear' chat?" I asked.

"Tank sat him down and was very explicit—I know because I sat through every word—but Crum put his own spin on it. He's going to look like a homeless person that probably killed the dude for the cash in his pocket."

I pointed to each woman individually so there wouldn't be any misunderstanding. "Too late for any excuses; you're all coming with me." I walked sideways to make sure that none of them got the bright idea to cut and run. I heard the music before we rounded the corner to the pool. Crum was gyrating around, a woman under each arm, each of whom had a hand in the back of his hot-pink speedos. I turned to Mother. "Don't look below his chest and your eyes won't get scorched."

Despite the warning, Mother took a quick peek anyway and slapped her hand over her mouth to cover her laughter.

Mac opened the gate for us. "Crum's got another five minutes, and then he'll be done with the class."

We filed through the gate and sat at the tiki bar. Fab played bartender, and we all requested water.

"How is it your responsibility to get involved in what the man wears to court?" Mother asked.

"It's not. And not my area of expertise." I smiled at her. "That's why I'm going to fluff it off on you, and my best advice is to get your bestie, Fab, to stick her nose in his wardrobe. Who better to ask, since she loves to tell people what to wear? Crum might actually listen to her…that's if she can refrain from getting up in his face and telling him to stop being pigheaded before the conversation even gets started."

"It's going to be impossible to outfit the man in something suitable when he won't part with a nickel." Fab shook her head. "If he didn't have a gillion dollars, I'd offer to help, but in this case, his rich ass can buy his own suit."

"Let's take a vote—raise your hand if you think Fab should handle this dilemma." All hands except Fab's went up. I ignored her hissing. "It's unanimous then—it's your job to convince him to show up looking his best." I turned to Mac. "Crum also needs to leave his 'you're a snot hole' attitude at home. I'm sure you won't mind calling Tank and giving him a heads up that the talk would be better coming from him."

The pool gate opened, and Joseph entered, his rubber girlfriend, Svetlana, hanging on his arm and a beer in the other hand. He waved and grabbed a lounger, and the two sacked out.

"Joseph's hung over," Mac whispered conspiratorially. "He's been cutting back on the sauce, but he whooped it up with his buddies at Custer's last night. They were celebrating two-for-one night."

Custer's was a neighborhood bar that didn't have the best reputation, but those who hung out there didn't care and neither did the owner.

When the class was over, Mac whistled and hooked her thumb at Crum, who strutted over.

"I wonder if he can breathe in those; they look a little tight," Mother said.

"I dare you to ask him." I got the stink eye. "You brought it up."

"Hello, ladies." Crum bowed.

"Have a seat." I pointed to a chair.

"What have I done now?" Crum grumbled as he sat down.

"Can you take advice from the women at this table, keeping in mind that we all care what happens to you?" He looked skeptical. "So you know, Fab and I haven't stopped digging around in West's life, and we're not going to stop until we figure out who killed him or come up with evidence to clear you."

"West has security cameras at his mansion, and we wondered if the cops have gone over the tapes," Fab said.

Crum grunted. "When I see Tank at my appointment this afternoon, I'll mention it to him."

"Now, about what you're wearing to court…" Fab said.

"Tank sent something over in a garment bag," Crum said, disgusted. "I've got something else picked out, so I'm handing it back and making sure he deducts it from my bill."

"Before you do that, why don't you try on whatever he sent over and I'll give you my opinion?" Fab pinned him with a stare, daring him to do otherwise. "I'm certain you want to show up looking your best."

"If you think I'm going to trot around here in a monkey suit, you can forget it."

"Since you asked so nicely, I'd be happy to come inside while you change." Fab stood.

Crum snapped his mouth shut.

"You guys can wait here," Fab ordered imperiously and went off with the man in hot conversation.

"If anyone can change that man's mind, it would be Fab," Mother said.

"We hear a gunshot, we'll know how the makeover is going. Kaboom." Mac keeled over in her chair.

"What else? We can't hang around all day; Mother needs her rest." I patted her head.

She smacked my hand away.

The gate flew open, and Rude came barreling in, her grey hair standing on end—pretty much the same hairdo her almost-husband, Cootie, sported, but he only had a few tufts. Her dress was hanging on her like a sack, flip-flops slapping the ground.

"Just the woman I wanted to talk to." I waved as she sat down.

"I don't have long, since Crum and I are co-teaching the next class. I had to chew his ass for taking over and not leaving me anything to do."

"Glad you got that worked out," I said. "I need you to return Kitty because Miss January wants to get another one, and this one would be alive. She's not competent to take care of it, and Captain's not animal-friendly. I've got it headed off for the moment, but the issue might come back up."

"Furrball isn't going to like it. He's rather attached, and the next time she forgets to bring Kitty inside, he'll just snatch her up again. No problem, I've got this."

Furrball was a hefty Maine Coon that had adopted her and Cootie. He'd taken a shine to Kitty, not seeming to care that she was no longer among the living, and had a history of catnapping her.

Rude looked around. "Where's Crum?"

"You might want to start class without him," I said as a couple of guests strolled through the gate. "He's talking to Fab, and then he'll be out."

Rude jumped up and went to greet everyone. They were all happy to see her and spoke over one another.

"You don't need to worry about Miss January coming back with a kitten this time. I'm one step ahead of those two." Mac preened. "I made a deal with Harbor at the gas station and bought the whole boxload of kittens. I wasn't happy that he couldn't come up with a straight answer as to where he got them, but they were all healthy, so I quit the interrogation. They were hanging out in the office until I found all of them homes, which I did…except for one, and I'll take it home if no one steps up."

Crum's door opened, and Fab and he came out and headed back to the pool, where Crum waved and joined the yoga class in progress.

"The suit Tank sent over didn't fit. I told Crum to burn his recycled items, then called a local men's clothing store—which I know isn't ridiculously expensive and where I know the owner—and made an appointment. I threatened to hunt Crum down and kick his butt if I heard that he was a no-show or an insufferable client." Fab laughed at Mother's shocked face and added, "It didn't go that badly. I just put to him all the reasons why he should show up looking his best, and he listened."

"Any more problems for today that you might've overlooked?" I asked Mac.

"Nopers."

"We're going to lunch," Mother said. "Come with us."

"Next time. I've got some guests arriving, and it's their first time."

"You want to be more popular than you already are?" I asked.

Mac nodded with a big grin. "You know I do."

"Organize an impromptu welcome party for all the guests, call Jake's and order a buffet of items to be delivered and, of course, take all the credit."

"That's a good one. If it goes over well and the guests enjoy it, then I'll put it on my list of tricks."

"Okay Mother, you get to choose the restaurant."

"I'll think about it on the way to the car. You know, this wasn't as bad as I thought it would be. It was fun hanging out with everyone."

I side-hugged her.

Chapter Twenty-Nine

We'd dropped off Mother, who told us several times that she expected to be called the next time Fab had a job *and* that she also expected to be backup, since she needed to hone her skills.

Spoon would kill me and Fab if he could hear her.

Fab's phone rang, and she held it away from her ear while Gunz grumped. "Tomorrow then," she said, and hung up.

"I'm afraid to ask what he wants."

"He mentioned Tracy's name a couple of times, and that was it, no other details." Fab sighed. "You're coming with me, and no excuses."

"Did he ask that I be in attendance?"

"No, but you can still be in the office and eavesdrop. Whatever it is he wants, you can help me come up with a plan."

"The good news is that we haven't had any emergency calls from Tracy, so that's a positive. Maybe it means they've worked out their issues."

* * *

Despite the fact that we'd gotten an early start, when Fab turned into the parking lot of the office and cruised around the back, taking a car count, we were the last to arrive. That included Gunz, who was sitting in his SUV on his phone. I hadn't faced the man since I bought the house and wondered if the subject would come up.

"I'm going to grab a smooch from my husband, since Gunz is busy doing whatever," I said and cut over to the Boardwalk offices.

Fab was hot on my heels. "Don't dawdle, because he knows we're here and he'll be getting off his call."

Lark waited under the rollup door for the two of us, and Arlo came tearing across the grass to get a head scratch.

"Gunz is doing whatever." I motioned over my shoulder. The guys had told me that Lark made it clear to Gunz she wasn't interested.

"You don't need to worry about me—I wasn't that invested. And if Gunz gets too pushy, I have the guys' permission to shoot him." Lark grinned.

"Mine too," I whispered conspiratorially.

Creole walked up behind me and leaned in. "What are you up to now?"

I pasted on an innocent smile. Judging from his raised brow, it might need some work.

"Excuse us," he said to Lark, then walked me

into his office and laid a big kiss on me. "Back to my question."

I told him about the pending meeting. He didn't like that I didn't know what was on the agenda. "Didier and I find that man barely tolerable, and that's quickly fading with all his issues." He continued to mumble-grumble.

I pointed my finger at him. He leaned forward and nipped at the tip, but that put an end to him getting worked up. "I'm only going for Fab, and with any luck, I'll blend into the wallpaper—" Which we didn't have. "—and it'll be a quick meeting."

He enveloped me in a hug that would have ended in a smooch had it not gotten interrupted by a shrill whistle.

I looked up at Creole. "Gunz is here." I attempt to imitate the whistle, which made him laugh. "Gotta go." I patted his cheek. He pulled me in for another kiss before I raced off to the stairwell.

Gunz's rump was disappearing into the office as I got to the third floor. I slowed and followed, keeping a wide berth, and was about to sit behind Gunz while they exchanged pleasantries when Fab, with her own agenda, pointed to my usual chair in the corner behind her desk.

The big man stuffed his oversized frame into a chair, and his beady browns zeroed in on me. "I suppose congratulations on the purchase of the rooming house are in order."

So, he'd found out, and I was still alive. "Thanks. It was a good fit, since I own other properties on the street."

"You make it sound like you own the block." Gunz sniffed. "It's just the two, isn't it?"

"I wouldn't mind owning the whole block." I smiled benignly and ignored his question. "I'm sure you've heard the news that there was a fire at the property. It's been ruled arson. You heard anything about that, by any chance?"

Gunz gave me an assessing glare meant to scare me. If I hadn't been treated to his ferociousness in the past, I'd be out the door. "Of course, I heard about it," he gritted. "I hear about most everything that goes on in this town." He shifted in his chair. "Would you mind giving Fab and I a moment to go over a case?" Sounded more like, *Beat it*.

"Hold on." Fab and Gunz engaged in a stare-down. "If this is a new job, I can't take it on by myself, and you know the reasons why." Didier would flip. "It's easier if Madison hears everything first-hand." Leaving off, *That way I don't have to repeat everything*. "Unless you want me to use Toady, and if so, I'll give him a call."

Gunz shook his head vehemently. It wasn't a secret that he thought Toady was a cretin. The feeling was mutual. In a butt-kicking contest, I'd put my dough on Toady, despite the size difference. After a long pause that bordered on awkward, he said, "I need you to convince Tracy to come back to town and bring the children,"

"Where is she going to be living?" I asked and got the *behave* stare from Fab. Okay Mother.

"As you're aware, Tracy and your sisters didn't get along, and I feel confident in saying that she won't agree to go back and live with them," Fab told him, holding her own despite his simmering anger.

That was a polite way of saying the sisters scared her enough to grab her purse and run.

"I tried to talk Tracy into giving the living situation a second chance, pointing out that there isn't anything my sisters wouldn't do for her and the children."

Oh brother. Anything is the problem.

"Since she's being difficult, I've arranged for her to live in one of my buildings here in town," Gunz said.

Hopefully not one of the flophouses.

"Does Tracy know about this new living situation?" Fab asked. He shook his head. "My advice is to drive to her grandmother's and tell her what you have in mind. That way, she can feel like she's part of the decision-making."

"If Tracy would just spend more time around my sisters, she'd see how loving they are."

I looked down, so he wouldn't notice me making faces.

"Talk to Tracy, and if she's on board, call me. I'll take care of the rest. But know that I'm not bringing her back unless she wants to come. Are we agreed?"

"Don't forget to tell her what a great guy I am." Gunz smiled at Fab.

"I know you think it's a good idea to have me be the one convincing Tracy, but trust me on this one—it would be way better coming from you."

I thought my eyes would roll back in my head.

My phone rang, and I stood, said, "I've got to take this," and walked away. Sitting at my desk, I shot Xander—who sat across from me clicking away on his laptop—a smile of relief. "Thank you for rescuing me." I'd pushed a button that sent a tone to his phone to call me, another clever app he'd installed.

"You just make sure no one finds out it's me." Xander laughed. "So you know I haven't been slacking on your requests…"

"When have you ever slacked on anything? Never," I answered for him.

He smiled. "I'm still running down information on West. I've discovered that his office was a front—more like a mail drop. I got friendly with the receptionist over there, and she told me that it was rare for West to have a client. Most of their clients use their service the same way—claiming it as office space to appear legit. Before West died, a couple of men came in—checking out the place, dropping his name. Neither has come back. Since he died, a private investigator and a cop both came around asking questions."

"That's impressive. How did you get the information out of the receptionist?"

Xander chuckled. "I drove up there and turned on the charm. Showed up right as she was locking the door and took her out to dinner. I may have misrepresented myself, telling her I was working on a story in the hopes of using it to get a job working for a local online news site. In lieu of cash, she wanted help finding an old school friend, and that was easy to deliver on."

"Are you two going to, uh…"

Xander laughed. "No, we're not. It's a long drive to be dating someone."

"You know my mother would love to fix you up."

He held his hands up in front of him. "No, thanks. If you even hint that to her, I quit. After hearing about Lark's date, not on your life."

I groaned. "I didn't know that she'd come through on a date. I haven't heard a word. Now I'm not asking."

"Lark's words were: 'Hairy like an ape and an IQ to match.'"

Both of us laughed.

"Where did Mother find him? That description doesn't sound like anyone I've met."

"How did this go…?" Xander teased. "One of the neighbors…her best friend has a son who was looking for looove." I shook my head. "To your mother's credit, she wanted to request a resume, but with Spoon laughing in the background, she changed her mind and instead interviewed the guy's mother."

I covered my face and laughed. "Great idea. Everyone's mother thinks they're perfect when it's clear they're not even close. What was I thinking? I just didn't want Lark to date some galoot. Now she'll quit."

"No way is that happening. Lark loves her job. And she gets to bring her dog to work. No other job would allow that. Maybe a few, but they're hard to find."

Fab stormed into my office and sat on the corner of the desk. "Who called?" She held out her hand.

Ha! If she thought I was handing over my phone, she could think again. I wasn't ten years old. I pocketed it and fast. "Wrong number. Now, what's got you in a state?"

"After you ditched me, I again tried to suggest that Gunz fix his own love life. Said that it wasn't a job for a fixer. I told him it would mean more to Tracy coming from him, but the words didn't register." Gunz liked things his way. Any deviation, and he slammed down one of his massive hands and demanded that his edicts be followed.

"I was happy that he didn't seem irked about me buying the property. He's probably relieved, now that it has fire damage and needs a partial rebuild in addition to updating."

"Gunz is annoyed all right. He thought he had

the inside track and the deal all but signed. He can't figure out how he lost it, and since he's like a dog with a bone, I don't expect him to give it up just yet."

"I was about to update you on that property." Xander clicked furiously on his laptop. "I attempted to run down the renters, and they all scattered—not one left a forwarding. A couple of the names didn't check out, so I'm assuming they're aliases. Vicky Prell, the woman running the place—she split, and it's anyone's guess whether she'll resurface. If she wants to follow through on her lawsuit, she'll have to show up at some point. I'm not an investigator, but Vicky looks the guiltiest to me, and I base that on her rap sheet of petty crimes. Nothing arson-related, and no arrests in more than ten years."

"Good job, as always," I said. "Interesting that they would take off. Let's hope they stay gone." I turned to Fab. "Back to your dilemma. What's your plan?"

"You're going to call Tracy, pretend to be me, and find out what she wants."

"Which I'm not going to do, but it's a good idea."

Chapter Thirty

Fab cruised down the highway, and not in her usual "eat up the road" style. We'd decided to try somewhere new for lunch, and I got to pick. I warned her it would be an interesting hole in the wall. I'd seen a write-up online about a new seafood shack with great reviews that had opened on the outskirts of town and pulled up their website to make sure that they had outside seating.

In the side mirror, I caught sight of a black Escalade pulling up alongside the Hummer and turned toward the window. It was hard to make out the driver through the tinted windows. The SUV was close enough that I could have reached out and opened their door. "Not certain what's going on, but try to avoid damage to the Hummer." Whoever it was wasn't swerving, so I ruled out drunk. If they wanted our attention, they had it.

Fab honked at the car poking along in front of her, and I was relieved when the Escalade moved back over into the center of its lane. I then watched in horror as it flew back at us, ramming into the passenger door with a shriek of ripping metal. The back window of the SUV inched down, and a handgun appeared.

Fab jerked the wheel and hit the gas.

Two shots rang out, and the Hummer swerved violently, Fab's grip on the wheel tightening to keep it under control. The Escalade weaved and roared off.

Fab coasted gently to the side of the road with no further damage to my SUV, which was limping along on what felt like at least one flat tire.

"I got a brief glance at the shooter, and I'm telling you—it was Kettle Q with her finger on the trigger." I struggled to control my temper. "I know what you're going to say. Did you happen to notice that the Escalade is a match for the one that Gunz drives?"

"Why would she—"

"It was my car that picked up Tracy," I cut Fab off. "If Gunz knew it was mine when he called, then the sisters know too." I pulled my phone out of my pocket.

"Who are you calling?"

I ignored her question, making a mental list of the calls I needed to make.

"911," the operator said as I put the call on speaker.

"I want to report being shot at on the highway headed south out of Tarpon Cove."

Fab looked surprised, but didn't ask me to hang up.

I answered the operator's questions, and she assured me the cops were on the way before hanging up. "Once I find out whether the cops are going to tow my coach off to impound or not, I'll know whether to call Spoon."

"Are you absolutely certain about what you saw?" Fab asked.

"I'm certain enough to file a police report. It's their job to figure out who was behind the wheel—which I'm guessing was Watusi—and whether I'm right about the shooter or not."

A cop car rolled up behind us. I got out and moved to the back bumper as Kevin got out of his car.

"You two okay?" he asked.

"Happy that Fab was behind the wheel—she's always calm," I said as he got closer, then told him what had happened and what I'd seen.

"How sure are you that it was Kettle?" Kevin asked. "Met her a few times, and I know she's an excitable woman, but no arrests I'm aware of."

"I'm fairly certain. Unless she has a twin." I shuddered at the possibility of there being two of her.

"Any reason why she'd want to shoot at you?"

I told him about relocating Tracy at her own request and added that she and Gunz had reconciled.

"You're telling me that Gunz has a kid?" Kevin rolled his eyes. "Seriously?"

I nodded, not knowing what to say.

Kevin shook his head and turned his attention to Fab, who'd gotten out of the Hummer and stood a foot away. She had nothing to contribute, as she hadn't seen anything, too busy making sure we didn't end up wrapped around a tree.

"It's none of my business what clients you chose, but Gunz has quite a history of shady dealings. Before you tell me what a goodie two-shoes he's turned into, my answer is: there've been rumors. Nothing provable." Kevin got down on the ground and checked out the tires. "Unfortunately, the bullets went through the sidewalls. You're going to have to have this towed. You're lucky that... Just lucky. If I have more questions, I know where to find you." He waved and walked back to his car.

I flicked through my phone, and when Spoon answered, I said, "I need a tow truck out on the highway headed south, just past the lumber place."

"You okay?" he growled.

"Just annoyed." I hit the highlights and left out that I had ID'd the shooter.

"You're going to need a ride."

"If whoever is driving the tow truck could drop us off on the highway close to home, it would be appreciated."

Spoon snorted. "I'm sending Billy, and I know he'll get you to your door."

By the time I hung up, Fab had gotten our personal items out of the SUV. "Once Gunz hears that the cops paid his sister a visit, I'm certain he'll have questions of his own. When he asks why I didn't call: 'I was too busy getting the car hauled off to call you or anyone else.'"

"Did you call Didier?" I asked.

"For once, I did. Although I may have left off one or two things, the most important point is that they both know we weren't hurt. Neither is happy, but that's to be expected."

Thankfully, Billy Keith didn't let grass grow under his work boots and got to us in short order. He waved out the window as he rolled up, then backed up the flatbed and got the Hummer hooked in place. The three of us got in the truck, me in the middle.

"Good to see you." I smiled at Billy. "Heck of a way to catch up."

"Xander keeps me updated and mostly laughing."

When Xander first hit town and needed a place to live, Billy stepped up and offered to rent him a room. They didn't get on each other's nerves and decided to make it a permanent arrangement.

Spoon called it when he said Billy would make sure we got home. He drove up to the entrance to the compound, and we hopped out.

"Free food at Jake's. Anytime," I said.

"Heck, they never even let me pay for drinks." Billy laughed.

"Good."

We both waved as he pulled out.

"I kept my eyes peeled, and we weren't followed," Fab said as we hiked up the road to our houses. "I'm going to tell Gunz that this is unacceptable. If Kettle's got a gripe, she has to talk, not shoot. Thank goodness she didn't aim for the windshield."

"It's going to be my pleasure to present Gunz with the repair bill."

Chapter Thirty-One

It took an extra day to get the Hummer back. Besides getting tricked out with new tires, it was serviced and spit shined inside and out, making it look like new. The day I went to pick it up, Fab called, saying that she was indulging in a drama-free day. I was tempted to whine loudly in her ear but managed to contain myself, as I planned to take several of those myself, and soon.

All appeared quiet as I pulled into The Cottages, except for Crum backing out, leaving for another court date. He'd ended up taking Fab's suggestion on where to get a new suit, and Mac had driven him. She'd called and reported that the shopping trip had been a big success and he looked like a new man. Crum and the tailor had hit it off, going on about some subject that came close to putting Mac to sleep. Not a snotty word between the two. To Mac's surprise—and mine when I heard it—he didn't complain about having to shell out for new duds.

I parked in front of the office, and Mac was standing at the bumper when I got out. I swear, she must have had her head stuck out the window to scope out the neighborhood. Or she'd had a camera installed, but she always denied it when asked. Her lime-green crocs were fairly tame for her. I did wonder if she was the one who glued the flowers to the toes or if it was the manufacturer's idea.

"In case you didn't know, this is national drama-free day," I told her.

"I'll spread the word, but I'm telling you now that it won't make the guests happy." Mac smirked. "They're sleeping in after last night's bus trip. After dinner, Rude rounded them up, and they hit up a couple of bars and got their drunk on. Rude likes it when they're tanked; she claims then they don't question the nonsense she spouts."

We both caught sight of Kevin slapping our way in a pair of flip-flops and shorts.

I lowered my voice and said, "Let's hope he's in a good mood."

"He always is on his day off."

"Hello, officer." I saluted. "Good to see your friendly smirk. It is friendly, isn't it?"

"I've got some news for you that you're probably not going to like."

I groaned, noticing that he didn't look upset to be relaying whatever it was. "Let me guess—this is a heads up that your toilet is on the fritz and you've taken to peeing out the window?"

"I had a talk with that tenant of yours and, in legal terms, told him to knock it off. How do you find these people?"

"Not the same way that I got you. My brother didn't move this one in; he came with the building."

"Is that the end or is there more?" Mac asked.

"There's always more." I pasted on a smile.

"Problem taken care of, though he disputes there ever was one. Says it was nothing more than wild gossip. He did admit to watering the plant he has growing up there and says that's what people saw and misconstrued."

"That plant is plastic." Mac whispered, but both of us heard her.

"So sad that I miss all the good stuff." Thankfully. "Very kind of you to take care of that problem, officer."

"Your other problem..." Kevin appeared to be waiting for acknowledgement, so I nodded. "We're continuing to investigate the shooting, though we don't have much to go on. In addition to having an alibi, Kettle doesn't own an Escalade. Before you tell me that Gunz does, I know that. It was in the shop. Another officer checked it out."

"Got to hand it to Kettle—she pulled off a shooting and managed to make it a 'she said, I said.'" No kidding, it was in the shop—smashing into the Hummer would have thrashed the Escalade too.

"Free advice: stay away from the sisters. In fact, the whole family." Kevin grimaced. "So you know—I believe you, but neither of us can prove it."

"I appreciate the update." I nodded toward the end of the block. "Anything new on the fire?"

"If one of the previous tenants shows up, give me a call. I have a few questions I'd like to ask."

"If I could be of more help, I would, but I haven't owned the property long enough to meet any of the tenants. Not that they were interested in exchanging hellos. Vicky Prell is the only one I'd recognize."

"If you do..." he said, and I nodded. "I came up here to raid the snack bowl." He winked at Mac.

"On my desk is a blue-handled bag, special for you," Mac told him, and he took off as though someone might beat him there.

"No wonder you're everyone's favorite around here. In addition to solving their problems, you provide junk food. Just so you know, I'm not complaining."

Mac steered me toward the barbecue area—the best spot for watching the action in the driveway...if it weren't empty at the moment.

"Why do I feel as though my moment of 'all is well' is about to evaporate?" I asked as we sat on one of the cement benches. "Where's that ratty plastic pool you scored? We could be soaking our feet."

"Poof." In addition to the sound effect, Mac threw up her arms. "Gone in the night. I came over for my morning stroll, and the eyesore wasn't waiting on me to dunk my feet."

"What does your security footage have to say about that?" I knew she'd had someone other than Fab rig up a camera at her house.

"A couple of hooded figures skirted through the bushes, snatched it up, and ran out the front. The only shot I got of their faces was blurred."

"That's too bad. We could've sent Fab to kick butt and gone along to watch."

Mac and I laughed.

"My news... I should've told Kevin but thought you should hear it first."

"News. Kevin. Can't be good."

"I caught that Vicky woman going into the house. 'To check it out one last time,' she said. She wasn't quite skunk drunk, but she'd tipped a few and was laughing it up about the fire. I don't think she knew who I was." Mac shook her head. "If you can't control your mouth when you're drunk, you shouldn't drink. Or stay home. She confided that she got a heads up to pack and get out and was paid to keep her mouth shut. Said the man wanting to buy the property wasn't happy when it sold to someone else. Thank goodness no one got hurt or died."

I nodded in agreement. "Gunz?"

Mac shrugged.

"What would he get out of burning it down? Didn't work out that way, but it needs plenty of work. Maybe he, or whoever it was, thought I'd sell at a discount. Must not know my husband is in the construction business." Maybe Gunz didn't have anything to do with the fire after all.

"Vicky didn't elaborate, but when I showed her a picture of Gunz, she looked wide-eyed and said, 'Forget I said anything,' then ran off down the street. At least she wasn't driving."

Which meant that she was still in the neighborhood somewhere.

"I shopped his picture to the busybodies in the neighborhood, and one thought maybe she'd seen him once but waffled so much I discounted her. No one else copped to even seeing him around." Mac pulled out her phone, bringing up the picture and handing it to me.

It was a great frontal shot; no doubt it was him. "How did you get this?" I tried to make out the background. It wasn't taken on one of my properties.

"I saw him coming out of the Smoke Shop and snapped his picture without thinking. Good thing he didn't catch me."

"Were all the tenants paid off?" I asked.

"Vicky didn't come out and say specifically but hinted that they were."

"Four to six people know that a crime was committed. It's hard to believe that one of them won't talk eventually, even if just to brag." I eyed Mac. "You going to drop this tidbit on Kevin? I'd do it, but since I wasn't the one to hear it firsthand, he'd be wanting to know my source."

"I'll catch him when he's alone. I don't want anyone finding out that I snitch for him on occasion. You know, but I trust that you won't tell."

"No worries there." Her confidence that I'd have her back pleased me. "No wonder you're his favorite, with everything you do for him, plus keeping him up on what's going on in the neighborhood."

"Having learned a trick or two from you, I'm going to negotiate a favor, but only if it turns out my info is useful."

"If it's proven that Gunz was involved…" I winced. "Kevin already said he wants to talk to Vicky. Hit up Xander, and if he finds anything new, turn over the info and take the credit." Mac clearly liked the idea. "And if you hear anything else, I want to be the first to know." I turned and craned my neck. "I'm surprised I didn't see Kevin leave the office."

"I did. He cut down the back walkway. He'll drop the bag off and head to the beach. He's the biggest user of the water bike. Says it's a chick magnet." At my doubtful look, she added, "No, really."

"I don't want to ask, but anything else that needs my attention?"

"The excitement begins when the guests start rolling out of their cottages. Since they're hungover, it'll be a while. But no worries; it's barbecue night and party on."

Chapter Thirty-Two

The next day, Xander emailed an extensive report on everything he'd found on the drives Fab turned over from the West mansion. I called a meeting at The Boardwalk offices and asked that he hit the highlights of the information he'd uncovered.

On the way in, I stopped at the Bakery Café and loaded up on breakfast items and danishes. I'd asked Lark to get orange juice and coffee and said, for the latter, to get a blend that would please everyone and good luck with that. She took a "drink what we have or go without" stance, and I hadn't heard a word about her being a meanie regarding that policy.

Lark was sitting at the picnic table watching Arlo chase after something when I arrived. She jumped up to help me carry in the pink boxes.

"As you requested, I put out the invite to the Chief and Casio and told them there'd be food. You know that's a seller." She chuckled. "Also warned against either of them sneaking in after the fact and helping themselves. Not happening."

I laughed, and we went inside and set the

boxes on the counter. I noticed that she hadn't removed her oversized dark glasses. "Let's leave these here, and everyone can help themselves." Lark already had plates and utensils sitting out. "Have a seat."

"I have to check on Arlo." She ran out the door and disappeared in a snap.

If she thought her mad dash would stop me from finding out what was going on, she was wrong. I followed her and watched as she stood in the middle of the parking lot and stared off in the opposite direction of Arlo, who was peering between the fence slats into the water below. After some whimpering, he turned away. Whatever had caught his eye had gotten away.

"Lark," I yelled and pointed to the picnic table. She shuffled over, taking the smallest of steps, and sat down. "One thing you should know—I'm not easily deterred. What the heck is going on with the glasses?"

She pushed them to the top of her head, revealing that she was sporting a nasty shiner. "I fell."

"That's bull-oney. Who the flip hit you?"

"It's nothing." Her cheeks turned red.

"You wanna play hardball? Fine. I'll snatch up Arlo and hold him hostage until you talk."

"That would be just plain old mean." Lark frowned. "I'm pretty sure you wouldn't do anything that cruel. At least, I don't think so."

"I'll be taking Arlo to my house. The two of us

can work on my dog rapport, and when you decide to talk… Hope he gets along with cats."

"He chases them," Lark said drily. "I'm not caving." She jutted out her chin, and we engaged in a stare-down. When I didn't look away, she sighed. "Fine. I decided to moonlight…short-lived."

"You need money?"

"I need something to do. It gets old sitting at home." Lark studied her fingernails. "There was this guy at the trailer park…"

Bad start, and from the looks of her eye, it wasn't going to get better.

"We had a couple of drinks and hit it off…sort of, I guess. Anyway, Chip is a private investigator, and he hired me to come along on a job as his girlfriend. The pay was decent, and part of the job was going out to dinner. How hard could that be? His client wanted him to get the goods on her cheating husband so she could negotiate a better divorce settlement."

"I'd think that the pre-nup would cover that."

Lark shrugged. "Anyway…" Her finger tapped the table. "When we got to the restaurant, the man was sitting at a table by himself. Chip wanted me to go over, get friendly with the guy, and get some information. Just as I got to the table, I realized that I didn't have a clue what kind of information. I turned and looked over my shoulder, and Chip was taking pictures. I figured out that he was setting the man up and exited through the patio."

"Chip blacked your eye?"

Lark shook her head. "I got an Uber back to the park, and when Chip got home, I went over, banged on his door, and told him he could stick his jobs and not to speak to me ever again. He just laughed; he couldn't have cared less." She unleashed an irritated sigh. "Unbeknownst to me—although I should've figured—Chip did get a couple of pictures of me standing at the table and gave them to the wife, who showed her husband. It was my bad luck to run into the two of them in Homestead. The man recognized me, got in my face, and told me whatever I had planned wasn't going to work, that he was back with his wife. She stood back the whole time, a big-ass smirk on her face. That's when I blurted, 'If you weren't such a turd, your wife wouldn't be having you followed.' I could see that was news to him. He erupted with, 'Liar,' and pushed me. I pushed back and landed on the ground, my face making contact with the concrete. He mumbled sorry and grabbed the wife's hand, and the two ran off."

"You got names? I'll take Chip's last name. And how about the client?"

Lark shook her head vehemently. "No way. I know that look, and you're not going to go beat either of their behinds. I never asked the husband's name, and I was a party to setting him up, however unknowingly."

"That doesn't mean he gets to hit you."

"He probably wouldn't have flipped his stick if his wife had confessed her part in the whole thing, but then they might not have gotten back together. No happy ending, or some such." Lark smiled like a mental patient, then laughed at herself.

"If you change your mind, text me their names," I said, and she shook her head. "On another subject, my humblest apologies. I thought Mother had a better than even chance of setting you up with someone decent—didn't think she'd completely miss the mark. She had some convoluted plan, and you know how it worked out."

"Two dates." Lark held up her fingers. "Both lame... You get the point. No more. Your mother has been very sweet to me, so this conversation stays between us. I don't want her thinking I was complaining behind her back."

"Plans run in the family... I've got one. Did you just groan?" I bit my lip so I wouldn't laugh. "I don't have a particular man in mind, but if I meet one... In the meantime, I have a friend who's always looking for someone to bar hop with and grumbles when she can't find anyone. Doesn't mean you need to get your drunk on—go for the entertainment. Jake's is full-service—food, drinks, and fun."

"I got up and sang at amateur night." Lark's cheeks turned pink. "I didn't get booed like the guy before me. Didn't seem to bother him. I'd have died."

"I've got an idea," I mused.

"Please no."

"Text me what you're looking for in a man. If it sounds like anyone I know, I'll casually hook the two of you up. Arrange for you to meet and check each other out, no stress. Stop shaking your head and send the list. You never know."

"You don't have to—"

I waved her off. "I may not know anyone." Lark didn't believe me, but whatever. "Does the PI know about your eye?"

"Chip packed his trailer and hit the road. If I'd known he only booked the space for a week, I wouldn't have bothered."

A convoy of cars pulled into the parking lot, everyone attending the meeting arriving at once. Not sure how they pulled that off.

I stood and motioned Lark up. "Anyone asks about your eye, you ran into a door. Make sure to use a 'mind your own business' tone, and that should take care of any further questions."

Lark laughed, then turned and whistled for Arlo, who raced over and eyed the cars as they parked and everyone got out.

"Let's go inside before they eat everything."

Chapter Thirty-Three

The usual suspects gathered around the conference table, and Mother and Spoon were the last to arrive. I corralled her before she got to the door, told her no questions about Lark's eye, and informed her that I was taking over introducing Lark to a potential or two.

"You just go ahead with that silly little grin; you're about to find out that it's not easy," Mother grumped. "Take my advice—don't take someone else's word about their male relative's attributes. Check them out yourself. I should've listened to Spoon and not gotten involved. The Madeline Spoon dating service is closed."

"My husband is of the same mindset as yours. But it's hard for Westin women to mind their own business." We both laughed.

The food got inhaled. Thankfully, I was well-trained to over-buy. Lark made sure that the coffee pot was never empty.

Once the table had been cleared, I stood and slapped my hand down. "Call this meeting to order. Xander's in charge. Anyone gives him a hard time—Fab will shoot you." No one contradicted me, but a few eyebrows went up.

Xander's cheeks flamed.

Spoon raised his hand. "I want my name added to the agenda."

"Done." I scribbled in the air. "Anyone else?" No hands, so I guessed not. "Let's have a warm welcome for the Chief and Casio. They've been scarce of late, off doing who knows what," I said and got an even-eyed stare from both men.

I plunked down next to Creole, who put his arm around my shoulders.

Xander cleared his throat and stood.

I gave him a *kill it* nod.

"As you all know by now, Travis West was murdered and Crum, who didn't do it, got arrested. I've been digging into West's background. He got his law degree and worked for a couple of big firms up until three years ago. He quit suddenly, and as far as his law license went, all he did was keep it current." Xander picked up his water bottle and downed about half of it.

I felt bad because I knew he was nervous and smiled encouragingly.

One last swig, and he continued. "West interested me because I couldn't find a record of any big cases he worked on. He couldn't have supported himself for long without a job, and no record of him being a trust-fund kid. Then I came into possession of some of his personal files, which answered the question of how he was supporting himself—blackmail."

"You're telling us that West left a paper trail? And you somehow got your hands on it?" the Chief barked.

I was the only one at the table that already knew and didn't have a surprised look on my face. "Let him finish."

"I received three drives and found the files all identical, so it was easy to conclude that two were used for backup," Xander continued. "West manage to dig up some explosive dirt on three high-profile men, then hired a private detective to get pictures. Once he had proof, he made initial contact with the men, concocting a reason that they needed to meet—in one case, under the guise of becoming the man's client. He demanded cash to buy his silence and arranged for it to be deposited in a special account. I know this because he kept records of all his meetings and correspondence. As for the cash, I'm not certain why the transactions weren't flagged by the bank. Another assumption on my part is that he had a connection at his bank, who ensured the large cash deposits weren't reported."

"Blackmail is certainly a good reason to murder him," Creole said.

The Chief and Casio nodded.

"You can cross one of the three men off the list—Harmon Lane. Tired of being blackmailed, he called West's bluff. In the email exchange, he reminded West that blackmail was a crime that could result in prison time and said he'd happily turn him over to the authorities." Xander sat back down.

"Then what happened?" Fab asked. "We already know that West doesn't have a criminal record."

"Wouldn't you like to know why he was being blackmailed?" I smirked at Fab, knowing she wanted every iota of information. I'd gloat later that I knew before her.

Fab glared with a slight shake of her head.

"A prominent businessman and pillar of the community who owned several car dealerships, Lane was having an affair with his niece. Although she was of legal age, it was, well…incest."

"Was? So the affair's over?" Casio asked.

Xander nodded. "Not in the way you think. Not sure of West's reasoning, but he gave the photos to a newscaster at a television station in Miami, and it made headlines for days. They were brutal. When Lane killed himself, that fired up the story even more. Though at least then, he garnered more sympathy from reporters, who were excoriating him before he turned up dead."

Clearly, no one had expected that outcome. I hadn't when I read it.

"What happened to the niece?" Mother asked.

"Lane took care of her before he offed himself. He set up a bank account for her, and after the reading of the will, she immediately moved to Los Angeles and is living under another name."

"Now we're down to two men?" Brad asked. "Wonder if they knew about one another. Either way, bet they weren't sad to hear of West's demise."

"I called Fab's funeral friends." That made everyone laugh except her. "They used their connections to check with the funeral home that hosted the sendoff and ask for the names of those who showed up, if they could be had." I ignored Creole and Didier shaking their heads. "Bet you didn't know that it's like a fraternity among the funeral directors; they all seem to know each other." Who snorted? I looked around. "West's brother, who lives in New York, made the arrangements by phone. As for guests, no one that actually knew him showed up. The affair wasn't an entire no-show, as several regulars came—the ones looking for free food. The sandwiches aren't bad."

Creole twisted his head sideways and rolled his eyes. I gave him the mean-girl stare and tried not to laugh. "Sounds to me like there are two better suspects than Crum, as the dude in his underwear didn't even punch back."

"Not that he didn't want to… I was there," I defended him.

That brought groans from family, who were once again putting The Cottages in the "sell" column.

"Blackmail is a messy business, especially if the victim thinks it's going to go on forever, without an end in sight, which is usually the way it works," Casio said. "If these men are high-profile, then they'd likely hire someone to pull the trigger."

"Finding out which one it was and proving it would be damn difficult," Creole said.

"In order to use the information you just shared, should it be necessary, the DA would need to show where he got it," Casio said, assessing me with a flinty stare. He obviously knew I knew where it came from, but I wasn't copping to anything just yet.

The Chief raised his hand. "How did you get these files?" His question was laced with sarcasm.

Xander made a shocked face. "I could never out my source."

I practically shrieked when all eyes turned my way. "Me? Anyway, the question of how isn't as important as who killed West and how to get Crum off."

The Chief snorted. "Spoken like a shifty criminal…or his defense attorney."

"You're the Chief of Police here. Ex, anyway," Fab reminded him, as though he'd forgotten. "Wouldn't you treat this evidence the same as information handed over by a snitch?"

Although Didier stared at her with a raised eyebrow, he tugged her to his side.

"Yeah," Creole and Casio said, almost in unison, as they turned their attention to the man.

Both men had worked for the Chief as detectives when they'd been on the force.

"Three men, now two, were being blackmailed for their indiscretions, and you have the proof?" the Chief asked Xander.

"The other two are a little more involved. I have a disc, if you want to take a look at it." Xander picked up his briefcase, snapped open the locks and retrieved a square black box, which he held it out to the Chief, who took it. "You'll find that West was good at digging up dirt."

"To get a sniff of that kind of information, he would've had to run in the same social circles as his victims," Casio said. "It's not the kind of dirt you just stumble on. It wouldn't be far-fetched to assume that he paid someone for the information."

"How did a nobody lawyer rate high enough to mingle with the hip and happening?" I asked. "They don't allow just anyone to walk up and join the party."

"West made the gossip pages when he lived in Miami, always on the arm of a rich woman." Xander scanned his notes. "I found out that he paid his way through college by working for a dating service that catered to a select clientele."

"Why not just find himself a rich older woman and mooch off her happily ever after?" Mother asked.

"For a lawyer, he was incredibly stupid to keep detailed files on every exchange he had with his victims," Xander said. "It seemed like he was enjoying his game of blackmail. In addition to gathering the information, he ran background checks and financial searches and knew to the penny what they were worth."

Spoon broke the silence that followed. "This is where I should speak up and tell you why I'm here."

"I figured Mother corralled you. You know she's not one to miss any excitement." Brad winked at her.

"I see now." I shook my finger at Mother and Brad. "There's hot news, and Mother tells Brad, but not me," I said in a faux sulk.

That had everyone laughing.

"I tracked down Mike Stone, the private investigator who harassed Madison and Fab at the café the other day." Spoon eyed us as though we'd withheld information, when he was there and knew exactly what went down.

Creole and Didier growled.

"Big man to the rescue." Arms over my head, touchdown. "Spoon kicked his ass—sorry, I mean butt—to the other side of the road." Not quite, but it sounded good.

"Anyway..." Amusement flickered in Spoon's eyes. "Me and one of my guys paid Mike a visit."

I'd put cash on Billy accompanying him, never one to turn down excitement.

"It surprised me that we didn't have to beat the hell out of the man to get him to talk. A bit disappointed," he added with a grin.

Mother beamed at him.

Hell, I mouthed at her and got the *behave* stare.

"Turns out Mike doesn't have any real training. Surprised me he could get a license…if he's got one—I didn't ask to see it. He boasted about attending online PI school and getting a certificate, which he took to mean he was free to flash a badge he picked up at a uniform warehouse."

"No wonder he copped an attitude when we made fun of his badge," Fab said.

"Mike has a high opinion of himself and his abilities, but let it slip that it was his first job," Spoon told us. "You mentioned that West's brother arranged the funeral and no other relatives put in an appearance." He looked to me for confirmation and I nodded.

"Peter West contacted Mike and hired him to make sure the cops didn't overlook any evidence, saying he didn't want the murderer to walk," Spoon said, skepticism in his tone. "Mike told us that he went to the mansion, figuring there was no harm since West was dead and the cops had released the scene. He assumed it wasn't trespassing since he had the brother's permission."

"Wonder how many break-ins there've been since the cops released the mansion." The Chief's stare included Fab and me oozing anger.

We stared back benignly, as did our husbands.

Good thing they knew everything that went down ahead of time or they'd be oozing anger.

"He was caught off guard when he came upon another man in the act of tossing the office," Spoon continued. "Mike thinks the reason he got away without being shot was that he told him he'd seen two people running down the beach to a boat parked at the dock. The man took off in hot pursuit. Not knowing how much time he had, Mike hid in a space behind a cabinet and stayed there watching as the man came back and ripped the office apart. Judging by the swearing, it's Mike's opinion that he didn't find what he was looking for."

"Surprised that Mike didn't confront the other two," Creole mused. "Did he by chance offer up a description?"

"The pictures he took weren't the best, but it wasn't hard to ID both parties if you'd ever met them." Spoon stared at Fab and me. "He also got pictures of the boat and, from the banner advertising, knew it was a rental. He paid the clerk at the dock for the information on the rental card, which included the license number of the Hummer. There aren't many of those in town, so it wasn't hard to spot. Finding it parked at the bakery was a fluke."

"Mikey catches up to us, and his bright idea is to impersonate a cop. Then, when that doesn't work, he whips out a little blackmail of his own, threatening to call the cops unless we turn over anything we found in the house. That's if we'd been there in the first place." Fab held up empty hands and flashed crazy-girl smile around the table.

Mother and I grinned at her.

"So how did you leave it with the man?" Didier asked.

"Told Mike that he lucked out getting away with his life after confronting the two of you. Let him know that you had friends that would feed him to local rodents, who are a hungry bunch, as they haven't been fed in a while." Spoon reached in his pocket and pulled out a business card. "Had to pay Mike for this one. The other intruder was either this man, Kirk George, or he dropped his client's card while crawling around. I already gave the name to Xander to check out."

Making a startled noise, Casio took the card.

"This George guy is one of the men West was blackmailing," Xander said. "He's a prominent businessman whose son likes to hook up with rich women and clean out their bank accounts, then move on to the next one."

"What about the other victim?" Creole asked.

"Frank Craig," Xander said. "He owns a restaurant in Miami, and the partner got them involved in a money laundering scheme. When West informed the two men what he'd found out, the partner skipped town, leaving Craig to answer West's demands. Once he found out what his partner was up to, he put an immediate stop to it, but West didn't care. 'Tell the authorities' was his response."

"It's been a while since I've seen George. I believe I'll pay him a little visit." Casio pocketed the business card.

"I've got a better idea." I smiled at him.

Brad laughed. I attempted to elbow him, but he moved away.

Creole snorted, thinking clearly not. "That's hard to believe."

"How about we dump all the information Xander's compiled in your lap?" I raised an eyebrow at Casio. "As long as you can guarantee me that you won't be influenced by your friendship and leave Crum to twist. If that's agreeable, I'm happy to put a dozen IOUs on the table as an incentive. New ones. Not returning any from the stack that you owe me, which I don't expect will run out in my lifetime."

"Good idea," Fab said, like it was my first one. "Casio's the one with Miami contacts, more than anyone else at this table. Except the Chief, and he'll be needed to boss Casio around so he won't get off track."

"Better than Fab or Madison," Didier grumbled.

"The exception would be if you need backup; then we're available," I offered, knowing there was zero chance he'd take me up on it.

"That will be a cold day in…" Creole leveled a glare at Casio, who grinned. Creole then eyed me, letting me know, *No way*.

I pouted, even though I was happy not to be chasing a killer.

"You have another of those drives?" Casio asked Xander, nodding at the one sitting in front of the Chief. "I want to look over everything myself."

Xander reached into his briefcase and handed another one over.

"Show of hands." Mine shot in the air. "Aren't you all happy to be updated at the same time?" Not a single hand went up.

"I have a couple of questions," the Chief said, engaging in a stare-down with Fab. "Sizing you up as the ringleader. How is it that you were able to find these files? Especially since I know the cops did a thorough search."

"A false bottom in one of his desk drawers." Fab's smile didn't inspire confidence that she was telling the truth.

The Chief didn't say it, but his face said, *Yeah sure*.

Before the Chief could ask another question, I stood, knowing it wouldn't derail him for long. "This has been fun. I'm sorry to inform you all that there are no leftovers." I made a sad face.

Chapter Thirty-Four

The next morning, Fab had a meeting scheduled with Gunz at the office. I let her know that I planned to stay downstairs, so as not to start a fight. I'd asked Spoon to send me an invoice for the repairs to the Hummer, with no family discount pricing. He'd emailed it, and I'd printed a copy.

"What's that?" Creole pointed to the paper in my hand.

"Just a little something I had Spoon fax over." I held up the invoice.

Creole gave it a once-over. "You know that Gunz is fifteen times bigger than you?"

"That's why I carry." I lifted my skirt.

"I'm coming with you." He stood.

"That won't be necessary, since my goal is not to pick a fight. Just looking to clear the air."

"You're too late." He indicated behind me with a nod. "Meeting's over. It will make Didier happy that Gunz is out of here with no added drama. Unless you start something."

"Gunz," I yelled at the top of my lungs. He turned, and I motioned him over. He stared, as though trying to decide, his lips tightening, then finally ambled over. "Let me handle this," I said to Creole, who glared back and whispered, "Whatever you're up to…you've lost your mind."

All eyes shifted to the middle of the room as I handed Gunz the invoice.

"What's this?" He glanced at the sheet, then wadded it in a ball.

"You might want to save that. Or I can email you another one. It's the invoice for repairing the damage Kettle did to the Hummer and the detailing that makes Fab happy." I ignored Fab, who stood out of range, rolling her eyes.

"Kettle was cleared by the cops," Gunz practically spit, his ears turning pink. "To be clear, I'm not paying you one damn cent. And I want you to get over to the police station and retract your statement. You can say you were mistaken, or however you want to frame it, since you were. I'm sure you'll come up with something."

"Now you listen to me." I struggled to keep my voice calm, losing the battle as my voice went up a few notches. "I'm very clear on what I saw, and it was your sister Kettle sticking her head out of your SUV and shooting at us. If she says different, then she's a liar." I ignored his face turning red, anger pouring out of his orifices. "It's obvious that you don't give a flip what happens to me, but what about Fab? She was driving and could have been hurt or killed if the

SUV had gone into a ditch. Let me repeat—your sisters are liars. Watusi had to be driving, who else? You know that I'm telling the truth and you and whoever you've paid are covering for them. Now pay the damn bill."

Gunz threw the invoice on the floor.

"Fine. Be a dick." Now I was yelling. "Warning: Kettle or Watusi ever shoots at me again, and I'll shoot back. And believe me, I don't miss."

"You're not to go on any more of my jobs," Gunz seethed.

"That's sad." My voice dripped with sarcasm.

Gunz pivoted and had parting words for Fab, which I couldn't hear, then stomped out.

Once he cleared the door, I said to her, "I came very close to banning him from this property, and you're the only reason I didn't. But that's subject to change if he doesn't pay up, along with an agreement to corral his sisters. If not, then you'll have to conduct business at a taco stand."

"Both of you need to calm down, and when that happens, I'll be brokering a truce," Fab said.

"What did Gunz want?" Didier asked.

Fab took a seat in the reception area and motioned for the rest of us to do the same. "After I made it clear that this was an issue better dealt with by him and that I was out, Gunz and Tracy finally sat down and talked. She's not moving back to the Keys."

"Smart decision," I mumbled.

"It turns out that her grandmother has a guest house in the back of her property. It's big enough for Tracy and the kids, and they have a yard to play in."

"Gunz didn't come here to tell you that. He wants something." I struggled to contain my sarcasm.

"He wants me to get Tracy and his sisters together to sit down and talk out their differences."

"You?" My mouth dropped open. "Has he forgotten that Kettle loathes you and the feeling's mutual?"

"If you'd let me finish…" Fab simmered with frustration. "I told him it was a terrible idea, that he needed to stop pushing and give it some time before demanding that they kiss and make up. Not only did I tell him it would never work, but that rushing Tracy could have her digging in even more."

"That was good advice. Be interesting to see if Gunz listens. If he doesn't, I hope you turn down the job." Didier gave Fab an even stare.

"When he gets an idea, he digs in his heels and won't listen to the alternatives. What he needs is time to come around."

Chapter Thirty-Five

Brad, who'd been sitting at the conference table listening to every word and chowing down on his lunch, wadded up his trash and dumped it, grabbing a drink.

Before he could disappear into his office, I called, "Bradford."

He turned with a smirk. "Don't know anyone by that name."

I'd teased him with the name off and on as a kid, and it didn't irritate him as much as I'd have liked. "Since we're in share mode, what's going on with you and Logan?" I pointed to a chair.

"Got some work to finish before I leave."

"I'll call Mother and we'll track you down."

The guys laughed, knowing that involving Mother was a threat that always worked.

Brad moved closer but didn't sit. "Seriously, I don't have time for your antics when I've got a home visit in a couple of hours. I've got to make sure it goes well so they'll give me guardianship of Logan. The last thing I want is for him to think that no one ever wanted him."

"According to Emerson, your case worker

likes you, so don't worry so much about these visits; you'll do great." I smiled at him. "Logan's very lucky."

"Mila and I already think of him as family. I'll be happy when it's official."

"And Mother is horribly upset to have another grandchild to spoil," I teased.

"You didn't hear this from me, and when you do hear it, you better act like it's the first time." I nodded. "Mother knew about my last home visit and stopped by, all 'I was just in the neighborhood.' Yeah sure. She hijacked the interview, and the two women talked like old friends. And before you ask, I sat there with a stupid look on my face, thinking 'do I interrupt or…' I opted to keep my mouth shut. After the woman left, thankfully all smiles, Mother stopped me from telling her a thing or two with, 'Now she knows what a supportive family you have.'"

"Just know that I'm here to do whatever you need."

"Since you offered…" Brad flashed a sneaky smile. "Arrange a playdate with my kids and Casio's. They've been reminding me how much fun the compound is, and we haven't visited for a while. I plan to take all the credit."

"I'm thinking big bash." I threw my hands wide. "Combine playtime with Emerson's housewarming party and throw in food, drinks, and fun."

"Emerson's all moved in and loves living there. You may have seen her running on the beach, since she does it every morning. She laughed about how quiet it was, considering you two live down the block."

"I know she never said any such thing." Over Brad's laughter, I said. "We'll drag out the water toys and bikes, organize a race or two."

"Keep your eye on her, Brad; she cheats." Creole winked at me.

I made a face at him. "All's fair, and you only say that because I've figured out how to beat you."

The elevator doors opened, and Xander rushed into the office. "I just got a news alert."

All eyes turned to him; I was probably the only one that didn't want to know.

"Fire at the West mansion," he announced. "One of the news sites uploaded a video showing flames shooting out the windows. Another showed the firefighters getting it under control. Didn't appear to be a pile of rubble."

"When was the last time the Cove had a fire? Now two in a few weeks," Creole mused. "Probably not connected, but it would be nice to not to have any more."

"You have any details?" Didier asked.

Xander shook his head. "I was surprised videos had already been uploaded. The headline was 'Murder, now fire.' So far, no suspects; at least none mentioned."

"Thanks for the heads up, Xander," Creole said, then turned to Fab and me. "I hope you two are listening. Since you don't know who has eyes on the place, the last thing you want to do is attract attention by driving by the property. Or, knowing you two, getting out and trespassing. So stay away."

"That includes parking another boat at the dock. If you're caught walking up the beach, no one's going to believe that you're looking for your cat." Didier zeroed in on Fab.

"I agree," Fab said, and she sounded sincere.

Fine with me. I refused to go back for any reason.

"It really was a great house; would be sad if it was a total loss," Fab said. "Depending on the buyer, it might get bulldozed anyway."

"I'd be interested to hear what the fire marshal's report says. Not sure if it's public record; if not, I can hit up a friend of a friend," I said.

"It wouldn't surprise me, considering what a criminal West turned out to be, if it was someone making sure that no evidence is ever found," Fab said.

"It won't take me long to find out what the verdict is," said Xander, who was clicking away on his phone.

"This is a good time to ask what you're doing with your burned-out property, since you haven't mentioned it." Brad wrinkled his nose.

"The upside is that it's not a complete loss," I said with more enthusiasm than I felt. "My partner and I are in negotiations on the rebuild, with the goal of making it cuter than ever." Tearing it down and replacing it with multiple units would never be approved, and the street already had enough apartment buildings. I looked to Creole for confirmation.

"I'll admit, I was slow to get on board, but after surveying the damage, I knew a Boardwalk construction crew could get the work done in a couple of months." Creole shot me a smirk. "You ready to get started?"

"This is going to be fun." I ignored the groans.

Chapter Thirty-Six

A week passed, with all staying quiet. Fab and I were at our respective houses catching up on paperwork. It was a good time to get organized, since neither of our phones was blowing up with calls.

"Anyone home?" a male voice shouted from the open sliders. "If you're not, you really should lock your doors."

I looked up as Lilli Famosa skirted around her brother Alex and ran over, giving me a hug. "We stayed home from school today."

The twins ran inside. Not following their sister, they jumped on the couch and stared at the television with an expectant look.

Finding the remote, Alex held it up.

I nodded. "Make yourself at home."

He grinned and found an animal channel for his brothers to watch.

Larry strolled in late, plopped down in the doorway, and stretched out. Good luck stepping around or over him.

As Lilli ran over and joined her brothers on the couch, Alex joined me at the island, slipping onto a stool with a pondering look on his face, as though figuring out what to say next.

"Whatever it is, just blurt it out," I said, knowing it was something big, or otherwise, he wouldn't round up his siblings and bring them over for an impromptu visit when they should all be in school.

"My dad didn't come home last night," he blurted out in a whisper. "If that's not bad enough, our nanny called in sick. She wanted to talk to Dad, but I put her off, telling her he was on a business call. I didn't have a way to get us all to school. Even though I know how to drive, I didn't think it was good idea, even aside from not having a car or license, and my dad would kill me. We had that talk."

"Back to the part where Casio didn't come home… That's not something he would do," I said with confidence, knowing he wasn't an irresponsible father.

Alex nodded, worry etched on his face, casting glances at his siblings. "My dad always says to think before I act, so…" He huffed a breath. "After calling his phone several times and getting voicemail, I called the hospital, and thank goodness, he's not there. As for calling family, forget that; I don't want you-know-who involved because frankly, I don't trust a one of them. Dad feels the same way."

I only knew one other family member, though it was rumored there were hundreds of them. "Your uncle and his wife?" I asked, and he nodded. My stomach clenched at the thought of those two getting word that Casio was a no-show. The custody battle they'd initiated the last time he went missing was ugly, the wife in particular thinking Casio wasn't fit as a human. And I'd bet that she wasn't over losing the court case, as she was used to getting her way with no interference from anyone.

"My Uncle Brick doesn't give a dip about us kids, but his wife…" Alex scrunched up his nose like a smell had permeated the room. "If she knew we were alone last night, she'd snatch up my brothers and sister and haul them off to Miami. Me, she'd ship off to who knows where. We can't stand the sight of one another. I'm incorrigible, you know." I expected a smile at the latter, but his face grew more serious.

"I'm aware that you may have a slight flaw or two, but I like you anyway." I gave him a big smile and a wink. "Knowing your dad, he'd want us to get this figured out before we call anyone else." Except maybe the cops, and that meant the Chief. I pulled a notepad in front of me and scribbled a couple of notes, taking the time to take a couple of calming breaths, hoping with everything in me that this wouldn't turn out badly. "You appear to be a teenager with a plan. If I'm wrong, go ahead and tell me. If not, spit it out."

"Since you owe me…" When my brows went up, Alex amended that to, "I don't have all the details on that scam because I didn't eavesdrop hard enough, so I'm here to cash in on future favors."

So much like his dad, I was smiling. "For starters, pack up your siblings and move in here until your dad gets back." Where the heck was Casio? He'd never leave his kids. I attempted to maintain an unworried smile, but a rock had settled in my stomach.

"That would be a lot of lugging stuff back and forth, and you can bet we'd forget something." Alex shook his head, discarding that idea. "If the nanny hadn't called in sick, it wouldn't be a problem. If you could take us to school and make sure we don't run out of food, that would be great."

I didn't think it was a good idea. His siblings were too young not to have an adult in the house, and Alex might be a teenager going on forty, but he wasn't old enough.

"I really want to help find my dad." His voice was filled with anxiety. "But he'd flip, so I'll leave it to you, as long as you keep me updated. I've put my siblings off, telling them that he's off on a job. I can get away with that for a short time before they get suspicious."

Casio's wife had died of cancer, and he'd stepped up to being a full-time father. The proof he'd done an excellent job was the four bright, intelligent, well-behaved children sitting in my house. He'd promised his wife that he wouldn't screw them up and had made good on his word.

It hadn't escaped my notice that Alex's leg was swinging back and forth in a manic gesture. "I'm happy that you chose me to help you figure out what's going on. I promise—" I held up my right hand. "—to corral a group of doers to turn over every rock. Another promise: we'll find him."

"I knew you were the right person because my dad says you're a nervy chick and I know he means it in a good way."

"I'm going to make a few phone calls and round up a crew. First call is to the Chief—he may be able to answer the question of where your dad is without us having to go any further. The next call is to Creole; they worked together, and your dad respects him. In the meantime, I've got a job for you." Alex sat up straighter, already liking whatever I was about to suggest, even though he had no clue what it was. "Go next door and tell Fab to get the heck over here. Don't take any excuses about her being too busy. If she starts to give you too much trouble, trot out a sad face. I'm certain you have one."

Alex made one face after another at me.

I almost laughed. "Pick one—you've got a minute or two to get it perfected before you're standing on her doorstep."

"I'm going to take Larry and run down the beach, burn off some worry." Alex slid off the stool. "Please do whatever it takes to find Dad."

"You've got my word." I picked up my phone and watched as Alex raced to the patio doors, signaled to Larry, and they disappeared down to the beach. I called Creole, and when he answered, I lowered my voice and said, "Casio's missing—he didn't come home last night. His kids are here, and the three young ones have no clue. I need you to put on your detective hat, come home, and work some magic." I relayed what little Alex was able to tell me.

"The Chief is here raiding the cupboard again. I'll see if he knows what's up, and if not, I'll have him in tow. Either way, I'm on my way home."

"Call me back if he's on some job for the Chief."

"Will do."

We hung up. I didn't have to wait long before my phone pinged with a message: "Chief has no clue."

I called Xander. "Are you able to track Casio's phone?" I asked when he answered, then told him that Casio hadn't come home last night. "I'm not sure what kind of information it will yield, but anything at all would be helpful."

"If he hasn't removed the battery, it won't take me long to figure out where the signal's coming from. I'll call you back."

The kids were beyond cute, their attention glued to an episode of Animal Planet: bears and their offspring romping through the jungle. There was no way I'd allow them to stay by themselves, even if it meant I had to sleep at Casio's. I wasn't sure that Creole would readily agree to stay with me, but I had a few hours to come up with a plan that would work for all of us.

Alex came through the patio doors, arms in the air: *Score.* Both he and Fab had smirks on their faces. Larry plunked down inside and took a watchful pose.

"Does Larry need water or anything?" I asked.

Alex whistled the dog over and showed Larry the cats' bowls. One sniff, and he finished off the dry food and water.

"So we're in agreement…" I eyed Larry, then Alex. "The dog pukes, and you're cleaning it up."

"Larry eats anything," Alex said with a snort.

"Honored that you sent me an escort," Fab said, slipping onto a stool. "Since you don't have a phone—" Which she eyed. "—and I don't know my way."

"One of these days when my eyes roll back in my head and stick there, you get to explain it to Mother."

"Good one." Alex shot me a thumbs up.

"How much do you know, so I don't have to repeat myself?" I asked Fab's back, as she'd gotten up and was digging around in the fridge like she didn't know where everything was. She grabbed a water and held it up to Alex, who shook his head.

"You and your sibs are welcome to help yourself," I told him.

"So you know, Fab threatened to shoot me if I didn't tell her everything," Alex said, lowering his voice and using the snooty tone Fab favored. The two of them grinned.

Fab came back and sat opposite me.

"Seriously?" I turned to her. "It pains me to have to ask, but one can't be sure with you."

"Alex takes a joke better than you do." The two knuckle-bumped.

The front door opened, and Creole poked his head inside. "Alex," he called, motioning him over. He waved to me before the two went out the door.

"Wonder where he and the kid are off to?" I stared at the door as though it would answer.

"It would be easy enough for you to follow them."

"Creole would flip."

"I'll pull Alex aside when they get back and question him. He'll answer just to get me to go away."

I shook my head. "No way Casio would disappear on his kids and leave them alone all night. I don't want to think about the possibilities."

"Just stop. No need to conjure up trouble. If anyone can handle themselves in a bad situation, it's that man, and he's got plenty of experience," Fab reminded me. "I'm afraid it has something to do with the West case, since the last time we saw him, he was headed out to investigate. And remember, he mentioned knowing one of the men being blackmailed."

My phone rang, Xander's pic popping up on the screen. "Casio's phone is in Miami," he said when I answered. "It's still turned on and the battery hasn't run down, so I was able to track it to the Venetian Islands—San Marco, to be exact."

"Would you continue to track? In case it changes location."

"I'll keep in touch," Xander said. We hung up, and I relayed the conversation to Fab.

"It's possible that Casio had a case in that area," Fab mused.

"The Chief doesn't know anything about Casio's disappearance. I guess we'll know for sure when they come back inside, since Creole said he'd be bringing the Chief," I added, cutting Fab off before she could toss out a suggestion that we hit the road to Miami and do our own search.

The front door opened, and Larry and Arlo flew inside and romped through the living room and out to the patio. They were followed by Lark and Alex.

"Lark offered to be our nanny until ours gets better and can come back to work," Alex announced.

That caught me off guard, since I couldn't remember when they'd met. But it made sense that they knew each other, since Casio and Lark worked in the same building. "I take it you've interviewed her and she meets your requirements?"

"Lark always has good snacks at Dad's office," Alex said. "We definitely need more of that at the house."

"The dogs? They gave their paw of approval?"

"Larry's been to the office, and he and Arlo play together and get along good. They both like to chase squirrels."

Swell. I tried not to grimace.

"We're going outside," one of the twins said. They both jumped up off the couch, and one turned off the television.

"Hold up and I'll go with." I slid off my stool, then stopped, noticing Lilli had fallen asleep on the other end of the couch.

"I've got this," Lark assured me. "We'll take the dogs." She turned to the kids and whistled. "Listen up. No going near the water."

The little heads nodded, including Alex's, and they went out the door.

"Let's go out on the patio in case they run wild on her," I said. "I have to sit where I can see into the living room."

"Where's Creole?" Fab asked.

"I have the same question, but between the dogs and the kids, I didn't get a chance to ask."

We barely took a seat before Creole and the Chief trooped inside. They grabbed drinks and joined us.

"Casio's car is in the garage. No sign of foul play," Creole said.

"That's not good news," I said.

The front door opened and closed. Didier came in with his laptop, handed it to Fab, and sat next to her. "I knew you'd want to check the compound security feed."

Fab opened it and began tapping away, Didier hanging over her shoulder.

I told the guys about Xander's call.

"Casio wasn't working a case up there for me," the Chief said. "When we talked yesterday, he was asking questions about the West case. I told him he shouldn't stick his nose in that case. We all know the local police won't be happy."

"He knew one of the men, and I did ask him to check it out," I reminded him.

"I told him it was a bad idea to get involved. That anyone with information should take it to the cops or the DA and let them deal with it." The Chief gave me a flinty stare. "He said he was just going to ask a few questions and was doing it because his kids like the professor and he doesn't want to have to tell them that Crum's permanently residing behind bars."

"A silver Mercedes pulled into the compound yesterday morning," Fab said, staring at the screen. "Casio met the car at the end of his driveway and then vanished from view. No front license tag. This is where the state requiring one would come in handy."

"I'll ask Alex if he knows that car," Creole said.

"Whoever it was left within ten minutes," Fab said. "I got a partial plate—WOO."

"Forward me everything you have on West," Creole said. "Not sure there's a connection, but I won't know until I investigate. I still have a few connections in Miami, but the Chief has more, so however you want to handle this…" he said, deferring to the Chief.

"I'm going to file a missing person report with the current chief," the Chief said. "I'll ask that they handle it quietly."

"Won't you have to contact his family?" I grimaced.

"Alex told me that Casio and his brother are back on speaking terms, but the wife doesn't know since she hates his guts," Creole said. "Alex wanted me to promise that Cruella wouldn't snatch them away. I told him we'd do our best."

"I'll reassure Alex that we won't pull any surprises on him or his siblings," I said.

The Chief stood. "I say we go back to the office, talk to Xander, and decide what to do next."

"I sent you the video of the Mercedes," Fab told Creole.

"I'm going to change and meet you back at the office," Creole said, nodding at Didier.

Once the Chief left and Fab and Didier went back to their house, I headed to the bedroom. Creole had tossed aside his suit pants and dress shirt for well-worn jeans and a t-shirt and tucked a revolver into the back of his waistband.

"I take it that you're... uh..." I wondered exactly what he was planning on doing.

"If I'd gone missing from my house, Casio would do the same for me. We know that he was interested in the West case once he realized he knew one of the players. So that's the best place to start. It's possible that Casio asked one too many questions, or got caught snooping, and that was motivation for one of those men to figure out exactly what he knows."

"You need to be careful." I gave him a long kiss and a hard hug, then walked him to the door. "If you don't check in regularly, you're going to have one hot wife, and not in a good way."

Chapter Thirty-Seven

The next morning, I lingered over my coffee. Creole had come home late and left early, which left me feeling annoyed. I understood, but felt that I could be used behind the scenes. There was still no word regarding Casio. The more time that went by… I stopped those thoughts.

Fab came through the open sliders, wearing a cheeky smile that said she was up to something and carrying a small thermos. She came over to the island and plunked down the container, grabbed a mug out of the cupboard, and poured herself a cup of swill. "If you made decent coffee, I wouldn't have to bring my own."

"And here I was, thinking 'if only Fab would show up with food.'" I checked her over as though she might pull something out of her pocket. "You're here early, so that must mean Didier is off with Creole again."

"I had plenty of objections, which Didier cut off as soon as I mentioned his lack of a cop background." Fab blew out a frustrated sigh.

"If Creole thought Didier was going to get his butt shot off… I'm sure it won't come to that," I added at her angry glint. "It's not the first time

Didier's had his back. The times we've been to the shooting range together, Didier's been every bit as good a shot as the rest of us."

"None of that makes me feel the slightest bit better," Fab huffed and looked around. "It's quiet. Did you take the kids to school?"

"Who knew that school started at almost the crack of dawn? Kind of happy that the Famosa kids took a vote, and it was unanimous: Lark got the nod for temporary nanny. She spent the night at Casio's, got the kids to school, and no clue what she's doing with the dogs, but they're with her. I called, offering any help that might be needed, and was politely turned down."

"All the kids are mature for their age, Alex especially. Casio isn't a slacker in the parenting department."

"The other three are much more laid back than Alex was at that age. He was a bundle of trouble and enjoying every minute. I'm thinking the first one is practice for the rest."

"Let's just hope—"

"Don't say it," I cut her off. "I know you're up to something besides complaining about the coffee. I'm all ears." My phone rang, and I flipped it over to see that Mac's name had popped up. I groaned. "Let's hope that everyone didn't go crazy at once. I don't have the energy." I answered. "I only want to hear good news; bad news can wait until next week."

"It's good, I suppose. Not bad anyway. How's

that?" Mac said. "It's more like news."

Fab jabbed her finger at the phone.

"You're on speaker, and you-know-who is listening."

"Your house that burned down—"

"Does Madison have another one that we don't know about?" Fab snapped.

Be nice, I mouthed.

"I'm ignoring you." Mac mimicked Fab's tone. "Anyway, where was I? Oh yeah. One of the dudes that lived there—and should you need his name, I've got it on my phone and can text you. Where was I?"

Fab rolled her eyes.

"I'm thinking Dennis, but that could be the other guy. Let's go with Dennis... He got pulled over for a traffic violation. Very stupid on his part, since he had an outstanding warrant and the car wasn't registered. Sad about the previous owner being dead; makes you think there's a story there. I placed a small wager on stolen."

"Why don't you hustle to the good part?" Fab said in a faux grouch, grinning.

I shook my head at her.

"We all know how annoyed you'd be if I left out the slightest detail, so hold your water. Where was I? I'm doing a lot of forgetful this morning; should've had my coffee before I called. It's your fault, and you know who I mean, since you keep interrupting."

"I'll help you out," I said, shooting Fab a

smirk. "I'm guessing that Dennis was hauled off to the county jail until he rustles up bail."

"That reminds me… I need to give Frack a jingle. I get a referral fee for anyone that uses his services. Don't know if Dennis's got collateral, but I figure what the heck." Mac stopped her incessant rustling of papers. "Xander can find out what the warrant was for. I don't have a clue and couldn't very well ask, since Dennis was in cuffs when I arrived." She took a long slurp of something. "Melba's grandson, who lives on the next block over—Melba does, that is—told me that Dennis is going to broker a deal in exchange for information on the fire."

"If this just happened, how does the grandson know anything?" I asked.

"Dennis bragged he had an ace up his sleeve if he ever got hauled in. If you ask me, the grandson would've brokered the same deal, giving up Dennis. He's a sneaky sort."

"Done yet?" Fab asked in exasperation.

Mac ignored her. "As for Vicky, who brags she's the manager/owner of the house, although there're times she can't remember which one…turns out Vicky is a name that she borrowed from a dead friend. I guess you can call yourself anything these days."

"Not legally," I mumbled.

"I don't suppose they picked her up?" Fab asked.

"The reason she went with Vicky is that she's

got warrants. She gave the boarders a heads up that trouble was coming and they should get out while they could, sealing the deal with five hundred dollars apiece. Before you ask… Word is that she disappeared shortly after I last saw her and hasn't been seen since."

"What's Vicky's real name?" Fab demanded.

"Don't know that one yet, but I know…hand it over to Xander the second I find out."

"Any more names to hand over? In particular, the one that fronted the cash?" I asked.

"Vicky would be the one to talk to, and that's if she turns up. If she's smart, she's long gone."

"As always, you're on top of the latest and I appreciate you passing it along. I'm suggesting you be careful who you ask questions, in case the firestarter comes back peeved, wanting a second shot at turning it to ashes," I said.

"That's why you need to light a fire under Fab's…and have her get her security guy to install a camera or two down there so I can keep an eye on it from my living room."

I slapped my hand on the counter. "Got that?"

Fab plugged her ears.

"She's writing it down as we speak, and oh look, she scribbled 'rush.'" I grinned at her.

"One of the guests is waving like a lunatic. Gotta go, but know that it's all quiet around here. For now," she added in a rushed tone and hung up.

"If it gets out that the cops know Gunz is

behind the fire, don't be surprised if he disappears," I said.

"I asked him point blank. He strenuously denied it, and I believed him. Let's face it—there's always another real estate deal." Fab reached down her top, pulled out a wad of money, and slapped it down in front of me. "Speaking of Gunz… This is payment in full for the SUV repairs. He didn't admit that his sisters were involved but did say he didn't want any hard feelings and that as far as he was concerned, it was a dead issue."

I didn't bother to count it, knowing that Fab had and probably in front of him. "That's surprising, since he was so adamant that his sisters were unfairly accused despite my ID."

"You'll be happy to know that I got assurances out of him that it won't happen again. I warned him that if it did, we would get even and it would be messy."

"That was nervy of you." I smiled at her. "Reassure me that Gunz's promise means we don't have to look over our shoulders."

"No worries. I believe that he put his oversized foot down." Fab's phone signaled an incoming text. It was either the longest message ever or she read it several times. "It's from Casio."

"Since when do you trade messages with him? What does he want? Why didn't he come home? Is he home now?"

"One at a time, please." Fab reread the message. "I've forwarded addresses a time or two, and that's about it." She continued to stare at the screen. "Casio wants me to deliver the drive and any hard copies with the West information to an address in Miami; he needs it for evidence." She flashed me her phone.

I took the phone out of her hand and read the message a couple of times. "Why would he call you 'Honey?' Since when? He's looking to get his butt kicked by a French dude I happen to know. You need to look up this address." I read it off.

Fab turned my laptop to face her and entered the address. When she turned it back, it showed a two-story older brick office building in an area with other businesses a couple of blocks down from a main street.

"No way he wrote this. If not him, then who?"

Fab had picked up her phone and was tapping away. "I just informed him that I wasn't his errand girl and if he wants me to drive to the other side of the world, he needs to call and ask nicely." She put the phone on the counter between us.

"That's the first time you've admitted the Miami area is a hike."

We both stared at her phone, willing it to ring. It took several minutes before it finally did. Fab put it on speaker, and it couldn't have been a worse connection.

"Casio here," he said, as though she wouldn't

know after his name came up on her screen. "It's imperative that I get the information to bring the West case to a conclusion. I just need you to deliver it to the address I texted and text me back when it's done."

It was a man all right, but not Casio. I shook my head at Fab, and she nodded, agreeing with my unspoken thought.

"Depending on traffic, it could be a couple of hours," Fab said.

"It's a secretarial services office and open until five. You can leave it with the receptionist."

"I'll call you when it's done." Fab hung up.

I picked up my phone and called Xander. "Fab just got a call from Casio, and although it was a staticky connection, we highly doubt it was him. Whoever it was was trying to pass himself off as Casio, but the voice wasn't close."

"I'll call you back in a few." Xander disconnected.

Catching a brief glimpse of the excitement that danced in Fab's blue eyes, I couldn't help but groan inwardly. "As much as you want to jump into the middle of whatever's going on, it's my job to be the voice of reason. Keep in mind that we have no clue what any of this is about. I'm suggesting that we call Creole and share what just happened. And not leave out that neither of us thinks it was Casio on the other end."

"Go ahead and call Creole."

Fab gave in a little too easily, but I was taking

it and picked up my phone.

"If the guys are in Miami, as I suspect, there's no reason for them to come back down here to pick up the drive. We can handle a simple delivery job." Fab's sneaky smile was firmly in place.

Yeah, sure. I called Creole. "Voicemail." I left a message.

Fab made a call. "Didier's also went to voicemail."

My phone rang, and I answered with a glance at the screen. "What do you have for me?" I asked Xander.

"The phone hasn't changed location. It's giving off a strong signal, so Casio or someone is keeping it charged. Not very smart if it isn't Casio; you'd think they'd toss it after running over it a few times."

"The men being blackmailed in the West case—do either of them live up in that area?"

"Both of them. Not that particular island, but close enough."

"If anything changes, let me know." We hung up.

"I've come up with a plan," Fab said, looking pleased with herself.

No surprise there.

"We make the delivery and wait to see who shows. In the meantime, we continue to call the guys. All that's left to decide is—do I deliver a drive with all the information or a blank one?"

"On the off-chance it was Casio, I say we deliver the information that was requested. And if it wasn't him, then whoever it was might hurt him if they don't get what they want." Casio already had a copy of the information (he asked Xander for a drive). That's another clue that this isn't legit.

Fab slid off her stool. "I'm going home to change into that workout outfit you got me, and I suggest you do the same. I'll be back to pick you up in fifteen minutes."

I locked up, changed into the navy workout pants she suggested, and took my Beretta out of a lockbox, knowing that it would fit in the concealed pocket on the side of the leg. I opted for the matching top and slid into tennis shoes. I grabbed my phone and go-bag and made it out to the front with barely a minute to spare, and of course she was waiting.

Chapter Thirty-Eight

We cruised slowly out of the compound, pausing to check out Casio's driveway, but nothing had changed. She took Highway One north until we connected with the Interstate, which was the fastest route to the Miami Beach area. Once there, she veered over and down the off-ramp, then wound through the streets a few blocks from where we exited and turned onto a non-descript street of strip malls boasting a variety of businesses.

Fab pulled into the half-full parking lot of a two-story office building and cruised the driveway that looped around the building. The signage boasted doctors, lawyers, and a variety of others, including the business we were looking for, and she checked every one of them out before pulling into a space on the far side. The secretarial place on the end had a list of services painted on the picture window, including bail bonds.

"I'm going to drop this off." Fab reached over the seat and picked up the padded envelope containing the drive, which she sealed closed. "Once I'm inside, I'll check out the place. That way, I'll know if someone else had the same idea and is watching me."

"I'm going to sit here and what? Stare out the window? I'm coming with you, since you don't know what you're walking into. I'll hang around outside and try not to appear shifty. When you come back out, I'll continue to hang back while you get back to the car and park it in the best place to watch everyone entering and exiting that office."

We got out and walked around the side of the building.

"I'm going to go sit on that bench over there and pretend I'm smoking."

Fab shook her head at my idea but didn't come up with a better one. I cut diagonally across the parking lot and took a seat on the lone cement bench on the other side, which was damn uncomfortable. I never glanced back at Fab, but saw out of the corner of my eye that she'd entered the business. After a quick scan of the parked cars, I knew that none of them were occupied. Fab was in and out faster than I expected, having figured she'd hang around for a few questions. She disappeared back the way we came and came cruising into view a minute later, parking under a tree at the opposite end. On the way back to the car, I stopped at the group mailbox. Nothing to see—none of them were marked. I hopped in the SUV and scooted down in the seat, same as Fab.

"Not a single car came or left," I said. "What happened? You were faster than I thought you'd be."

"Turned out to be a one-woman office on the bottom floor with office space for rent upstairs. The woman was on the phone when I came in. She put the call on hold and told me, 'Mr. Famosa is expecting the delivery. I'll call and let him know it arrived.' She barely gave me a glance before getting back on the phone." Fab picked up her phone and sent Casio a text.

"This place isn't that far from the Venetian Islands, so if the caller is still over there, it shouldn't take too long for him to get here." I took out my phone and called Creole. Voicemail again. I left a message to call me. "This is boring."

"We haven't even been here five minutes." Fab eyed the clock on the dash. "Get ready to take pictures of any car that cruises into the lot and of whoever gets out. If they do what we did and park on the other side, we'll follow them once they leave the office. We'll know it's the right person if they have the padded envelope."

"Once we're done here, I get to pick the junk food." I leaned back and scrolled through my phone.

For a long time, it was quiet. One car had pulled in and parked, and a woman got out and went into the hair salon. An hour went by, and then a silver Mercedes pulled in and parked in front of the secretarial office. A casually dressed sixty-something man got out and went inside and was right back out, opening the envelope and withdrawing the black protective case as he walked. It wasn't Casio, not even close. Fab had her camera out and was busy snapping pictures.

"It's the same model and color as the car from the compound security tapes." Fab peered over the steering wheel. We both waited to see what the man would do next. "A little too coincidental, isn't it?"

The man behind the wheel finally backed out. Fab thrust her camera at me, pulled out, and followed at a discreet distance.

"The last three of the license plate match up to the ones on the security tape," I pointed out.

Fab followed him, while I made sure to get good pictures. I didn't have to ask what she was doing; I'd known this was how the trip would unfold before we left the house. I texted Creole again.

The driver was familiar with the streets, avoiding all the busy ones and instead opting for a couple of side ones that took us to a street that linked all the islands. I'd have enjoyed the blue waters of the Intercoastal Waterway much more if I knew what was next on Fab's agenda.

"What are you going to do when the driver gets to where he's going?" I asked. "You know there's nothing but million-dollar mansions out here."

"That just means we'll have to be more careful while staking it out and waiting for the guys to show."

The man turned north onto San Marco. No guard shack but plenty of personal security who'd notice two women parked on one of the residential streets, since all of them probably had parking restrictions. The houses ranged from luxury mega-mansions to smaller houses that had yet to be snapped up and bulldozed to make room for larger ones.

I called Xander. "Can you track my phone and let me know if I'm in the same vicinity as Casio?" I asked when he answered. "And have you seen the Chief around?"

"Nope. I can go downstairs and double-check; it's quiet here today." After a pause, he said, "You're sitting on top of one another."

Just great. "If you see Creole or Didier, have them call."

"You be careful." We hung up.

"Casio's close, but exactly where? Don't know," I told Fab. "What now? This isn't the kind of neighborhood where we can loiter without attracting attention."

The Mercedes had looped around the island, turned onto a side street, and took an immediate turn into the driveway of a white stucco fifties-style house. The garage doors went up, he pulled in, and they closed. The front entrance to the house was around the corner and faced the main road. The entire property was surrounded by a thick, leafy ten-foot hedge that, to its credit, was green and lush, and provided coverage from prying eyes.

Fab backed up and around the corner, and into the driveway of the house across the street. According to the sign, it was undergoing remodeling, and not a truck or car in sight.

Chapter Thirty-Nine

I hadn't been timing it but knew it wouldn't take long for Fab to get restless and need more action than sitting and staring over the steering wheel at a solid fence built into the massively tall hedgerow. I called Creole several more times and left "call me" messages. In case he hadn't gotten the first six. I also called Xander and gave him the license number of the Mercedes to run.

"I'm going to go have a look around." Fab threw open the car door.

"Hold up." I grabbed for the back of her top and got air, but at least she sat back down.

"What are you going to do, climb the fence? You don't know what's on the other side, a dog perhaps. The roofline tells us that the front door is set back a few feet."

"You can't tell anything from where we're sitting. I need to get up close." Fab scanned the mile-high hedge that ran along the front of the property and around the corner, ending at one side of the garage.

"What a good way to get shot."

"I just want to know the layout of the house," Fab whined.

"Trust me, you're not going to figure that out by peeping through the bushes. Even if you get on the property, what are you going to do, peek in the windows like some perv? Think about your reaction if you caught someone doing that."

"Gotcha, no trespassing. I'm still going to check out the property, but I'll stick to the street. I won't be gone long."

"I'm coming with you." I reached for the door handle.

"What you're going to do is get behind the wheel and be prepared to pick me up if you see me being chased or whatever."

"If you minded your own business, you wouldn't have to worry about 'whatever.'"

"I'm dressed for jogging, and that's what I'm going to do—from this end of the property around the corner—and find out where it ends on that side. Even if I'm seen, no one's going to give me a second look."

"So I don't go out of my mind with worry, let's hook up our earpieces and you can give me running commentary on what you see." I pulled mine out of my pocket and hooked it over my ear.

It was a fast hook-up, and Fab tested it to make sure it worked. The ringing of my phone stopped her from slamming the door.

"Xander," I said upon answering and put him on speaker.

"The car is registered to Kirkman George, one of the men West blackmailed."

That was the guy Casio mentioned knowing. He'd never said how well.

"George lives in Miami Beach. I texted you the address. The address you're at is in the name of an LLC. I can do some more digging to see if I can get the names of the officers," Xander said.

"That's the one who was being blackmailed over his son's activities," Fab mused.

"I was able to find out that he made restitution to a couple of the women George Jr. bilked."

"The man we followed to this house was older, so it must have been George Sr.," I said. "Let's hope he didn't do anything to Casio to protect his son."

"Just be careful, you two," Xander said and disconnected.

Fab had stuck around and heard every word. "I'm thinking that Casio's the only one who could tell this George character how to contact us, so it's my guess that he's not dead. Yet. Now that George has the drive, that could change. Which is why my plan to check out the property can't wait." Fab cut off any argument on my part by closing the door and crossing the street.

I climbed into the driver's seat and watched as she jogged along the curb. She stopped several times to eye the hedge, then kept moving.

"I don't know what kind of shrubs were chosen for this barrier, but it was designed to keep people from trespassing and it's effective," Fab said over the mic as she inspected it closer, turning at the property line where a cement wall separated the house from its neighbor. She changed direction and curved around on the side street, following the same track as the Mercedes, and disappeared from sight.

"What are you doing now? I can't see you." I didn't yell but close.

"Calm down. Just checking out this side of the house. The only difference is that on the far side of the garage is a walkway, which would make sense because it goes past the trash area and into the backyard."

"Just be careful." I picked up my phone and called Creole again. This time, he answered.

"I was just getting ready to call you. What's going on?"

"If I can't turn off my phone, then neither can you," I snapped.

"I'm sorry; we were in a meeting with the Chief and a couple of local detectives. I'll make it up to you, I promise. Now, take a breath and tell me what's going on."

"If Didier's close by, you should put me on speaker." Which he did. I filled the two men in on everything that had happened, not leaving out a detail.

"Where's my wife?" Didier grouched.

I lowered my voice and said, "I'd ask her, but she just shushed me."

Didier groaned. "You tell her to get her butt back to the car."

"Hey Fab, your husband wants you to crawl back out of the bushes and get your a-s-s back to the car," I said in a sickeningly sweet tone.

Creole chuckled.

"Tell him I'm on my way back," Fab whispered.

I repeated what Fab said. "My guess is that she'll get here when she's done snooping around."

"You're a horrible friend," Fab hissed.

"Or a really good friend that doesn't want anything bad to happen to you."

"If you're done now," Creole cut in. "We're on our way. Depending on traffic, it won't take long."

"Once you get to the island, don't get off the main road," I said. "You'll see the Hummer in the driveway of an ugly green L-shaped house, and there's room to park next to me." I heard the truck doors shut and the engine start.

"Creole and Didier are on the way," I whispered to Fab.

Fab whispered back, "The backyard is huge—there's a guest house back here."

A door slammed, which had me sitting up and staring at the house. "Say something."

"I'm on my way back, but it will take a few so

don't freak out." I heard a crashing sound, followed by an unidentified noise. "I'm almost out of here."

My phone rang again, and it was Xander. "I'm afraid to ask," I said on answering.

"George Sr. owns the property on San Marco. A corporation that he set up for the transaction."

"You're the best."

"Anything you need, I'm a phone call away." He hung up.

My eyes darted back and forth from one end of the street to the other. For someone on her way, she was taking long enough.

Finally, Fab came jogging around the corner and across the street at the same time as Creole's truck came into view. He parked next to me as Fab got back in the SUV. The two men got out and climbed in the back.

"Tell us what you found out when you trespassed on the property," Creole said to Fab.

"Before everyone gets all grouchy." I held up my hand. "Xander just called and…" I relayed the short conversation.

"You might want to dial down the attitude, since we didn't know when you two were showing up." Fab crossed her arms and glared at Creole. "What would you have had me do different, except the trespassing part?"

"Just tell us," Didier said, short on his usual patience.

"Casio's here and still alive; he's tied to a chair

in the guest house."

"How did you get back there?" Creole asked.

"There's a pathway along the side. I hopped on the trash cans and over the fence section between the hedge and the garage. Getting out wasn't as easy, as something caught George's attention—probably me moving around—and he stationed himself at the front window. I had to double back and around and found a thin spot in the hedge where the trash cans were lined up and wiggled behind them…after knocking a couple of them over." Fab made a face.

So that was the noise.

"We should probably hurry it up, before George does something stupid now that I've delivered the information he wanted," Fab said.

"Didier and I will go," Creole said.

"That's what you think," she hissed. "I do all the work, and you get the takedown? No way."

"I'm not getting left behind." I ignored the big eyeroll from Creole. "How about I ring the bell at the front gate? That'll give you guys cover to go sneaking in the back way."

"Unless the housekeeper answers," Didier said. "Which is likely."

"Go ahead, leave me sitting in the car. I'll be seeing you sooner than you think," I said.

"You're lucky…" Creole started, then stopped. "Go ahead and see if your dog has wandered onto their property."

"It's a cat," I said.

The three got out, and I jumped out myself and headed for the front gate, surprised that Creole would let me go by myself. When I got there, I wondered if he already knew that there wasn't a bell or any way to get the attention of someone in the house. No just stopping by for a friendly hello, not without calling first.

I eyed the palm trees and picked the closest one to the road, then got down on my hands and knees, crouched low to the ground and crawled through the hedge, making sure my face didn't make contact with the dirt. I got up, rubbed my hands on my pants, and decided not to waste time knocking on the front door. I went around the side of the house and made my way towards the back, skirting around the pool area as the threesome trooped into the guest house like they lived there. Shooting a glance to the side, I noticed that they'd gotten the side gate open and left it that way. I broke into a run and threw open the door of the guest house, barging into a large open space. The living room had large windows overlooking the pool and a door on one wall that I assumed led to the bedroom. It had a musty air of not having been used for a quite a while.

"Hope I didn't miss anything," I said, louder than necessary.

Casio was tied to one of the chairs at the kitchen table, spitting who knew what out of his mouth. "Took you long enough," he grumbled.

Creole and Fab had their weapons trained on George.

"You want to tell your friends to calm down? If that's who they are, since they didn't announce themselves as cops. I got what I want; you're free to go." George started for the front door.

"You're not going anywhere," Fab growled at him, and he stopped short.

Creole tapped her on the shoulder. "George doesn't have a gun, so if you shoot him, it wouldn't be self-defense."

"Shoot me?" George squeaked.

I made my way over to Casio and eyed the knots. "This isn't my forte. You might want to whistle for Fab."

"Casio, your call," Creole growled.

"Someone untie me," Casio snapped, barely controlling his anger. "I'll deal with George. I have a few questions for him after I rearrange his face; then I'll call the cops and have him booked on murder one."

"What the hell are you talking about?" George sputtered, stomping over to Casio but maintaining his distance. "You know damn well I didn't kill anyone. All I'm admitting to is being an overprotective a-hole."

"How about kidnapping and assault?" Casio snarled.

Didier motioned to Fab and pointed at Casio. She crossed the room and had the knots undone in short order.

Casio shook out his hands and rubbed his wrists. "Convince me you're no killer, because I've got evidence that says otherwise. And that evidence will put you away forever."

"I didn't kill West, if that's what you're thinking. I heard you were investigating the case and figured you'd gotten your hands on the information he used to blackmail me. I know I wrecked our friendship." George squeezed his eyes shut, letting out a shaky breath. "I was desperate to stop shelling out money and willing to do anything short of sending my son to prison. But no, I wouldn't have stooped to murder." He backed up and dropped into one of the chairs across from where Casio was still sitting.

The others grabbed the chairs scattered around the room, and I sat on the arm of the couch.

"How did you end up here, tied to a chair?" Creole barked at Casio.

"My kids?" Casio's eyes shot to me.

"They're fine. Except for Alex, they think you're on assignment." I smiled reassuringly. "As soon as they're out of school, you should call. They'll be excited."

Casio nodded. "Thanks."

"I kind of like them." I winked at him.

Some of Casio's frown lines smoothed out.

"Back to my question," Creole said, less annoyed this time.

George barely lifted his hand. "My fault. I

used our friendship, saying I had information on the West murder, since I knew he was digging around. He's a damn good cop, or was, and I knew he'd unravel the whole mess. Casio met me in the driveway, invited me into the house, and that's when I hit him over the head."

Casio rubbed the back of his head and winced.

"Managed to heft his big ass into the car and brought him here. Figured it made sense to tie him up, or he'd be gone soon as he woke up. When he came around, I made a bargain—he gets me the information and he can go," George related with little remorse.

"Who would believe that you didn't kill West after that story?" Fab asked with a shake of her head. "I don't."

"You weren't listening—I'm no killer."

"You could've come to me and asked for help, not beat my brains out," Casio simmered. "I would've helped you. Not the way you hoped, as I wouldn't cover up Junior's criminal activities. My advice would've been and still is to let him face the music. If you don't, he's not going to stop his criminal ways until he gets caught…or is stopped by a bullet from an outraged lover or husband."

"I can't send my kid to prison," George moaned.

"Yeah, because then he might grow up and leave the criminal life behind," Casio practically spit.

Creole broke the stare-down between the two men. "If you didn't kill West, then who did?"

"Why do you care who killed West? Good riddance." George shook his head, conveying that he thought Creole was nuts.

"Because an innocent man is going on trial for a crime he didn't commit and could end up in prison for the rest of his life." Creole stopped just short of yelling.

"My guess is it was another of West's victims—Frank Craig. Ran into him one night when he was drunk, and he ran his mouth on and on about how much he hated West and that he was going to get what was coming to him—he guaranteed it. Next thing I heard, West was dead. I was surprised when I saw the name of the man arrested—never heard of him before—but I figured he was another of West's targets. Honestly thought it was Craig, since he made the threat, but good luck proving anything against the man; he's got connections up the chain."

"If you don't want me to press charges against you for kidnapping, what you're going to do is repeat everything you just said to my old boss, Chief Harder," Casio threatened, "who I happen to know is in contact with the current chief on this case."

George snorted. "You're out of your mind. I'd have to be an idiot to turn myself in to the cops for kidnapping."

"Look, there's more than one copy of the dirt

West had on you, and at some point, it will come out." Casio's anger bored into the man. "I suggest that you get a lawyer and prepare for a bumpy road. As for your son, if you want him to ever be any kind of decent human, let him face the consequences of his actions. It'd be better for him to get a lawyer and turn himself in before the cops come looking for him."

"If you'd keep your flap shut, this would go away," George yelled. "You holding out for money like West?"

"I'm not the only one with a copy of this information…" Casio said with a tight smile. "I got it from a third party, so you can assume that others have it."

"What are the cops going to do?" George's shoulders slumped, the fight draining out of him.

"They'll assign detectives to the case, and those named on the drive will be investigated, along with anyone else they discover that West might have been blackmailing," Casio informed him. "Even if you convinced us that you didn't do it, which you haven't, there's still an innocent man on the hook."

"The Chief is in Miami, so I'm going to have him get over here." Creole took out his phone and walked outside. It didn't take him long to come back.

"Sorry about how I handled this," George said to Casio sheepishly. "I didn't see another alternative with my son involved."

Casio nodded and stood. His fist shot out and made contact with George's nose, blood flying everywhere. "You deserved that, so no whining because no one here cares that you're hurt."

George crumpled up, grabbing his face. Blood running through his fingers, he stumbled over to the kitchen sink and hung his head over it. "Did you have to break it?"

"Yes," Casio barked, cradling his knuckles.

I'd had enough and walked outside, Fab not far behind.

"Now what?" she asked.

"No clue. I just needed some fresh air," I said.

George came out the door, a towel pressed to his face, his phone in his hand.

Casio and Didier joined us.

Casio nodded in George's direction. "My guess, he's tipping off his son, who'll make a run for it if he hasn't already." He turned to me. "Are the kids really okay? I tried to tell that asshat that I needed to get home, but he didn't want to hear it. Then tried to get him to at least let me call my kids. That fell on deaf ears."

"Alex is a lot like his old man—calm under pressure. He's something for a teenager. Oh yeah, your nanny called in sick, but got that covered. Don't forget to call them and let them know you've finished up 'the job' and are on your way home." Casio enveloped me in a hard hug.

"Ouch, you galoot."

"Sorry." He grinned, so clearly not. "I knew you'd step up and not go off half-cocked."

Creole's phone rang, and he stepped away.

"Fab wants to know if we can go home," I said.

Didier raised an eyebrow but didn't object.

"Stick around for the Chief," Casio ordered. "He'll probably be bringing a couple of the Miami detectives assigned to the case. They won't be happy to find out what went down."

"There's an easy fix—have them take the credit for everything," Fab said.

Chapter Forty

I eyed the stack of chairs off to the side of the patio, helped myself to one, and dragged it to the far end—a good location to watch everything unfold, though I'd rather have been on the road home. I watched as George stalked back to the main house. No one suggested that he stick around or not leave the property. Apparently, I was the only one who thought he might make a run for it.

Fab, who'd been in the thick of things, finished talking to the guys and dragged her own chair over, sitting down with a sigh.

"We never told the Chief the whole truth about how we got our hands on the drive," I said, a *now what?* look on my face. "A little wager?" Fab was already shaking her head. "It's going to come up again, and dancing him or the Miami detectives around isn't going to work, so what are you going to say? As for myself, I'd like to speak to a lawyer before admitting to a crime."

"I'm going with..." She paused.

I inwardly groaned.

"An envelope was dropped off at my door. No

clue who left it."

If she was expecting applause for that one, she wasn't getting it. "Except that more than one person knows that's not true. And did you forget that the compound has cameras? The snoopy owner has to know everything." Not even a smile. "Free legal advice, and you know what that's worth..." I made a zero with my fingers. "You can probably get away with being less than truthful to the Chief, since he's no longer on the force, but it's not going to be long before official folks want a sit-down."

"Don't worry so much. We'll figure it out."

"One of us has to." I struggled not to snap at her. My eyes swept the backyard and found what I was looking for—the three men were now standing next to the pool. "Casio," I shouted. That caught everyone's attention, and all eyes pivoted to me. Casio stared me down, and I crooked my finger. He headed my way. Creole started after him, but his phone rang and he stopped short. As soon as Casio got close enough for no one else to hear except Fab, I said, "I'd like to call in a few favors in exchange for a big one from you. Whether you decide yay or nay, I want a guarantee that you won't rat me out."

"You don't have to worry about that." Casio snorted. "Anything you say stays between us unless you tell me otherwise. I expect the same in return."

"You might want to get yourself a chair." I

pointed to the stack.

Casio went and procured one and carried it back over his head. When he sat down, I ignored his grunt of impatience.

I told him exactly how we'd gotten our hands on West's drives. "I don't want to go to jail. Or lie, which would only delay jail until it was found out. I'd like the same for Fab." Surprisingly, she'd been suspiciously quiet. I'd figured that she'd guess what I was going to ask him and expected her to raise an objection, but it didn't come.

Casio's hard stare bored through me for so long that I began to wonder if he was going to say anything. "Happy that you filled me in on *all* the details. I've got this covered, and when I'm done, you won't be on anyone's interest list."

Creole joined us, towering over us all and staring us down, attempting that mind-reading trick of his. I'd have to ask if it worked on anyone other than me...and in my case, it only sometimes did.

Didier moved behind Fab's chair, hands on her shoulders.

"The Chief's here." Creole chuckled. "Frustrated that he had to call and find out how to access the property. Told him to hike around the block and up the drive, the side gate's open."

"Let's hope George didn't take off. Didn't hear a car, but then, we probably wouldn't." Casio jumped up as the Chief and two other men walked in, looking around. "I've got this." He jogged over to the trio.

Creole bent down and brushed my cheek with his lips. "You behaving?"

"Sort of."

He grinned at me. "I'm sure that bunch is going to have more than a few questions for us." He motioned to Didier, and they headed to the other side of the pool.

"For once, I'm happy not to be part of the discussion." Fab eyed the men, who were deep in conversation and checking out the main house.

"You feeling okay?"

Fab ignored me. "I've got our escape planned," she whispered, though no one but me could hear.

"Whatever your idea is, I like it already. But we might want to hold off until we're certain we're not needed for questioning."

Fab tilted her head toward the house. "Look who just made another appearance. Guess George didn't beat it down the block after all."

I followed her gaze as he came through a pair of sliders, his nose taped, holding an ice pack. A man in an expensive suit was at his side. "Want to wager that the suit is a lawyer?"

Fab gave me a disgusted look—she wasn't taking that bet. "Incoming." She jerked her head. "Remember: short answers. If it gets too intense, we play the 'we need to call our lawyer' card."

A muscled hardass nodded at us. "Ladies.

Detective Titan." He grabbed the chair Casio had vacated and sat down. "Casio says that he contacted you to deliver the drive." He gave Fab a once-over.

"Fab Merceau, licensed private investigator." She stuck out her hand, then went on to tell him what had gone down in the past couple of hours in concise terms.

"And you?" Titan shifted his attention to me.

"Madison Westin." I didn't extend my hand. "I was along for the ride, and everything happened as Fab just laid out."

"Should I have more questions, I can get ahold of you both through Casio?"

We nodded.

Titan stood.

"That was interesting," Fab said as she watched the detective join the other men, who were now seated around a table by the pool. "I expected a lot more questions. I'd say that Casio more than delivered on keeping our names out of the discussion."

"Don't go all attitudinal on him if turns out that he made himself the star of the case and takes all the credit for bringing in a murderer. Especially if it keeps us from needing a lawyer."

Fab and I watched as Creole and Didier made their way over to us.

"We need to hang around and answer a few more questions, and I'm not sure how long that's going to take," Creole told us.

"Does that mean Fab and I are free to crawl through the dirt to the car and blow on out of here?" I asked.

Creole and Didier shook their heads, but both sported a slight smile.

"Interestingly, Casio diminished your role to a couple of sentences," Creole said. "I was happy but surprised." He stared down at me.

"Why isn't George in cuffs for kidnapping Casio?" Fab asked.

Didier snorted. "More creative storytelling on Casio's part. His story was that he came willingly as part of his investigation. He admitted to a heated exchange of words, but brushed it off as two friends disagreeing."

"George, who hadn't been asked a question up to that point and was clearly hiding behind his lawyer, appeared grateful. But his troubles are far from over." Creole stared as the men all stood up.

"What happens with the case?" Fab asked.

"I imagine that the DA isn't going to be happy to hear about a couple of new suspects," Creole told us. "The detectives told us that in their opinion, her case against Crum wasn't that strong. It was a crapshoot what kind of verdict a jury would have returned."

"That's good news for Crum," Fab said.

"I'm certain he'll appreciate being cleared of murder," Didier said. "Although even with new evidence, it won't happen overnight."

"Be interesting to see how he plays it," I said. "If it gets him more women, he'll happily be known as the one that got away."

Creole and Didier chuckled, much to their disgust, I was certain.

Fab stood and tugged on my arm. "We're going to sneak out of here. See you guys back at home."

I stood and turned to Creole for a hug and a quick kiss. "Let Casio know that I'm going to tell his kids I talked to him and he'll be calling them as soon as he has a minute."

* * *

Fab and I rode most of the way home in silence. I broke it by asking, "Are you wishing you'd stayed and were a part of whatever is happening?"

"I'm happy to not be facing any criminal charges. Should that change, know that I won't be mentioning your name…or our husbands."

"Just promise not to lie; it would only make things worse. We should contact Tank and see if he's willing to represent us should we need it."

Once we got back to the compound, we eagerly went to our own houses. I took a shower, got something to eat, and curled up with a book to wait for Creole. He didn't show up for hours, and I fell asleep waiting. Eventually, he climbed in bed and was asleep before his head hit the pillow. I curled up next to him.

The next morning, I got up early and made coffee, having it ready when Creole came out dressed for the office.

"It was a long night and there were a million questions." Creole came close to draining his coffee mug in one gulp. "It was Casio's show, and we only had bit parts. He's got a jones to solve this case, and from previous experience, nothing will get in his way. On the way home, I asked him, 'What the hell?' and he shot back, 'None of your business.'"

"You could call in sick."

"I planned to do just that before I remembered the meeting Didier and I have scheduled at the Boardwalk. But soon, we'll take a couple of days off. No interruptions."

"I'd like that a lot." I refilled his mug.

"Do I dare ask what you have planned for the day?"

"You're going to be happy, because I plan on working from home, the cats curled up on my feet. It's my intention to keep a low profile until there's a resolution to this case."

"Be sure you tell your friend, or she'll come up with an emergency."

I laughed, knowing he was right.

"So you know, Casio explained your involvement by saying that you and Fab were neighbors and he asked you to deliver the drive. End of story."

"No one questioned that?"

"Casio pretty much monopolized the conversation in his typical fashion. I'm used to it, but the other men were looking a bit bulldozed. It came out that the detectives would have liked another crack at searching the mansion from top to bottom. But as you know, it's been reduced to ash. It would behoove you to stay out of the neighborhood."

"I have no intention of even glancing in that direction." I grimaced.

"I shouldn't be surprised by how Casio handled the Miami detectives. He was never one to do things by the book, but because he was so good at his job, he rarely if ever got called on it." Creole's phone dinged with a message, which he read. "Didier will be here in two minutes." He stood and put his mug in the sink, then came around the island and kissed me. "Remember, low-key."

"Same to you."

Chapter Forty-One

It had been a couple of weeks, and all had been quiet. Fab and I had kept our promise to maintain a low profile. Getting an update on the state of the case was near impossible. Casio hadn't been around much, and when he was, he was with his kids. "Patience" was Creole's mantra.

That day, an early morning meeting had been set up at The Boardwalk offices, attendance mandatory. As usual, Creole and Didier had left early.

Fab stormed through the open sliders and took a seat at the island. "Happy to see you're dressed."

"Hey, I made an effort." I twirled around in my hot-pink sundress and low-heeled slides, noting that Fab had chosen a black sundress and heels. "I'm assuming that you got the same admonition not to be late. Mine came with a kiss and stink eye."

"I got a kiss. Didier was short on patience, so I didn't ask what was on the agenda."

"Hmm…" I tapped my cheek, which garnered me an eyeroll. "Our safety. No more doing illegal stuff. Look attentive. If they think you're not listening, they'll repeat themselves."

"There's no reason we couldn't have this meeting here or at my house," Fab snarked. "If there's more coming than our foursome, we just order more food. We've had plenty of practice at that."

I picked up my phone and called Lark, hitting the speaker button. "How's the mood around the office?"

"Grouchy," she sing-songed in a low tone.

Fab and I made faces. "Did you bring sweets this morning?" I asked.

"If someone had tipped me off that they all apparently fell out of bed and hit their heads, I could have."

"No worries. I'm going to hit up the bakery on the way."

"Plan for extras." Lark was back to singing. "Toodles."

I looked at the screen, and sure enough, she'd hung up. "That was rather abrupt. She didn't give me a chance to ask the head count and find out who exactly is going to be in attendance."

"Let's be surprised."

"Not only is sarcasm going to get you in trouble, you've apparently forgotten that you don't like surprises."

"We've got time for a triple shot of caffeine, and then we won't care who's doing what." Fab grabbed my purse and handed it to me.

We headed out the door and got in the SUV. Fab drove slowly out of the compound, eyeing each house as she headed to the gate.

"What are you looking for?" I turned in my seat to see if I'd missed anything.

"Just making sure that the neighbors are obeying the rules."

"Apparently it slipped your mind that there aren't any."

"I guess I'll have to get on it." Fab smirked.

She headed straight to the bakery, and traffic cooperated. It didn't take us long to make enough selections to fill a couple of boxes.

Back in the car, I said, "You might want to hit the gas, lest we be late."

"That's a first." Fab took one of her shortcuts, and we got to the office with minutes to spare.

"You have a meeting with Gunz?" I nodded at the SUV a few spaces over.

"Just great." Fab groaned. "Didier's going to think I made an appointment on purpose."

"That's why you're going to hustle upstairs and deal with whatever problem he thinks needs your immediate attention, then boot his big backside. You've got a good excuse: you can't keep your already scheduled meeting waiting. I can buy time by waving the boxes under their noses."

"After the sister incident, Didier pretty much doesn't want him around."

"I'll tell your husb and mine—since he feels

the same way—that his appearance is unexpected and you're on your way. So don't make a liar out of me."

"You're the best." Fab hopped out and raced across the parking lot and upstairs.

I grabbed the boxes and headed inside, Arlo greeting me at the door, tail thumping on the floor. "Head scratch later," I promised him.

Brad jumped up and relieved me of the boxes, taking them over to the kitchen counter. "Good news. Gail wanted me to thank you and Fab for everything you did, finding her sister's kids. Allison finally showed up at the motel, found out her sister took the kids, and gave her a call. They're working things out."

"I wonder what that means." I'd known a drug addict or two, and that wasn't going to be an easy road.

"I didn't ask." He grimaced. "Wished her the best and got off the phone."

"I'll tell Fab."

Brad brushed my cheek with a kiss.

I waved to the men at the conference table—the Chief at the head, Creole and Didier on one side, Casio on the other, and empty chairs on both sides. "Everyone needs to grab a plate and something yum to eat. It will give Fab time to dispense with a client who showed up without calling for an appointment."

Lark had made coffee and was busy refilling everyone's cups. I winked at her.

You never had to tell the guys twice. They got up and helped themselves, then took their seats back around the table.

"I have an update," the Chief said, devouring his muffin. "The local DA has recused herself due to her brother being a suspect in the case, and the case has been moved to Miami."

"How does that affect Crum?" I asked.

"The charges against him were dropped, but they could be refiled on the off-chance that more evidence comes to light in the future," the Chief said. "There's no anticipation that will happen."

"The two men being blackmailed were hauled in for questioning, along with the brother of the man that killed himself, and all lawyered up. As of now, George's son is nowhere to be found." Casio snorted in disgust over the last part.

Fab was running out of time. The guys had inhaled their food, along with the coffee. As Lark cleared away the plates, I got up and asked, "Water anyone?" and delivered bottles to the show of hands.

"I saved this for Xander," I said to Lark, pointing to a plate covered in foil. "After the meeting, will you make sure he gets it?"

"Great minds." Lark pointed to a second plate.

"No wonder you're everyone's favorite."

Lark beamed.

Arlo barked and barked again. He'd jumped to his feet and stood in the doorway, getting everyone's attention, since he only barked when outside chasing something.

A scruffy thirty-something, scraggly brown hair hanging in his eyes, bounded through the door, kicking Arlo—who growled and bared his teeth—out of the way. The only thing that stopped me from shouting "bite him" was the gun in the man's hand.

You could hear a pin drop as he scanned everyone's faces and settled on Casio. "You couldn't mind your own business?" He cocked the gun.

A gun went off, but not his. He unleashed a scream, blood stained the sleeve of his shirt, yet managed to keep hold of his gun as he stumbled back into Lark, who'd run to her dog. She attempted to jerk away, but he yanked her forward and wrapped his hand around her throat.

Arlo charged with a growl.

"Sit, Arlo," Lark commanded when the man threatened to kill the dog. He reluctantly sat back. When the man loosened his hold on her throat slightly, Lark pulled her hand back, aiming for his ribcage, but he managed to evade the blow and slam her into the wall, then twisted her around and held her in front of him.

"I should've killed him," Fab lamented from where she'd moved to stand next to me, her gun at her side.

I nodded at her, telegraphing, *This is isn't over yet.*

Casio stood. "Don't be a stupid ass, George. You've got it in for me; we can handle it outside between the two of us. No one else needs to get hurt."

George Jr.? Now that I looked closer, I could see the resemblance—a few of the same facial features.

"You couldn't mind your own damn business," Junior seethed.

Lark gripped the arm wrapped around her throat and tried to pull it away. Junior said something to her that none of us could hear, and she stilled.

"Let the lady go, and then you walk out of here. No one will come after you," Casio told him.

Junior vigorously shook his head.

"You've got enough legal troubles without compounding them by shooting someone. Do that and you'll never get out of jail; even your father won't be able to fix it for you." Casio held out his hand in a placating gesture.

"Now you give a damn." Spit flew out of Junior's mouth. "After your chat with my father, he disowned me. Finding out that I murdered West was pretty much the final straw. He ranted that he'd had my legal issues covered, but did he? I don't think so. As long as West was alive, he was going to continue milking dear old Dad for money. There goes my inheritance."

Lark weaved back and forth and slowly

slumped in Junior's hold, slamming her elbow into the man's groin as she went down. He folded in on himself but managed to keep hold of her wrist. She let out a bloodcurdling scream and slammed her fist into his nose. Junior hit her with his gun, dropping it in the process.

Another shot went off, and Junior stumbled back, then fell to his knees.

Lark crawled into a sitting position, and Arlo leaped on her, licking her face.

"Told you so." I winked at Fab.

"I suppose my Walther is headed for an evidence box." Fab smiled fondly at her handgun.

Casio raced over to Junior and knelt at his side.

"I'm dying," Junior moaned.

"Let's hope not. You hang in there. If you die, your father will be madder than a hornet." Casio ripped off his shirt and pressed it to Junior's upper chest.

"I'm calling 911." I fished my phone out of my pocket and held it in the air.

"I'm on it," the Chief yelled.

Fab and I bolted over to Lark and each took an arm, helping her to her feet.

"I'm fine. But for a minute there, I thought I'd pass out." Lark rubbed her head.

"Have a seat on the couch and kick your feet up. There's plenty of room for Arlo to lie next to you." I pointed, as though she didn't know it was in the middle of the reception area.

"Go to hell." Junior attempted to jerk away from Casio, pain showing in every line of his face.

"You need to stop moving around. Paramedics are on the way." Casio looked to the Chief for confirmation, and he nodded. To the room at large, he said, "This is George Jr., if you haven't guessed it already. I need to call his father."

"Don't bother," he rasped.

Creole moved to Casio's side and took over holding the cloth to the man's chest. It had barely made a dent in the blood flow. Casio pulled out his phone, presumably to call Junior's father.

Both Fab and I sat on the coffee table in front of Lark to make sure that she didn't go anywhere until the paramedics gave her a quick check.

"What did Gunz want?" I asked.

"To have me check out an apartment building where he admitted upfront that drugs were being sold out of the front entrance." Fab waved me off. "Before you get all huffy… I told him Toady was the man for the job, that the only way I could do it was to lie to my husband and that wasn't going to happen."

"Gunz isn't stupid. He had to know that would be the answer, so why not get someone else to start with?" I asked.

"I think he wanted to use Toady but has badmouthed him to the point where he doesn't want to ask for the man's help. So better to have me do it."

Lark sniffed. "Serve Gunz right if Toady told him to shove off."

Didier ran under the roll-up doors to meet the cop car that had pulled up and parked.

We watched as Kevin got out and walked to where Didier was waiting. The two talked, and Didier pointed to the building. A minute later, an ambulance arrived.

"Can I get up now?" Lark asked me.

"The paramedics just got here, so no."

"They don't need to waste their time on me; not when he's bleeding all over the floor." Lark sighed and sat up straighter. "Hey Junior," she bellowed. His eyes fluttered in her direction. "You get out of jail for some reason, don't come back here. You do, and I'll shoot you for kicking my dog." She stroked Arlo's fur.

Kevin—who'd come inside and overheard Lark—winked at her.

Didier showed the paramedics inside, and they came in rolling a gurney, dropped their bags, and knelt beside Junior.

"Kevin's never that nice to Madison and me," Fab grumbled. He must have had bionic ears today, as he looked at Fab and laughed.

Catching sight of the Chief, he said, "I suppose you're the one in charge of this crew?"

"The short of it is that the guy on the floor came here to kill that one." The Chief jabbed his finger at Casio. "Fab shot him, he grabbed Lark as a shield, and Fab's second shot put an end to the drama."

Kevin turned toward Fab and me and flashed a faux frown, looking pleased with himself. "I'd have been disappointed if the two of you hadn't been involved."

The paramedics loaded Junior up and wheeled him out.

Kevin talked first to Casio and then Creole, before coming over to talk to Fab.

I interrupted before he could start. "What about Lark? Are the paramedics going to check her out?"

"Didn't know she needed it," he said.

"I don't really. I'm fine," Lark assured us. "If I start to feel off, I'll call the doc. We've got one that makes house calls."

Kevin nodded. "I'm surprised you didn't kill Junior."

"Madison is rubbing off on me." Fab flashed me a faux frown. "I'm hoping it means less paperwork."

"I'm happy there's now been an arrest in the West case and, better yet, that it's been transferred north. For all his moaning and groaning, Junior didn't appear worried that he'd be putting his fate in the hands of a jury." Kevin shook his head.

"Even though he's on the outs with his father, he'll probably get him the best lawyer money can buy," I said.

"Are you talking about Cruz Campion?" Kevin snorted.

That would surprise me, as Cruz claimed he didn't represent those who were actually guilty. And this one had confessed in front of a room full of witnesses. I groaned, hoping that I didn't get a subpoena to testify.

When Kevin was done questioning us, Lark told him, "Be sure and grab a drink on your way out." He nodded.

"I think he was actually nice to us," Fab said as we watched him cross the room to talk to the guys.

"That's because we're growing on him."

Chapter Forty-Two

A week had gone by, and there hadn't been a single urgent phone call. George Jr.'s arrest had made plenty of headlines. He was still in intensive care, his condition listed as "guarded." The press had hounded his father, who gave them a terse "No comment," along with the finger.

Creole left the office early, announcing when he walked in the door, "Lark's singing at Jake's tonight, and we should go show our support."

I got on the phone and reserved the deck. With the doors open, we'd be able to see and hear Lark, no problem. Then placed one call after another to anyone I thought would be interested. Mother's hot idea was for her to grandkid-sit, and she called Brad and Casio and made the offer. All the kids, except for Alex, were hot to stay on the beach and play.

Another reason for celebration: Brad had been approved for guardianship of Logan.

Creole and I were the first to arrive, and I made sure that everything had been set up per my request, starting with the tables being pushed together so we could sit together.

Fab and Didier were minutes behind us.

"We'll drive ourselves so we can leave when we want," Fab had informed me when I called her.

"If you cut out early, you can bet something will go down. Don't expect a replay."

"You're annoying."

I heard Didier laughing in the background before she hung up.

Kelpie, who I'd called and given a heads up, had chosen a variety of beers that she put on ice in a large enamelware bucket. The busboy carried it outside and set it on a side table.

Brad, Emerson, Casio, and Alex arrived en masse, coming through the front door. The Chief came through the kitchen, stopping for a chat with Cook. How they'd become friends was a state secret. He walked behind the bar and planted a big kiss on Kelpie's cheek, and she turned and threw her arms around him.

Mac and Frack came through the front, his arm slung around her shoulders. She waved and introduced him to the others lounging around, drinks in hand. His background check had come back with no red flags.

"Is romance in the air?" Fab motioned to the Chief and Kelpie, then Mac and Frack.

I flipped an imaginary coin. "You go ahead and be the one to ask demanding questions about their intentions."

"Who uses that word?" Fab sniffed.

"What I was thinking was downright vulgar, so be happy I cleaned it up."

Creole leaned in and laughed in my ear. "I want to hear later."

Didier nudged Fab. "Yeah, hon, go ask away, and then come back with a report."

Brad and Emerson came through the patio doors, cutting off her response.

Looking into the bar area, I saw Casio and Alex in a three-way hug with Lark. I knew that the kids had had a lot of fun with her when she filled in for the nanny. She'd expertly covered for Casio with the kids, telling them he was on a job. Judging by the appreciative glint in Casio's eyes, he was happy with everything she'd done.

Tank came through the door with another man, and I did a double take—it was Crum…in clothes, and not trash finds, and he looked good.

I jumped up and walked inside to meet them. "Look at you." I checked him out with a wink.

"Now you listen here, girlie—don't get any ideas; this is for special occasions." He ran his hand down the front of his silk tropical shirt, which he'd paired with shorts and a pair of boat shoes that also looked new.

"I'm just saying you look hot."

Crum's cheeks pinkened. He stepped forward with a grin and patted me awkwardly on the shoulder. "I know you don't go for the touchy stuff but wanted you to know how much I appreciate you and that friend of yours sticking your nose into my case."

Tank laughed.

"I'm just happy that you weren't carted off to the clink." I smiled.

Alex came running up and engaged in a convoluted handshake with Crum.

"I hope you don't mind," Tank said to me. "Alex invited Crum, and I included myself in the invitation."

"Please come out and sit with us. There's plenty of room and lots of familiar faces. And if there's any legal news, you'll get to hear it firsthand." I beckoned them over to the bar. "Get a drink, then come out to the patio." I moved over next to Fab, who was standing by the bar, and peered over her shoulder, attempting to read her phone screen.

"My father finally made time to sprint into town," Fab read, looking up when Kelpie called to her. She placed an order for several drinks, including a pitcher of margaritas, and I knew she had me covered. "Tried to talk him into coming, but he wanted to stay at your house and herd kids with Madeline and Spoon."

Emerson came up behind me, sticking her head over my shoulder. "I came to warn you…" She nodded toward the pool table.

"Whatever it is, maybe you could handle it?" I teased, glanced around the room. Nothing stood out.

"Wait…" Emerson turned her head from side

to side. "They moved. They're over there now." She pointed to the jukebox.

A woman—forties maybe, in an orange tent dress and high-tops, a beer in hand—labored over her selection. Suddenly, a head appeared out of the top of her backpack and stared wide-eyed around the room.

"Is that a monkey?" My eyebrows went into my hairline.

"Brad and I had a hot debate about it for about a minute, then came to the same conclusion. His advice was to grab a drink and not get involved." Emerson laughed.

Brad showed up at Emerson's side and slung his arm around her shoulders. "No, and if that wasn't clear, N. O." He tugged on her arm. "Our drinks await us."

"But I didn't get a chance to ask..." I made a pleading face, knowing he'd never fall for it, and his eyeroll said it all.

"Please. This is out of my area of expertise, and I'm not interested in a crash course. So, sis, your monkey problems are your own."

"Just tell her no animals allowed," I said to Emerson, who laughed.

"Husbands to the rescue." Fab pointed with a laugh.

The monkey struggled inside the backpack. A couple of twists, and he was out, climbing up the woman's head and vaulting into her arms. He wrapped his arms around her neck and checked out the room with a wide-eyed stare.

Both Creole and Didier advanced on the pair. Whatever was said, the woman turned on Didier and yelled at him.

Fab caught his attention and made a gun finger. Didier shook his head.

More words were exchanged. Then Didier pulled out his phone, conveying, *Your choice*.

The woman cursed him, downed her beer, and stormed out.

Creole, who'd stood back, clapped him on the back, and the two men laughed.

The woman and her monkey had barely cleared the door when two men exchanged words—barely understandable, since they were drunk—and fists flew, barely connecting. The bigger of the two men jumped the other, wrapping his arms around his middle, and they hit the floor and rolled around. The men at the bar hooted and egged them on, nursing their beers.

I made eye contact with Doodad, who was lurking on the other side of the room, taking in the pitiful excuse for a fight. "Do something," I mouthed and jabbed my finger at the men. Before I could scream "No," he pulled his gun and put a bullet in the ceiling. That brought the fun and games to a halt. The two sat cross-legged, their mouths hanging open. Doodad marched over to the two men staring up at the ceiling and had a few words for them. They hustled to stand and went together to the bar, where Kelpie had beers ready.

"Your bartender is very pleased with herself," Fab said as all eyes turned to Kelpie. "I'm betting that she planned this floor show."

I groaned inwardly. I wasn't going to ask.

Creole stomped over to the bar and had a few words with Kelpie. The whole time, she was shaking her head and sending her lit tassels in a spin, a *Who me?* look on her face.

Didier was headed over, and I stepped in front of him. "I take it you weren't your sweet Frenchy self with that woman." I faux frowned.

He crossed his arms and stared a hole through me. "She was barely intelligible and reeked of beer; she'd spilled some down the front of her dress."

"If you ever need a second job, you're hired."

Fab laughed. "The women would be lined up." She winked at him.

Alex ran up. "That was the coolest. I followed her out, and she answered a couple of my questions. Wally is a support animal, and she's going to report you for kicking her out." He grinned at me.

"If you're going to make stuff up, you need to do a better job. Ask Fab for tips." I heard her snort from behind me.

"True story." He held up his right hand.

"You need to corral everyone out to the deck before another fight breaks out," I said to Alex, who shot me a thumbs up and started to spread the word. I wanted my choice of seat and headed out there, saving the one next to me for Creole. Across from me, Casio grinned. "Isn't Alex a tad young to be here?" I asked. I knew it was legal, but still, we weren't kid friendly.

"He cornered me, reminding me that he covered for me while I was off doing 'whatever.' I told him it was a complicated case and that I'd let my guard down and promised it wouldn't happen again. He pointed out that he wasn't a kid, though I disagree, and said that Lark's a friend and he was cashing in future favors that he planned to start stockpiling. Wonder who he learned that from?" Casio arched his brow at me.

"Probably from you."

He grinned, then turned his chair toward me and lowered his voice. "If anything happens to me, I want you to take my kids. You say you're fine with it and I'll make it legal. I ran it by Creole, and he said he was fine as long as you were. I had my brother listed but couldn't do that to my kids."

"There are a couple of stipulations." I pointed at him. "You're not to mention your demise again until you're ninety, and you super swear not to do anything that would endanger your life."

"Ninety. Can you imagine?" Casio chuckled. "I live that long, and I'm going to my reward with a cigar and a shot of whiskey." We both laughed. "I'm cutting back on the time I spend at the office, and when I do go in, I'll be taking the low-key cases—cheating spouses."

"Take it from me—some of those require a bulletproof vest." We laughed, as we both knew that to be true.

Everyone trooped out to the deck, drinks in hand, and sat around the table.

Creole sat down next to me. "You're my hero," I whispered. "You stepped up without hesitation and put an end to the madness."

He flexed his muscles. "Do you think the drama's over for the evening?"

"Probably not."

~*~

About the Author

Deborah Brown is an Amazon bestselling author of the Paradise series. She lives on the Gulf of Mexico, with her ungrateful animals, where Mother Nature takes out her bad attitude in the form of hurricanes.

For a free short story, sign up for my newsletter. It will also keep you up-to-date with new releases and special promotions:
www.deborahbrownbooks.com

Follow on FaceBook:
facebook.com/DeborahBrownAuthor

You can contact her at Wildcurls@hotmail.com

Deborah's books are available on Amazon
amazon.com/Deborah-Brown/e/B0059MAIKQ

PARADISE SERIES NOVELS

Crazy in Paradise
Deception in Paradise
Trouble in Paradise
Murder in Paradise
Greed in Paradise
Revenge in Paradise
Kidnapped in Paradise
Swindled in Paradise
Executed in Paradise
Hurricane in Paradise
Lottery in Paradise
Ambushed in Paradise
Christmas in Paradise
Blownup in Paradise
Psycho in Paradise
Overdose in Paradise
Initiation in Paradise
Jealous in Paradise
Wronged in Paradise
Vanished in Paradise
Fraud in Paradise
Naïve in Paradise
Bodies in Paradise
Accused in Paradise

Deborah's books are available on Amazon
amazon.com/Deborah-Brown/e/B0059MAIKQ

Made in the USA
Las Vegas, NV
16 October 2024

96913368R10212